Elizabeth Bennet's Deception

A Pride and Prejudice Vagary

by Regina Jeffers

Regency Solutions

Elizabeth Bennet's Deception

A Pride and Prejudice Vagary

Chapter 1

DARCY FROZE IN HIS STEPS.

"It could not be," he whispered to his foolish heart. He returned to Pemberley a day early to make the final arrangements for the surprise he meant for his sister. He left Georgiana in the care of his friend, Charles Bingley, and Bingley's sisters. Darcy experienced a twinge of guilt at his expecting Georgiana to contend with Caroline Bingley and Louisa Hurst, but Miss Bingley's effusions sorely wore Darcy's patience away, and so he made his excuses.

He cut across Pemberley's parkland to come forward from the road, which led behind it to the stables. Upon his approach, Darcy noted the unmarked carriage before the estate. Recognizing the possibility of visitors in the common rooms, he remained in the shadows, meaning to enter the private quarters through the back entrance; yet, the appearance of a young woman upon the rise leading to the river brought Darcy to a stumbling halt. From a distance, the woman had the look of Elizabeth Bennet, but he did not approach. Darcy acted the fool previously and refused to be found wanting again.

Perhaps a month after his disastrous proposal to Miss Elizabeth at Hunsford Cottage, Darcy spotted a young lady entering Hatchard's Books, and without thinking, he followed her.

"Miss Elizabeth," Darcy said as he came up behind her, but when the woman spun around to greet him, the lady was not the woman whose being haunted Darcy's thoughts for almost a year.

The girl's forehead furrowed in confusion.

"Pardon me, Sir. Do we hold an acquaintance?"

Darcy bowed stiffly.

"It is I, miss, who begs your pardon. From behind, I thought you a long-standing acquaintance." He stepped back to widen the distance between them. "I apologize for the inconvenience."

The girl's frown line deepened.

"Yet, you called me by my Christian name." The tone of the girl's voice spoke of her suspicions.

Darcy swallowed the blush of embarrassment rushing to his cheeks.

"If you are also an 'Elizabeth,' it is purely a coincidence," he insisted.

"I am."

Darcy rushed his apologies when he spied a matron marching to the young woman's rescue.

"Then I am doubly apologetic. My actions placed you in an awkward position. Please forgive me." He held enough experience with Society mamas to know when to make a speedy exit.

During his return to Darcy House, Darcy silently cursed his inanity for stumbling into what was a more humiliating situation. Later, in his study, he admitted to the empty room, if not to himself, that he missed looking upon Elizabeth Bennet's animated countenance.

"If it were she," Darcy warned his conscience, "Miss Elizabeth would have, in all probability, presented me the direct cut. The lady spoke quite elegantly upon her disdain, and you are imprudent to think your letter would change Miss Elizabeth's mind. Accept the fact the woman is not for you."

And so when Darcy noted another possessing Elizabeth's likeness upon the streets in the warehouse district of Cheapside a fortnight later, he turned away with the knowledge that as a gentleman's daughter, Miss Elizabeth would not be found in Cheapside. He strove to convince himself that he would soon replace Elizabeth Bennet's charms with that of another.

Belatedly, realizing he studied the woman standing upon the rise longer than was proper, Darcy slipped through an open patio door to escape the vision of Elizabeth Bennet at Pemberley, which so often followed him about. It was deuced frustrating to look for the woman wherever he his steps took him.

"Leave it be," Darcy chastised as he crossed the drawing room only to be brought up short a second time by the appearance of his housekeeper.

Mrs. Reynolds caught at her chest in obvious surprise.

"Mr. Darcy," she gasped. "I did not realize you returned, Sir."

Darcy caught her elbow to steady the stance of his long-time servant. Mrs. Reynolds came to Pemberley when he was but three. She, Mr. Nathan, his butler, and Mr. Sheffield, his valet, all knew the Darcy family's employ for over twenty years. "I noted visitors, and as I was not dressed properly, I thought to avoid the necessary greetings," he explained.

"I have just this minute turned them over to the gardener," Mrs. Reynolds assured.

Darcy swallowed the question rushing to his lips.

"Very well. Then I am free to seek the privacy of my quarters."

"Yes, Sir." Mrs. Reynolds glanced toward the entrance hall. "Should I have a footman bring up bath water, Sir?"

Darcy nodded his agreement. Again, he fought the urge to ask of the estate's visitors, but Darcy chose not to punish his pride with false hopes.

"Has Miss Darcy's gift arrived?"

"Yes, Sir. As you instructed I had the instrument placed in Miss Darcy's sitting room. It fits perfectly. Miss Georgiana will know such joy."

He smiled with the woman's kindness.

"My sister deserves a bit of happiness. After my ablutions, I mean to view the arrangement personally."

"Very good, Sir." Mrs. Reynolds started away to do his bidding. Yet, despite his best efforts, Darcy called out to her. "Yes, Master William. Is there something more?"

Darcy's eyes searched the staircase where he often imagined Elizabeth Bennet standing. Such yearning swelled his chest that he experienced difficulty breathing. *It is best not to know*, he cautioned his wayward thoughts.

"Would you tell the footman I will require his assistance in dressing. Mr. Sheffield and my coach will arrive later this evening."

"Certainly, Sir."

"And you and I should speak before Mr. Bingley's family arrives. Miss Bingley did not enjoy the vista from her guest room when last the Bingleys were here."

A scowl of disapproval crossed his housekeeper's features. Darcy knew many of his servants prayed he would not take up with Caroline Bingley. He expected if he were to act so foolish, he would receive a large number of notices of leaving from his staff.

"Perhaps before supper, Sir," Mrs. Reynolds said stiffly.

Darcy nodded his approval, and the lady strode away; yet, he whispered to her retreating form.

"Have no fear. Only one woman knows my approval as the Mistress of Pemberley." Darcy chuckled in irony. "And it remains unfortunate that even Pemberley's grandeur could not entice the lady to overlook its master's shortcomings."

Mr. Darcy's housekeeper consigned Elizabeth and her aunt and uncle over to the gardener, who met them at the hall door. As they followed the man toward the river, Elizabeth turned to look upon the gentleman's home. For very selfish reasons, she opposed her aunt's suggestion of the tour of Mr. Darcy's estate, but

Elizabeth was glad she came. In her future daydreams, she would picture him on the grand staircase.

If Elizabeth, when Mr. Darcy gave her the letter he wrote in *clarification* of his actions, did not expect it to contain a renewal of his offers, she formed no expectation at all of its contents. But such as they were, it might well be supposed how eagerly she went through them and what a contrariety of emotions they excited. No one observing her progress could give voice to her feelings. With amazement did she first understand that Mr. Darcy believed any apology to be in his power; and she steadfastly denied that he could possess an explanation, which a just sense of shame would not conceal.

With a strong prejudice against everything he might say, she examined his account of what occurred at Netherfield. She read with an eagerness, which hardly left her power of comprehension, as well as from an impatience of knowing what the next sentence might bring, so much so she could not attend to the sense of the written lines before her eyes. Mr. Darcy's belief of Jane's insensibility Elizabeth instantly resolved to be false, and his account of his real objections to the match brought such anger that she could not declare his actions just. The gentleman expressed no regret for acting upon his beliefs, at least none, which satisfied her. Elizabeth declared his style lacking in penitence, instead of naming it haughty and prideful and insolence.

But Mr. Darcy's account of his relationship with Mr. Wickham bore so alarming an affinity to Mr. Wickham's own narration of the events that astonishment, apprehension, and even horror, oppressed her. Elizabeth wished to discredit it, but every line proved that the affair, which she believed beyond the pale, could name the gentleman entirely blameless throughout the whole.

In hindsight, Elizabeth grew absolutely ashamed of her accusations. Of neither Darcy nor Wickham could she think without feeling she was blind, partial, prejudiced, and absurd.

"I acted the harpy," Elizabeth whispered as she implanted the image of Pemberley upon her mind.

When her relatives insisted upon touring the estate, Elizabeth convinced herself that viewing Mr. Darcy's property would prove just punishment for the pain she caused the gentleman.

"Of all this, I might have been mistress," she reminded herself with each new discovery of how easily she and Mr. Darcy could suit. They held similar tastes in architecture and décor. "So different from his aunt's ornate presentation at Rosings."

And so, although Pemberley's gallery sported many fine portraits of the Darcy family, Elizabeth searched for the one face whose features she wished to look upon again. At last, it arrested her, and Elizabeth beheld a striking resemblance to Mr. Darcy, with such a smile upon his lips as she remembered to have sometimes seen when he looked upon her. The viewing brought Elizabeth instant regret for she recognized the honor of Mr. Darcy, which led her to consider his regard for her with a deeper sentiment of gratitude than she ever admitted, even to herself.

Elizabeth wished she could tell Mr. Darcy that she found Pemberley "delightful" and "charming," but she quickly deduced the gentleman would assume her opinions mischievously construed: Mr. Darcy would think her praise of Pemberley a device to elicit a renewal of his proposal.

"Better this way," Elizabeth whispered as she turned to follow her aunt and uncle further into the woods. "I have memories of Pemberley, and no one else is the wiser of my presence under Mr. Darcy's roof."

Unable to quash his curiosity any longer, after supper, Darcy sent for Mrs. Reynolds.

"Yes, Sir?" The lady curtsied from her position inside the open door to his study.

Darcy motioned her forward.

"Would you see there is a vase of yellow roses placed upon the new instrument in Miss Darcy's quarters."

Mrs. Reynolds' countenance relaxed.

"I asked Mr. Brownley for fresh cuttings previously, Sir."

Darcy nodded his approval.

"I should not think to instruct you on providing for Georgiana's pleasure. You have been an exemplary member of Pemberley's staff for longer than I can remember."

The woman blushed at Darcy's kindness, but she kept a business-like tone.

"I also aired out the green bedchamber for Miss Bingley's use. I pray that will serve the lady's purpose."

Darcy understood Mrs. Reynolds' poorly disguised question.

"You may inform the staff I hold no intention of

seeing Miss Bingley in the family quarters. The green chamber is close enough."

Mrs. Reynolds closed her eyes in what appeared to be a silent prayer of thanksgiving.

"Will that be all, Sir?"

Darcy's heart raced, but he managed to pronounce the necessary words.

"Did we have more than one set of visitors today? Thanks to your efficiency, I so rarely encounter the estate guests, but I would not have you beset upon. Your first duty is to the running of Pemberley."

"No, Sir. Mr. and Mrs. Gardiner were the only ones we accepted in well over a week. It is no bother: I am proud of Pemberley."

"Mrs. Gardiner," Darcy's mind caught the name and rolled it through his body like a tidal wave striking a ship. *If the lady he observed was Elizabeth, had she married? Had she thought to compare what she earned to what she lost?*

Darcy's mind retreated from the possibilities, but he could not quite quash his fears.

"A young couple then? Perhaps on a holiday?"

Mrs. Reynolds shook her head in denial.

"Mr. and Mrs. Gardiner would be the age of your late parents. I overheard Mrs. Gardiner tell her niece a tale of the village oak. It sounded as if the lady spent part of her childhood on the London side of Lambton."

"Her niece?" Darcy's mind latched onto the one word in his housekeeper's tale that rang with hope.

"Yes, Sir. A fine young lady. Very kind to her aunt, offering her arm to Mrs. Gardiner's support. I believe the lady held an acquaintance with you. She and her aunt had a private conversation when they spotted the miniature of Mr. Wickham on your father's mantelpiece." Mrs. Reynolds' shoulders stiffened. "I am sorry to report, Sir, I could not give Mrs. Gardiner a civil account when she asked her niece how the young lady liked it. In truth, I quickly turned the conversation to your miniature."

"I appreciate your loyalty," Darcy said with a wry smile.

"My respect for the girl increased when she admitted she knew you 'a little' and that she found you 'very handsome,'" Mrs. Reynolds continued.

Darcy's eyebrow rose with curiosity. He hoped perhaps Mrs. Reynolds described Elizabeth Bennet, but he could not imagine Miss Elizabeth's declaring him handsome: The woman abhorred him.

"And how did this conversation come about?"

Mrs. Reynolds blushed, but she did not avoid his unspoken accusation, a sign of her long-standing position in his household.

"Do not look to place blame, Master William. I respect the late master's kind heart and his benevolence toward his godson, but I see no reason to display George Wickham's image in this house. Even the late Mr. Darcy could peer down from Heaven and see Mr. Wickham turned out very wild."

"We will discuss the future of Mr. Wickham's likeness upon another occasion. Speak to me of your conversation with the young lady."

It was Mrs. Reynolds' turn to raise an eyebrow in interest; however, she swallowed her questions.

"Mrs. Gardiner remarked of your fine

countenance when she looked upon the miniature, and then the lady asked her niece whether it was an accurate likeness. I then inquired if the young lady held an acquaintance with you. When she admitted as such, I asked if she found you a handsome man."

"Then, it was Mrs. Gardiner and you who placed words in the lady's mouth," he reasoned. Darcy felt the female likely agreed only to be rid of the conversation.

Mrs. Reynolds blustered.

"The girl's aunt and I stated the obvious," she declared with a tone commonly found among upper servants. "But neither Mrs. Gardiner nor I instructed the young lady to search out your portrait in the gallery nor did we lead her to it again and again."

Darcy's heart hitched higher.

"I count no one named Gardiner among my acquaintances. Did you overhear the young lady's name?"

"Her aunt called her 'Lizzy' several times so I would assume it is Miss Elizabeth or Lady Elizabeth."

"Miss Elizabeth Bennet," Darcy corrected. Remorse at not having met her today filled his chest. A glance to his housekeeper said Mrs. Reynolds wished an explanation. "The young lady's parents are neighbors of Mr. Bingley's estate in Hertfordshire. If it is truly Miss Elizabeth, we met upon several occasions. I believe I stood up with her at the Netherfield's ball."

"Then perhaps you might renew the acquaintance," Mrs. Reynolds suggested. "Mrs. Gardiner was to dine with friends before the family moved on to Matlock. I am certain Mr. Bingley would wish to behold Miss Elizabeth again."

An invisible hand squeezed Darcy's heart. Should he risk an encounter with Elizabeth Bennet? Had his letter softened the lady's disdain for him?

"Miss Bingley took a dislike for the Bennets," Darcy offered in explanation. "Mr. Bingley developed a regard for Miss Bennet. His leaving Netherfield was poorly done."

"I am sad to hear it, Sir, but your confidence explains the halfhearted air, which follows Mr. Bingley about."

Darcy nodded his acceptance: His housekeeper gave voice to what Darcy's pride denied. Darcy sorely wounded his friend by acting in partnership with Miss Bingley in separating Bingley from Miss Bennet. With a second nod, he excused his servant. For several long minutes, Darcy stared off into the emptiness, which marked his life.

"I cannot seek out Miss Elizabeth," he told the rise of expectation climbing up his chest. "Even if the lady might offer her forgiveness, Miss Elizabeth holds no interest in renewing our acquaintance. Furthermore, I do not deserve happiness when I robbed my friend of an opportunity to know it."

⟡

"You are very quiet this evening, Lizzy." Her aunt's friends invited them to dine in the evening, but once they returned to their let rooms, Elizabeth preferred to spend time alone with her thoughts of Mr. Darcy.

"Just a bit tired." Elizabeth made herself smile at her dearest aunt.

"Then you should retire early," her Uncle

Edward declared.

Her aunt ignored her husband's lack of intuitiveness.

"Are you certain what the Pemberley housekeeper said of Mr. Wickham did not upset you? I would venture the woman's loyalty to the Master of Pemberley colored her opinions."

Elizabeth expected her aunt to ask of Mr. Darcy, not of Mr. Wickham.

"Not in the least," Elizabeth assured. "While in Kent, I learned more of what occurred between Mr. Darcy and Mr. Wickham, enough so to acquit the former of any ill doing."

Aunt Gardiner's interest piqued.

"Would you care to elaborate?"

"I promised my source secrecy." Elizabeth would like to confide in her aunt and uncle for she wished someone would give her permission to beg Mr. Darcy's forgiveness, but she dug the pit of regret in which she wallowed. "As I explained in my letter before I departed for Kent, Mr. Wickham bestowed his affections upon Miss King, and I held no loyalty for the man when I arrived on Charlotte's threshold; therefore, I was free to accept other versions of the events." Hers was an exaggeration of what occurred, but it held some truth. "Although I still believe handsome young men must have something to live on, I pity whoever accepts Mr. Wickham's hand." *If only I did not previously express my opinions to the contrary*, Elizabeth thought.

"That is quite a transformation," her uncle observed.

"I am only aggrieved that I behaved with foolish

disregard for Mr. Darcy. I treated the gentleman poorly."

Her aunt's question came quickly.

"Is this revelation the source of your reluctance in viewing Mr. Darcy's home?"

Elizabeth swallowed the bile rushing to her throat.

"I rejoiced today when Mr. Darcy's housekeeper informed us that we missed his return to Derbyshire by a day. I would not wish to encounter the gentleman. Our last exchange of words was far from pleasant."

"If I knew..." her uncle began.

Elizabeth shook off his regrets.

"I asked the inn's staff of Mr. Darcy's being at Pemberley before we came to the place."

"We should be on to Matlock the day after tomorrow," her aunt declared. "Even with Mr. Darcy's presence at Pemberley we are not likely to encounter him. My friends do not travel in the same circles as Mr. Darcy. We shall be gone soon, and the gentleman will know nothing of our coming into his part of the shire."

Chapter 2

ELIZABETH STROLLED ALONG THE narrow road, which claimed the center of Lambton. Her aunt and uncle called at the church for Aunt Margaret wished to check the church records to verify the baptism of her late brother. Aunt Margaret had it her mind to create a sampler remembering James Montgomery, as a gift for the man's widow and children. Elizabeth begged off the task to say she required a bit of exercise.

After all the talk of Mr. Darcy and of Pemberley, Elizabeth slept little. She hoped after a bit of air, she could slip back to her quarters for a nap before supper plans with another of her aunt's former acquaintances.

"Tomorrow," she whispered to her reflection in the glass of what passed as a mercantile in Lambton. "Tomorrow, we shall be gone from this place, and Mr. Darcy shall be a distant memory."

The sound of a driver shouting to his team of horses had Elizabeth spinning around to view the spectacle. Ignoring the dangers to pedestrians and the strictures of good breeding, a chaise and four sped through the village streets. The driver's disregard for safety brought a quick frown to Elizabeth's features, and she thought to add her voice to those upon the street in condemnation of the man's actions, but the appearance of a familiar face through the carriage window clamped Elizabeth's jaw shut. *Caroline Bingley.* Wishing not to be noticed, Elizabeth dropped her head so her bonnet might disguise her features.

"What else could one expect from those who claim an entitlement not theirs," Elizabeth murmured.

A young assistant to the shopkeeper spoke from beside her. He leaned upon the broom he used to sweep the wooden walkway.

"I see the Darcys host company again." He wiped the sweat from his brow with a handkerchief. "Darcy's tenants pray that one will not become a permanent fixture at Pemberley." Realizing he spoke from turn, the young man bowed to Elizabeth. "Forgive me, Miss. I should keep my opinions private. Speaking poorly of ones betters is not acceptable."

Elizabeth blushed. Had she not possessed similar thoughts of Miss Bingley?

"I shall not relay your sentiments to others if you will promise me likewise." The young man nodded his agreement. "My aunt and uncle and I toured Mr. Darcy's estate yesterday, and we heard the housekeeper's praise of the gentleman toward his tenants and servants." Elizabeth held no idea why she punished herself with learning more of Mr. Darcy, but she could not seem to control her curiosity.

The youth appeared willing to share his opinions with her, so Elizabeth left the remark open.

"Those who serve Mr. Darcy give him a good name, and he treats my father fair. Pays his accounts regularly." The fellow gestured toward the store. "I heard some call him 'proud,' but I observed none of it."

Before Elizabeth could ask more of the young man's knowledge of Mr. Darcy, someone called her name. She spun again to observe Mr. Bingley striding in her direction.

"Miss Elizabeth." Bingley beamed with delight. "It is you. I thought my eyes played tricks upon me." He bowed and then accepted the hands she offered him. "I am so pleased to encounter you again."

"Mr. Bingley." She curtsied. "I thought..." Elizabeth glanced behind her where the shopkeeper eyed her with curiosity. Mustering her composure, she continued, "I saw a carriage pass through the village a few moments earlier. I thought Miss Bingley one of the passengers, and encountering you I find myself correct."

Mr. Bingley frowned.

"My brother Hurst's carriage. My coach out distanced his. Likely, Caroline fears she would offend Darcy if she arrives after me."

Elizabeth ignored Bingley's reference to Mr. Darcy.

"The driver appeared set upon reaching his destination," she admitted.

Again, Mr. Bingley scowled before schooling his features.

"Tell me what brings you to Derbyshire."

Bingley had yet to release her fingertips.

"I am on holiday with my aunt and uncle." Elizabeth's eyebrow rose with the approach of a young lady.

Bingley turned with a welcoming smile.

"Mrs. Annesley and I thought you deserted us." The girl slipped her hand about Bingley's elbow, and Elizabeth cringed inside. Had the gentleman truly abandoned her sister Jane?

"Nothing of the kind." Bingley patted the back of the girl's gloved hand. "Permit me to make the proper introductions. Miss Darcy, this is a dear acquaintance and one of my neighbors in Hertfordshire, Miss Elizabeth Bennet. Miss Elizabeth, I present Mr. Darcy's sister."

Georgiana, Elizabeth's mind filled in the blank. She curtsied in greeting.

"Miss Elizabeth!" The girl said with approval in her tone. "I long wished for your acquaintance. My brother spoke of you often in his letters from Derbyshire."

A bit of satisfaction shot through Elizabeth: Mr. Darcy spoke of her to his sister. Miss Darcy was tall, and on a larger scale than Elizabeth; and, though little more than sixteen, her figure was formed, and her appearance womanly and graceful. Although less handsome than her brother, Miss Darcy's face displayed sense and good humor, and her manners were perfectly unassuming and gentle.

"Something very ill I would assume," Elizabeth responded with her customary tongue-in-cheek tartness.

However. Miss Darcy's features crunched up in confusion. Elizabeth, who expected to find in the girl as acute and unembarrassed an observer as ever Mr. Darcy showed, knew relief by discerning such different feelings.

Mr. Bingley patted the back of the girl's hand and chuckled.

"Miss Elizabeth holds an odd sense of humor, one your brother often challenged. Their conversations were quite entertaining. A sort of verbal swordplay," Bingley explained. Turning to Elizabeth, he asked, "How long will you be in Lambton?"

"Not long. We leave tomorrow."

"So soon?" Mr. Bingley appeared disappointed. "I hoped we might speak of Hertfordshire. It has been a very long time since I had the pleasure of seeing you. And you have yet to share whether all your sisters remain at Longbourn." Something of real regret laced Bingley's tone, and before Elizabeth could reply, he added, "It is above eight months. We have not met since the 26th of November, when we were all dancing together at Netherfield."

It pleased Elizabeth to discover the gentleman's memory so exact. There was not much in Bingley's remarks, but there was a look and a manner, which gave them meaning.

"I fear there is little I may do. I am at the disposal of Mr. and Mrs. Gardiner." Elizabeth would love to know more of Mr. Bingley's feelings for Jane, but she could not face Mr. Darcy again: She unjustly abused Darcy in Kent.

Miss Darcy offered, "Why do you not join us for

supper at Pemberley? I am certain my brother would welcome your presence at his table."

The meal that Elizabeth earlier prayed not to attend with her relations now proved her salvation.

"My aunt holds long-time acquaintances in the area. I fear we are previously engaged for the evening."

Discontent crossed Mr. Bingley's countenance.

"Perhaps I might call upon your party after supper. I would be pleased to have the acquaintance of your aunt and uncle."

Elizabeth quickly analyzed the possibility of Mr. Darcy accompanying his friend. With a houseful of guests, Pemberley's master would not give offense by leaving them to their own entertainments.

"If you like, Sir. Mr. and Mrs. Gardiner would know delight in accepting you. We stay at the Rose and Crown."

"Mr. Bingley," Miss Darcy interrupted. "Mrs. Annesley returned to the coach. My brother will be anxious as we are so far behind Mr. Hurst's coach."

Bingley nodded his agreement.

"Darcy will be thankful I took such tender care of his sister." He bowed to Elizabeth. "Until this evening then."

Elizabeth curtsied.

"Thank you for the acquaintance, Miss Darcy. Deliver my family's well wishes to your brother." With that, they were gone. Elizabeth watched as Mr. Bingley assisted Mr. Darcy's sister to his carriage.

From behind Elizabeth, the shopkeeper said, "They would make a handsome couple."

Elizabeth swallowed the tears welling her eyes.

All along, she thought that Miss Bingley spread untruths when the woman swore Bingley would choose Miss Darcy to wife. Her dearest Jane's heart would break with the news.

"Yes. Yes, they would," she murmured. Elizabeth wished she could despise Mr. Bingley for considering an alliance to the Darcy family. Yet, if she could forgive Mr. Wickham's desertion of herself for Miss King's ten thousand pounds, how could she criticize Mr. Bingley's looking upon Miss Darcy's thirty thousand pounds with favor?

❧

"I thought to send out men," Darcy remarked as he assisted Mrs. Annesley and Georgiana to the ground.

"Mrs. Annesley needed to call upon the apothecary," Georgiana explained, "and then Mr. Bingley spotted an acquaintance in Lambton."

Darcy's heart stuttered, and he schooled his countenance.

"Miss Bingley spoke of no encounters," he said through tight lips.

Bingley stepped down from the coach.

"I doubt if either Caroline or Louisa saw much of Lambton," his friend grumbled. "As usual, Hurst ordered his driver to exercise speed over safety."

"Thank you for tending to Georgiana's sensibilities, Bingley." Darcy did not like the idea of the Hursts putting Lambton residents in danger. He would speak privately to the man. Darcy held a responsibility to the villages, which depended upon Pemberley for their survival.

Bingley shook off Darcy's gratitude.

"Your sister and Mrs. Annesley are excellent traveling companions. Did Mr. Sheffield arrive safely?"

"My valet and coach knew no difficulties," Darcy noted. "Now, why do you not speak of your fortuitous encounter upon Lambton's streets?"

Bingley glanced to the house.

"Caroline will not be pleased with my news, but perhaps you will be." Darcy knew what would come next. He hoped Elizabeth Bennt would be gone from Lambton before anyone discovered her presence and his connection to her. "Miss Elizabeth Bennet and her aunt and uncle are on holiday. After supper, I mean to call upon their party. The Gardiners will leave tomorrow."

"I extended an invitation for Miss Elizabeth and her relations to join us for supper, but the lady's aunt held previous plans," Georgiana added.

Darcy thought, *Very convenient.*

"I will be sorry to miss them. Now come along. I have a special gift for my favorite sister."

Georgiana wrapped her hands about Darcy's arm.

"As I am your *only* sister, what may I expect?" she said with a girlish giggle.

Darcy smiled down upon her. His sister survived the lies of a scheming scoundrel, and he was thankful to see new life in Georgiana's eyes.

"No hints," he teased. "This is to be a surprise."

Although she dreaded seeing Mr. Darcy again, Elizabeth knew disappointment when Mr. Bingley arrived without his friend. She quickly made the introductions to permit her aunt and uncle their say. Instinctively, Elizabeth knew her relations would not conceal their disapproval of Mr. Bingley's treatment of Jane.

"Do you plan to return to Netherfield soon, Mr. Bingley?" her uncle asked in what sounded of casual conversation, but Elizabeth recognized Uncle Gardiner leading Bingley into admitting what her relations wished to know: Had Mr. Bingley deserted Jane? "It seems a foolish waste of money to let an estate and never use it."

Elizabeth watched as Mr. Bingley squirmed in his seat, and she stifled the giggle springing to her lips.

"I hoped to do so. I found the company most agreeable," Bingley responded.

"We were of the understanding you had no intention of returning to Hertfordshire," Aunt Margaret observed.

Mr. Bingley glanced to Elizabeth, but she pretended ignorance of her aunt's assertion. She knew Jane's despondency after Mr. Bingley's withdrawal would not set well with the Gardiners.

"I assure you, Mrs. Gardiner, no such decision has been made."

"Really?" Her aunt's eyebrow rose in challenge. "Then your sister must have erred for when our dear Jane called upon Miss Bingley in London, she led Miss Bennet to believe you would not be returning to Netherfield."

"Miss Bennet was in London?" Mr. Bingley stammered.

Aunt Gardiner smiled knowingly.

"Yes, for some three months. Lizzy encouraged Miss Bennet to call upon your sister, but it was weeks before Miss Bingley returned the call, and then she stayed but the necessary quarter hour. I suppose calling in Cheapside made Miss Bingley uncomfortable."

Mr. Bingley turned to Elizabeth for affirmation.

"Caroline provided Miss Bennet a direct cut?" he demanded.

"I am afraid so, Sir," Elizabeth whispered. "I was sorry to play a part in bringing censure to my dearest sister. As you must be aware, your leaving Netherfield so soon after the ball took the entire neighborhood by surprise." Although she knew Mr. Darcy played a role in Miss Bingley's ploy to separate her brother from Jane, Elizabeth thought it best for Mr. Bingley's relationship with Mr. Darcy that Darcy disclosed his participation in the deception, rather than she.

"I had business in Town," he murmured.

Elizabeth watched Bingley closely as Bingley recalled the events.

"I knew surprise when Caroline and Darcy followed me. I planned to celebrate Christmastide at Netherfield."

Aunt Gardiner acted innocent, but Elizabeth knew her aunt a master manipulator. Aunt Margaret was one of the few who could dissuade Mrs. Bennet when Elizabeth's mother claimed a case of nerves.

"It is a shame you did not return, Mr. Bingley. We could have held a longer acquaintance for we spent our Christmastide at Longbourn. Yet, it is neither here nor there, we are acquainted now, and that is what is important. Is it not, Lizzy?"

Elizabeth swallowed her bemusement. Mr. Bingley's shoulders relaxed, and Elizabeth knew he erred.

"Certainly, Aunt Gardiner."

"Certainly, indeed. For now we shall have the opportunity to wish Mr. Bingley happy," her aunt proclaimed.

Mr. Bingley's confusion returned.

"Wish me happy?"

Elizabeth prayed Mr. Bingley was more astute in his business dealings than he was socially. No wonder the man's sister so easily influenced him.

"Yes." Aunt Margaret controlled the conversation. Elizabeth noted the look of pride in her uncle's eyes: Uncle Gardiner enjoyed his wife's display of aplomb. "You and Miss Darcy. Only today Elizabeth remarked on how you traveled together, and Miss Bingley told Jane in a note of parting of the match being desired by both families. Naturally, we thought you chose Miss Darcy to wife."

Mr. Bingley turned red, but not from embarrassment. His features announced that Bingley put all the blocks in order and now knew the truth. Whether the news brought about an end to Jane's misery, only time would tell. Despite finding him an amiable man, Elizabeth held little confidence in Mr. Bingley's taking control of his sister's vituperations.

"Although I think highly of Miss Darcy, there is no understanding between us. She has yet to know her first Season, and as the niece of an earl, as well as having family who can trace their roots to the thirteenth century, Miss Darcy can look far above my station in

Society."

Elizabeth's aunt patted the back of Mr. Bingley's hand.

"I am sorry to hear it. Elizabeth says you would make a handsome couple." Her aunt left the topic behind and turned Mr. Bingley over to her husband, who spoke eloquently upon several of his recent investments, but Mr. Bingley's expression said the man's thoughts remained divided.

"Ah, Charles, you returned at last," Miss Bingley called upon her brother's presence in Darcy's drawing room. "Please tell me your conversation with Eliza Bennet was worth your spending time from dearest Georgiana and your family."

When Bingley ignored his sister to pour himself a stiff drink, downing it and pouring a second, Darcy motioned Georgiana from the room. From the expression upon his friend's face, Bingley learned the truth of Miss Bingley's perfidy.

"Charles!" Caroline did not heed Darcy's silent warning. "What is amiss?"

"Absolutely nothing!" Bingley declared in cold tones. "Except I acted the role of fool."

Caroline spoke in a dismissive manner.

"If speaking to Miss Eliza…"

Bingley stormed in his sister's direction, effectively cutting off her protestation.

"The lady's name is Miss Elizabeth; you will speak to and of her with respect, or I swear I will tie up your dowry until you are too old to claim a husband."

"What did I do to deserve such censure?"

Caroline wailed. She fished a handkerchief from her sleeve to dab at her still dry eyes.

"Destroyed my chances at happiness," Bingley growled.

Caroline added a bit of a hiccup to her speech.

"What lies has Miss Eliza...Elizabeth spoken of me?"

Darcy did not wish to place a wedge of distrust between him and Bingley, but it was time for the truth.

"I suspect your brother holds knowledge of our keeping him from Miss Bennet."

"*Et tu, Brute?*" Bingley glared at Darcy.

"Yes, I schemed with Miss Bingley to deceive you. I should never have interfered in your affairs. My actions can only be termed absurd and impertinent, but I was not long in Hertfordshire before I saw, in common with others that you preferred Miss Bennet to any other young woman in the country; but it was not till the evening of the dance at Netherfield that I held any apprehension of your developing a serious attachment."

Bingley's expression said Darcy's explanation held little interest, but Darcy needed to free his conscience, so he continued.

"As your friend, I often observed you in love. At the ball, Sir William Lucas spoke of the general expectation among your neighbors of an expected engagement. From that moment, I studied your interactions with Miss Bennet. Your partiality for Miss Bennet was beyond what I ever noted in your behavior previously.

"I also watched your lady. Her manners and

look were open, cheerful, and engaging, but I detected nothing to define her regard. I came to the conclusion Miss Bennet would receive your attentions with pleasure, but she was lacking in sentiment. However, I erred. In Kent, Miss Elizabeth spoke of her sister's extreme shyness rather than her indifference. Miss Elizabeth swears her sister's attachment has not abated, and if you choose to act I hold no doubt of your happiness together." Darcy held Bingley's gaze with his steady one. "I will not ask for your forgiveness for I do not deserve it."

Darcy shot a glance to Caroline.

"I am obliged to confess one thing more. I knew Miss Bennet was in London for some three months last winter, and I purposely plotted with your sister to conceal it from you. With that damning information, I will leave you to your family conference." Darcy stood slowly. "If you should choose to end our relationship, although I will be sorry for the loss, I will understand." He despised the pain he brought to Bingley's door, and Darcy was glad to be done with the lies. He despised deception of any kind: His pride and his honor demanded he not repeat his actions.

Chapter 3

ELIZABETH KNEW A GOOD deal of disappointment in not finding a letter from Jane on their first arrival at Lambton; and this disappointment continued on each of the mornings thereafter; but on the third, her repining knew fulfillment by the receipt of two letters from Jane at once, one marked as "missent" elsewhere.

"Jane wrote the direction remarkably ill." Elizabeth examined the lost letter.

Her aunt and uncle planned to walk out just as the letters arrived.

"You enjoy your letters, Lizzy," Aunt Margaret declared. "We shan't be long."

Elizabeth thanked her aunt and uncle for their kindness. Once her relations made their exit, Elizabeth sat down beside the small table in the let sitting room to enjoy Jane's letters. She chose to read the missent one first. It was written five days prior. The beginning contained an account of all their little parties and engagements, with such news as the country afforded; but the latter half, which was dated a day later, and written in evident agitation, gave more important intelligence.

Since writing the above, dearest Lizzy, something occurred of a most unexpected and serious nature; but I fear alarming you–be assured that we are all well. What I must relate has to do with poor Lydia. An express came from Colonel Forster at twelve last night, just as we all claimed our beds. It informed us that Lydia went off to Scotland with one the colonel's officers– to own the truth, with Wickham! Imagine our surprise. To Kitty, however, it does not seem so wholly unexpected. I am very, very sorry. So imprudent a match on both sides! Even so, I am willing to hope the best, and that we misunderstood Mr. Wickham's character. Thoughtless and indiscreet I can easily believe him, but this step (and let us rejoice over it) marks nothing bad at heart. His choice is disinterested at least, for he must know my father can give Lydia nothing. Our poor mother is sadly grieved. My father bears it better. How thankful am I that we never let them know what was said against Mr. Wickham; we must forget it ourselves. He and Lydia were off Saturday night about twelve, as is conjectured, but were not missed till yesterday morning at eight. The express was sent off directly. My dear Lizzy, they must have passed within ten miles of us. Colonel Forster gives us reason to expect him here soon. Lydia left a few lines for Mrs. F., informing her of their intentions. I must conclude, for I cannot be long from my poor mother. I am afraid you will not be able to make it out, for I hardly know what I wrote.

Without allowing herself time for consideration and scarcely knowing what she felt, Elizabeth, on finishing the first letter, seized the other, and opening it with the utmost impatience, noted that it was written a day later than the conclusion of the first.

By this time, my dearest sister, you received my hurried letter; I wish this may be more intelligible, but though not confined for time, my head is so bewildered that I cannot answer for being coherent. Dearest Lizzy, I hardly know what I would write, but I have bad news for you, and it cannot be delayed. Imprudent as a marriage between Mr. Wickham and our poor Lydia would be, we are now anxious to be assured it took place, for there is but too much reason to fear they did not go to Scotland. Colonel Forster came yesterday, having left Brighton the day before, not many hours after the express. Though Lydia's short letter to Mrs. F. gave them to understand that she and Mr. Wickham were going to Gretna Green, Denny led the colonel to believe that W. never intended to go there or to marry Lydia at all. Colonel F. took the news as an alarm and set off from B. intending to trace their route. He did trace them to Clapham, but no farther, for on entering that place they removed into a hackney coach and dismissed the chaise that brought them from Epsom. All that is known after this is they were seen to continue the London road. I know not what to think. After making every possible enquiry on that side of London, Colonel F. came on into Hertfordshire, anxiously renewing them at the turnpikes and at the inns in Barnet and Hatfield, but without any success. No such people were seen to pass through. With the kindest concern the colonel came on to Longbourn and broke his apprehensions to us in a manner most creditable to his heart. I am sincerely grieved for him and Mrs. F., but no one can throw any blame on them. Our distress, my dear Lizzy, is very great. My father and mother believe the worst, but I cannot think so ill of Mr. Wickham. Many circumstances might make it more eligible for them to marry privately in Town than to pursue their first plan; and even if "he" could form such a design against a young woman of Lydia's connections, which is not likely, can I suppose her so lost to everything? Impossible. I grieve to find, however, that Colonel F. is not disposed to depend upon their marriage;

he shook his head when I expressed my hopes and said he feared W. was not a man to be trusted. My poor mother is really ill and keeps to her room. Could she exert herself, it would be better, but this is not to be expected; and as to father, I never in my life saw him so affected. Poor Kitty knows father's anger for having concealed the attachment between Lydia and Wickham, but as it was a matter of confidence, one cannot but wonder. I am truly glad, dearest Lizzy, you were spared something of these distressing scenes, but now, as the first shock is over, shall I own that I long for your return? I am not so selfish, however, as to press for it, if inconvenient. Adieu.

I take up my pen again to do what I just told you I would not, but circumstances are such that I cannot help earnestly begging you all to come here as soon as possible. I know my dear uncle and aunt so well I am not afraid of requesting it, though I have still something more to ask of the former. My father is going to London with Colonel Foster to try to discover Lydia. What he means to do, I am certain I know not, but his excessive distress will not allow him to pursue any measure in the best and safest manner. Unfortunately, Colonel Forster is obliged to be at Brighton again tomorrow evening. In such an exigence, my uncle's advice and assistance would be every thing in the world; he will immediately

comprehend what I must feel, and I rely upon
his goodness.

Elizabeth rushed to the cord to beckon her uncle's servant. Within minutes the man appeared.

"Please summon your master's return to the inn. It is a matter of urgency."

With the servant's exit, Elizabeth sank heavily in a chair.

"Ah, Lydia," she groaned. "How could you be so foolish? You subjected your family to ostracism."

Unable to wallow in her despair, Elizabeth was up and packing her things when her aunt and uncle returned.

"What is amiss?" Her aunt took the day gown from Elizabeth's trembling fingers. "What brought you such distress?"

Elizabeth gave herself up to the tears she denied earlier. Snuggling into her aunt's comforting embrace she gestured to the table where Jane's letters rested. Hiding her face in her aunt's shoulder, Elizabeth did not see her uncle take the offending missives into his grasp, but she knew when Uncle Gardiner came to the part announcing Lydia's folly.

"I will kill the dastard with my bare hands," he growled.

"We will go to London?" Elizabeth managed to ask. "My father has no means to understand Town rules of engagement."

Her uncle looked up from where he continued to read.

"A coach is too slow. I will let a horse. You and

Margaret may follow in the carriage. Mr. Bennet will have the good sense to call in at Gracechurch Street." He squeezed Elizabeth's shoulder. "All will be well. I will see to it." He handed the letters to his wife. "Assist me by packing a small bag. I must see to a mount."

"Should we not?" Elizabeth began but her aunt shook her head in warning.

Within a half hour, her uncle kissed his wife farewell, as well as placing a promise kiss on Elizabeth's forehead.

"I suppose we should finish packing our things. We could still cover part of the distance to London today," her Aunt Margaret said with lackluster.

Elizabeth watched, as the figure of her uncle grew smaller with this leaving.

"How will any of us find Lydia? None of us know anything of Mr. Wickham's friends or his haunts." Her words brought the glimmer of an idea as Elizabeth paused to permit the possibility root.

"Are you well?" her aunt asked in concern.

"Yes." A smile of satisfaction tugged at Elizabeth's lips. She turned to join her aunt, and with each step, her resolve grew equally as strong. "I may know a source who would assist us."

⁓⊙⁓

"Elizabeth, neither your uncle or your father would approve of your involving another," her aunt whispered as the door opened to reveal a familiar countenance.

"Miss Elizabeth Bennet and Mrs. Gardiner to speak to Mr. Darcy," Elizabeth announced to the stone-faced butler.

"Was the master expecting you, Miss?"

"No," she said baldly. "Just tell Mr. Darcy we are here. If he chooses to send us away, I will understand."

The butler opened the door wider, and Elizabeth stepped into the grand hall of *his* estate for a second time.

"Wait here, Miss."

When the servant walked away, her aunt whispered, "This is a mistake."

Elizabeth had not completely thought through how she would explain everything to Mr. Darcy, but she knew in her heart he was her family's only hope.

She looked up when she heard Mr. Bingley's voice.

"Miss Elizabeth? What is amiss?" The gentleman rushed down the steps to greet her. "You appear quite pale."

Elizabeth grimaced. Mr. Bingley was one facet of the equation she had not considered in her plan.

"I...I..." she stammered.

Before Elizabeth could form a response, as if from thin air, Mr. Darcy appeared upon the landing.

"Miss Elizabeth and her aunt are here at my request, Bingley. Perhaps you would be so kind to escort them to my study."

Mr. Bingley nodded curtly, but Elizabeth heard the strain in Mr. Darcy's voice.

"Perhaps this is not the best time," Elizabeth offered. "Mrs. Gardiner and I can wait for a more opportune time."

Bingley glared at Darcy.

"Do not permit my presence from keeping you

from your business with Mr. Darcy," Bingley said through tight lips.

Elizabeth shot a glance to her aunt, who nodded her head in silent agreement.

"You should hear what I must say to Mr. Darcy. Please join us."

Mr. Darcy's expression flared with annoyance, but he quickly recaptured his mask of indifference. Turning on his heels, he strode off to the left. Bingley extended his arm in Mrs. Gardiner's direction, and Elizabeth followed her aunt and the man her eldest sister loved. The room spoke of masculinity: dark mahogany floor, covered by a Turkish rug, a bank of windows with drapes the color of blood, an ebony desk, free of clutter, as well as books lining the shelves. Elizabeth's heart sighed with the thought of Mr. Darcy spending time in the room.

Mr. Darcy stood before the desk, appearing as formidable as ever. A scowl marked his lips, but a familiar look of what Elizabeth now interpreted as fondness rested upon her. She would give anything to turn back the clock, but once Mr. Darcy learned of Lydia's elopement, any regard he held for her would dissipate.

Once Bingley comfortably seated her and her aunt, Elizabeth spoke.

"Thank you for agreeing to speak with us, Mr. Darcy."

"Mr. Nathan indicated you appeared agitated. How may I be of assistance?" His words were clipped and laced with apprehension. Judging from his expression, Mr. Darcy was not happy to see her again.

Elizabeth cleared her throat. Her eyes fixed wide upon his features.

"I hoped you might tell us where Mr. Wickham could be found. I...I mean *we* must discover him quickly."

The expression of pain, which crossed Mr. Darcy's features, ripped at Elizabeth's heart. Even without his saying so, it was obvious Mr. Darcy made a logical jump: He thought Mr. Wickham seduced her. Although it grieved Elizabeth to realize Mr. Darcy thought so little of her, for once she permitted the gentleman his misconstruction. She would tolerate Mr. Darcy's disdain if it would bring her family closer to discovering something of Mr. Wickham.

"The Bennet family must learn of Mr. Wickham's whereabouts in a timely manner," her aunt began an explanation, but Elizabeth interrupted.

"Mr. Darcy understands our need, Aunt." She stared at him numbly. A dozen different emotions coursed through her, from outrage to bewilderment.

Mr. Darcy returned to his seat behind his desk.

"What makes you believe I hold knowledge of Mr. Wickham, Miss Elizabeth?" His expression turned as black as his tone.

"You know more of Mr. Wickham's habits than anyone." A painful tightness filled Elizabeth's chest.

"I thought him in Brighton."

Elizabeth kept the floor.

"He left some days prior without Colonel Forster's permission. The colonel traced Mr. Wickham to Clapham, but no farther. There, Mr. Wickham took a coach toward London. My father traveled to London;

this morning my uncle left Lambton to join Mr. Bennet. My aunt and I will follow in the coach. I thought you could provide me direction where they might search."

Mr. Darcy spoke in bitterness.

"Was this the purpose of your call upon Pemberley two days prior?"

"Mr. Darcy," her aunt declared, "I will have you speak to my niece in a civil tone."

"It is fine, Aunt. Mr. Darcy and I understand each other."

"We do, Miss Elizabeth." He picked up his pen to sharpen it. "Now, if you will excuse me, I have estate affairs to which to attend."

Bingley sprang to his feet.

"You call yourself a gentleman! I am ashamed to have called you friend. I should have realized you would take the high road and declare it benevolence."

Mr. Darcy placed the pen upon the well's lip.

"What would you have me do, Bingley? This is not my affair!"

Bingley leaned across Mr. Darcy's desk.

"Not two hours prior you asked me to name a task which would earn my forgiveness. It is named, Sir. If your finding Mr. Wickham to save the Bennets more heartache, then you will do so or never cross my path again."

Elizabeth knew she should tell both men that it was Lydia's shame, not hers, they defended, but she wished to know whether Mr. Darcy's disgust or his regard was the strongest.

Long moments where only the sound of both men taking the other's measure passed. Finally, Mr.

Darcy instructed Bingley.

"I suggest you call at Longbourn. I am certain Miss Bennet would welcome your sensibility."

"And what of Elizabeth?" Aunt Margaret demanded.

"If I find Mr. Wickham, it would be best if Miss Elizabeth were close at hand. I will escort the two of you to London."

"You have guests," Elizabeth objected. "Simply provide me the direction, and my uncle will see to the rest."

Mr. Darcy smiled without humor.

"Mr. Bingley sent his sisters on to Hursts' estate, and Mrs. Annesley is with Georgiana."

"I will order my carriage," Bingley declared as he started for the door.

"If Mrs. Gardiner will accept my presence in her husband's coach, I will travel with the ladies."

Aunt Margaret appeared disassembled, but she agreed.

"Elizabeth and I will wait below, Mr. Darcy."

"You should have told Mr. Darcy the truth," her aunt chastised. "Mr. Bennet will be most displeased that the gentleman holds you in contempt."

Elizabeth frowned. Her emotions were beyond her control at the moment, and the thought of spending two days in a coach with Mr. Darcy had her trembling in dread.

"Mr. Darcy never approved of me or my family." Boldly, Elizabeth claimed, "I care not for the man's opinions; all that is important is discovering Mr.

Wickham. At least, we may save Jane's connection to Mr. Bingley." Elizabeth's heart cried out in complete despair.

"And what of you, Lizzy? Are there no prospects you would accept?"

Elizabeth's gaze returned to where she last saw Mr. Darcy.

"No, Aunt. But there is the dream of someone."

"You sent for me, William?" Darcy looked up to find Georgiana framed by the open door. He worked hard to keep his expression calm.

"I wanted you to know I must return to London for a few days. I shan't be longer than necessary."

Georgiana took a tentative step in his direction. Her expression spoke of worry.

"Has this something to do with whatever upset Mr. Bingley last evening?"

Darcy wrapped his shaving brush and soap in a clean cloth.

"No. Mr. Bingley's dudgeon was my fault. I interfered in his life, and I should have kept my own counsel."

"Is that the reason Miss Bingley and the Hursts departed so quickly? When you sent me from the room I thought they learned the story of Mr. Wickham and found me in contempt. Did not Miss Elizabeth know Mr. Wickham is Hertfordshire? I overheard you saying something to that effect to Fitzwilliam." Her bottom lip trembled, but his sister stood tall: Another example of how Georgiana met her worst nightmare and emerged on the other side.

Darcy caught her to him. Gently he stroked Georgiana's back.

"No, my dearest. I sent you from the room to salvage a bit of honor. I knew I must apologize for wronging Bingley, and I did not wish to humble myself before you."

Georgiana's fingers caressed his cheek.

"Was what you did truly horrid?"

"Unforgivable," Darcy confessed. "That is the reason for my quick withdrawal to London. As part of my penitence to Bingley, he asked that I aid Miss Elizabeth with a family problem. The lady and her aunt wait for me below."

Georgiana looked up at him with such admiration that Darcy's pride ached.

"I would imagine you would act in the lady's behalf, even without Mr. Bingley's insistence."

"Would I?" Darcy released his sister to return to his packing. The idea he would deliver Elizabeth Bennet into George Wickham's arms ripped Darcy's heart into rough pieces. He was not certain he could act so bravely.

"Certainly, you would," his sister declared. "You are the best of men."

"The best of men never question their decisions," Darcy corrected, "and I cannot freely give myself up to this task."

"Mr. Bingley," Elizabeth cornered the gentleman while he waited for his carriage to be brought around. "I have something to confess to you."

He caught her hand with a tender caress.

"There is no need for you to explain to me. I would never think poorly of you."

Elizabeth blushed, and she lowered her voice.

"It is not I who has known Mr. Wickham."

Bingley's frown lines deepened.

"But you said..."

"I did not correct Mr. Darcy's assumption," she insisted.

Bingley shook his head in disbelief.

"No, I suppose you did not. Then why would you permit Darcy to think otherwise?"

"I do require Mr. Darcy's assistance, and I thought it would be easier if he thought he acted for my benefit. In truth, it is Lydia who ran off with Mr. Wickham. Mr. Darcy cares little for my family, but in hindsight, I find the gentleman always acted kindly toward me. Even so, what you must understand is if we cannot make Mr. Wickham marry Lydia, your return to Longbourn will be for naught. Jane will not accept a renewal of your attentions if she thinks doing so will ruin your family name. My sister understands the need for the Bingleys to move within the tiers of Society."

Elizabeth's declaration appeared to bring a serious notion to Mr. Bingley's features.

"Then I suppose it is best that you lead Darcy on a successful hunt for I plan to offer your eldest sister my hand, and I would prefer not to be denied."

Elizabeth's eyes twinkled with delight.

"But what of my omissions in seeking Mr. Darcy's assistance?"

Bingley shot a quick glance to Pemberley House.

"I would say Darcy deserves a taste of

interference in his most exacting plans. Play on, Miss Elizabeth, play on."

Once they settled in Mr. Gardiner's coach, Darcy asked, "Does Mr. Wickham know you are on holiday?"

Realizing she opened a bee's nest with her deceit, Elizabeth took her time in formulating a response. She would present Mr. Darcy with the truth, just not the complete truth. It would be necessary for her to maintain the pretense until her family found news of Mr. Wickham. *No more than a week*, she thought.

"As my youngest sister is a guest of Colonel Forster's wife, I would assume so. Why is that significant?"

Mr. Darcy stared out the window.

"I am praying Mr. Wickham did not follow you to Derbyshire. I would be displeased to learn he made an unexpected call upon Pemberley."

Elizabeth understood the gentleman's sentiments: Mr. Darcy left Georgiana unattended in order to assist a "fallen" woman.

"When Lydia traveled to Brighton with Mrs. Forster, my family and I were engaged to take a northern tour to the Lakes. Unfortunately, uncle's business kept us from so long a journey. We were obliged to forsake our journey to the Lakes for a more contracted tour. Despite what you may think, my uncle's desire to view Pemberley had more to do with your estate's reputation for fine fishing than it was to look upon another well-dressed sitting room. We saw our fair share of great estates on this journey."

Before Mr. Darcy could respond to Elizabeth's

challenge, her aunt interrupted. She realized belatedly her tone spoke of Elizabeth's rising ire.

"Do you believe Jane will be well with my children underfoot? Mrs. Bennet must be suffering from the shock of this situation," Aunt Margaret fretted.

"Jane will delight in having an excuse to leave Mrs. Bennet to Kitty and Mary," Elizabeth assured.

"When we reach London, I shall set a second course to Hertfordshire," her aunt declared.

"By then, Mr. Bingley will be at Netherfield," Elizabeth reasoned. "And perhaps, by then, uncle or papa will know success."

"Why has not Miss Lydia returned to Longbourn?" Mr. Darcy asked suspiciously.

"As you are well aware, Mr. Darcy, my youngest sister is not known for her sensibilities or her discretion when it comes to gossip."

Chapter 4

SHE ANSWERED HIS QUESTIONS, but something was missing from Elizabeth Bennet's responses: the fire–the innate bravery to face the unknown. Certainly it was possible her "condition" obliterated Elizabeth's resolve, but Darcy could not imagine it to be so. His eyes studied her form as Elizabeth slept in the seat across from him. He left her at Rosings after Easter, a little over four months prior. Enough time for Mr. Wickham to practice a seduction and her to find herself with child, but Darcy could not fathom Miss Elizabeth's succumbing to Mr. Wickham's pretty words of flattery. She would listen, but not fall into a compromising situation. Such was not in the lady's nature.

Moreover, Elizabeth's form was very much as it always was: small waist, slim legs and arms, full, round bosoms, but not engorged in preparation for a child. To know for certain she was increasing, Miss Elizabeth must be at least three months along. *But she remained in*

Kent for several weeks after my departure, Darcy reasoned. *Still long enough for her to become with child. Yet...*

Darcy shook his head to clear his thinking. Attempting to discern any signs of Mr. Wickham's print upon Elizabeth Bennet's body would drive him to Bedlam. For too many nights, Darcy dreamed of her beneath him and the idea of Elizabeth giving herself to another set his teeth grinding. Instead, he concentrated on the possibility of her succumbing to Mr. Wickham's questionable charms, and again he did not believe Miss Elizabeth possessed such pronounced insensibility.

Certainly, the lady took him to task for his supposed treatment of Mr. Wickham, but Darcy always thought she would be just as passionate regarding the injustice if Darcy kicked a stray dog or treated his tenants poorly. Miss Elizabeth often expressed opinions not truly her own. Although the woman preferred Mr. Wickham's practiced niceties to Darcy's stammering attempts at flirtation, Elizabeth Bennet possessed too much intelligence to accept a marriage without love. She refused a perfectly acceptable marriage with Mr. Collins and with him. *Surely she cannot love believe Mr. Wickham holds her with deep regard. He proved time and time again he seeks only enough funds to line his empty pockets. So why would Miss Elizabeth accept Mr. Wickham's professions of love. Furthermore, my former friend customarily directs his practiced pleasantries to naïve innocents, such as my sister.*

"Such as my sister." Darcy rolled the phrase over in his mind. "My fifteen year old sister." Darcy's eyes returned to the sleeping countenance of the woman he loved. *As I would do anything in my power to protect Georgiana so would Miss Elizabeth act to protect her family.*

The woman would accept rumors of ruination to permit her sisters an opportunity to know happiness. Darcy smiled for the first time since hearing Elizabeth's plea for him to assist her in finding Mr. Wickham. *If the lady wishes to locate the scoundrel, so be it. I am anxious to prove my theory viable. Yet, if she thinks our relationship is at an end, Miss Elizabeth erred. What exists between us is not finished until I say it is.*

∞∞

"Miss Elizabeth." Darcy waited for her in the upper storey of the inn in which they sought shelter for the evening. Having a late start from Derbyshire, the day passed quickly, but during their journey, Darcy came to several conclusions regarding Elizabeth Bennet: The most important of which was the complete impossibility of her having known George Wickham intimately. "May I have a moment of your time?"

She diverted her eyes, an action Darcy expected, but still found vexing. In the coach, he knew Elizabeth studied him, as he did her. With slitted eyes, he observed her looks of longing and of regret: The lady was not as immune to him as she once was.

"Can this not wait, Mr. Darcy? My aunt is below and desiring my company." Elizabeth's words were meant to chastise, but Darcy recognized the hint of desperation, which colored her speech throughout the day.

"Mrs. Gardiner is comfortably settled in the private parlor below. I tended to your aunt personally," Darcy assured.

With a deep sigh of the inevitable, Elizabeth squared her shoulders.

"You are most kind, Mr. Darcy. I apologize for my impertinence."

Darcy shortened the distance between them.

"It is I who should apologize, Miss Elizabeth. I once again permitted my pride to choose my path. My disdain for Mr. Wickham colored my initial response. You are blameless."

A grimace crossed her lips, and Darcy noted the expression of guilt that momentarily claimed Miss Elizabeth's features.

"A woman is capable of making choices, Mr. Darcy. She does not require a man to tutor her."

Darcy kept the smile from his lips.

"I believe you capable of many things, Miss Elizabeth, but even you would require lessons in intimacies." Darcy edged closer and dropped his voice to a raspy whisper. "In such matters, you are an innocent." He permitted his breath to caress her cheek.

A streak of red rushed up Elizabeth's neck, and Darcy knew the warmth of her body's closeness.

"We should not speak so familiarly, Mr. Darcy. It is unseemly."

Darcy ignored her protest. He planned to disassemble Elizabeth's resolve.

"I mean no offense, Miss Elizabeth." His lips brushed her hair, and her color deepened. "I confessed my feelings previously."

"Mr. Darcy," she murmured. "I must insist you..."

"Insist I what, Miss Elizabeth?'

With a great effort she took a step back.

"Your apology...is accepted, Mr. Darcy,"

Elizabeth stammered. "I realize my news was disconcerting. You must know I would not plead for your assistance if I possessed another alternative."

Darcy swallowed the desire present only seconds prior.

"But another choice exists," he said in sincerity.

Elizabeth's features crunched up in confusion.

"Even if I would choose to go off to Scotland or America, my actions would not change the fact my father means to confront Mr. Wickham. If Mr. Bennet loses his life to Wickham, Mr. Collins would drive my mother and sisters from Longbourn. They would know poverty and no future."

At least, Elizabeth thought through the ramifications of what Mr. Wickham's selfish perfidy would do to her family.

"Exactly. Such is why I offer another solution."

"Another?" Elizabeth asked in suspicion.

"Marry me," Darcy said in triumph.

His words had Elizabeth staggering backwards again.

"I cannot marry you, Mr. Darcy."

"Why ever not?" Darcy argued for Elizabeth's hand and attempted to ignore the deceit he practiced upon her. "My prospects are far better than Mr. Wickham's. You viewed my estate: You will want for nothing."

"Nothing except a contended husband," Elizabeth countered. "You did not consider your future. You would be giving Mr. Wickham's child your name. What if it were a boy? Pemberley would pass to..."

Darcy pretended shock.

"Needless to say, I cannot permit that to transpire." Darcy looked off as if searching for a solution. Finally, he asked, "What if I am unsuccessful in locating Mr. Wickham in time?"

"Then the Bennet name will know a black mark forever. A mark you will never experience upon the Darcy name."

"Thank God, Papa is safe." Elizabeth sank upon the settle in her aunt's drawing room.

Her uncle lounged in a high backed chair.

"Margaret insisted upon traveling on to Longbourn, and I previously convinced Mr. Bennet to leave this matter in my hands."

They arrived in Cheapside shortly after one, and Aunt Gardiner hustled Elizabeth's father into Mr. Bennet's waiting carriage. She meant to have her children in her embrace. All the talk of children rattled a long denied feminine urge in Elizabeth, and she encouraged her aunt to present an affectionate hug in Elizabeth's name upon her own mother.

"Now, explain to me this nonsense Margaret mentioned in haste. How could you permit Mr. Darcy to think you the one who succumbed to a scoundrel such as Mr. Wickham?"

"It was not my intention to mislead Mr. Darcy," Elizabeth began. She blew out a sigh of exasperation. "When I visited with Charlotte Collins in Kent, Mr. Darcy attended his aunt at Rosings Park. Our paths crossed often. In one of our conversations, I accused Mr. Darcy of abusing Mr. Wickham. In his defense, Mr. Darcy shared a privacy with me—one where Mr.

Wickham attempted to seduce another young innocent for her dowry."

"Mr. Darcy spoke of such depravity with you? My respect for the man sinks lower with each tale," her uncle declared.

"Please do not think ill of him, Uncle," Elizabeth rushed to say. "I wish I could describe my relationship with Mr. Darcy." She chuckled ironically. "We are both so stubborn, but as foolish as it may sound Mr. Darcy has become a dear friend. One with whom I often disagree," she added quickly. "But one who speaks the truth, even when it is unpleasant to hear. My initial trust in Mr. Wickham's goodness placed my family in a tenuous situation. I knew the length of his schemes, and I chose not to speak of it with my sisters and parents. I could have prevented this disaster."

"I would say the fault lies with your youngest sister," Uncle Gardiner insisted. He studied her features for a few elongated seconds. "Was the victim of Mr. Wickham's previous deception someone we know?"

Elizabeth gave a faint grimace.

"No one I could name without breaking confidences. Suffice it to say, as a result of their close relationship throughout their time at Pemberley and university, Mr. Darcy knew something of Mr. Wickham's less than savory past. He was able to bring an end to Mr. Wickham's plans."

"And you think Mr. Darcy can create magic again?"

"I think Mr. Darcy will serve as well in recovering Lydia. Needless to say, my youngest sister has no fine dowry to tempt Mr. Wickham to marry her.

I suspect Wickham required a quick exit from Brighton so the gentleman's creditors could not find him. Papa said Colonel Forster reported debts in Brighton and Meryton."

"And Lydia had a few coins Mrs. Bennet gave her before she left for Brighton." Her uncle quickly came to the same conclusion as Elizabeth.

"Yes. Mama always found coins for Lydia's whims, often at the detriment of her other daughters."

Elizabeth's bald declaration did not seem to surprise her uncle, who knew well his youngest sister's insensibility.

"Have you considered what will become of your *relationship* with Mr. Darcy when he discovers it is Lydia we seek."

Elizabeth closed her eyes to the pain of finality.

"At Netherfield, Mr. Darcy spoke of his temper being too little yielding for the convenience of the world and how he could not forget the follies and vices of others. The gentleman once his good opinion once lost to be lost forever. I hold no doubt Mr. Darcy will look upon me with disgust if I should ever hold his acquaintance again."

"Miss Elizabeth." Darcy bowed to her. "I apologize for the interruption. I asked the servant if I might speak to Mr. Gardiner or Mr. Bennet."

Elizabeth waved off his apology.

"I gave the instructions to see you through. My father escorted Aunt Gardiner to Longbourn, and my uncle is from home. He received a lead on Mr. Wickham. Uncle Edward seeks the truth behind the information."

Darcy considered Elizabeth's explanation before saying, "I see. In that cause, I will not keep you." He bowed to take his leave.

Elizabeth's expression held her astonishment.

"Do you have some news you wish me to convey to my uncle, Mr. Darcy?"

"No." Darcy experienced the customary flare of pleasure coursing through his body when he looked upon Elizabeth Bennet. Would he ever know this woman as his? "I intended to speak to your father." He shifted his weight to appear more casual than he felt. "I am surprised Mr. Bennet returned to Hertfordshire."

"You mean the fact my father does not plan to defend my honor surprises you." Elizabeth's tone spoke of a challenge, but she diverted her eyes from Darcy's gaze. "Papa has not the knowledge of London, as does my uncle, and we decided among us that if reputations cannot be saved, it would prove foolish for Mr. Bennet to sacrifice Longbourn. My mother and sisters depend upon him." Although Darcy knew Elizabeth's reasons logical, he could not think upon Mr. Bennet's actions with any degree of equanimity. A gentleman should never leave such business to others, especially not to his daughter. "Moreover," Elizabeth said with an attempt at a tease, "I have you and Uncle Gardiner."

"Yes," Darcy said quietly. "You have me…" He hesitated before adding, "and Mr. Gardiner."

Her eyes sparkled as if she found the notion most pleasing. Even so, Elizabeth kept a stiff smile upon her lips.

"I shall ask again: Do you possess information you would share with my uncle?"

Darcy heaved a weary sigh.

"I asked Colonel Fitzwilliam to speak to members of Mr. Wickham's militia regiment to determine if they can shed light on Mr. Wickham's activities."

Elizabeth's hazel eyes flashed with what appeared to be annoyance.

"I pray Colonel Fitzwilliam does not know the reason for your inquiries."

As if a moth to a flame, Darcy edged closer to her.

"I would never betray your confidences. You must know that. I told my cousin news of Mr. Wickham's creditors came to my attention, and I simply wished to make certain my former friend did not mean to bring more shame to Pemberley's door."

Tears misted Elizabeth's eyes, and her reaction warmed Darcy's heart.

"I do know your honor, Mr. Darcy." A hint of chagrin slid over Elizabeth's features. "It is nearly ten of the clock. I would imagine you busied yourself with this task since early on."

Darcy chuckled at her accurate evaluation.

"I began shortly after we separated yesterday afternoon."

"And you have only the news of Colonel Fitzwilliam's involvement to report?"

A gentleman could spend a lifetime learning the many facets of Elizabeth's expressive countenance. Darcy shrugged the inevitable.

"In truth, I thought to ask your uncle to accompany me on a journey across town. I went through my correspondence to find the directions for

Georgiana's previous companion. If you recall from my letter, Mrs. Younge was the one who manipulated my sister into accepting Mr. Wickham's attentions. The woman now owns a boarding house. I hoped Mrs. Younge knew something of Wickham's whereabouts in London."

Elizabeth rose upon hearing his explanation.

"Then I shall retrieve my bonnet and cloak."

Darcy's gaze narrowed.

"When did I say you would be traveling with me? My destination is not an area of London for genteel ladies."

A spark of annoyance flared in Elizabeth's eyes.

"First, I am not easily intimidated, Mr. Darcy, so do not speak to me of what you deem proper for my sensibilities."

"I am well aware of your determination, Ma'am," he said in amused contrition. Darcy found himself decidedly vexed by her stubbornness; yet, at the same time, he thought her decided manner remarkably admirable. "That particular fact does not change my opinion of your involvement in this venture."

"You have not considered all the ramifications, Sir," she reasoned passionately. "What if Mr. Wickham took residence at Mrs. Younge's establishment?" Elizabeth reasoned. "Because of your history, Wickham will refuse to speak to you, or he will leave Town before my uncle can press him into acting responsibly."

Darcy's eyebrow lifted in dismay. He did not know whether to be offended by Elizabeth's insinuation that Darcy might lose control of his emotions or to know a renewal of his estimation of Elizabeth Bennet as the most remarkable woman of his acquaintance. She would truly make him complete if Darcy could finally claim her loyalty.

"I assure you, Miss Elizabeth, I am quite capable of dealing with Mr. Wickham in your behalf. I do not believe Mr. Wickham will be at Mrs. Younge's house: He would never be so obvious."

Without further argument, Elizabeth started for the door.

"Your logic holds no sway with me, Mr. Darcy. I will leave Uncle a note as to our purpose."

"And what if I depart before you return, Miss Elizabeth?" Darcy challenged.

Elizabeth turned to smile at him in rueful humor, and Darcy found her tenacity beguiling.

"Then I shall follow you in a let hack," Mr. Darcy."

Darcy held no doubt Elizabeth would try.

"I have not shared Mrs. Younge's directions with you."

For a brief second, Elizabeth's confidence faded, but a squaring of her shoulders announced her determination knew no retreat.

"I will be only a moment, Sir."

With that, she disappeared into the bowels of the Gardiners' house. Darcy looked after her. Elizabeth Bennet's willingness to risk everything to protect her family reinforced his belief she was his perfect mate.

"Absolutely bewitching," Darcy murmured, "and I hold no desire to break the lady's spell."

Darcy nestled Elizabeth closer to his side as they

approached the run-down boarding house. They left his coach a block removed to avoid Mrs. Younge's spying a finer carriage in the area and sending up an alarm. As they approached, Darcy spoke softly for Elizabeth's ears only.

"Mrs. Younge will not be pleased of my appearance on her doorstep. I must warn you I will negotiate hard with the woman. You must not beg her for the information we seek for Mrs. Younge will operate to take advantage of your desperation."

"You wish me to be docile?" Elizabeth asked archly.

Darcy smiled down at her upturned countenance.

"You are to assume Miss Bennet's personality for the next hour."

Elizabeth rolled her eyes heavenward.

"Why did I not consider how manipulative you are? You will go to great extremes to have your way."

"I am all innocence, Miss Elizabeth," Darcy teased.

"We shall see, Mr. Darcy," she countered, as Elizabeth wrapped both hands about Darcy's elbow just as a maid opened the boarding house door a crack to peer out at them.

"Yes, Sir?" The girl's gaze slid across the cut of Darcy's jacket.

"Mr. Darcy to speak to Mrs. Younge," he said in his best Master of Pemberley voice.

"Be Mrs. Younge expectin' ye, Sir?"

Darcy placed a hand against the door and shoved his way past the girl. Even so, he kept Elizabeth close. Conveniently, Elizabeth responded to his lightest touch.

"Tell your mistress I mean a word with her."

The girl bobbed a quick curtsy and scurried away without showing them into a small parlor on the right.

With an amused shrug, Darcy gestured Elizabeth to lead the way into the room. They barely had time to take up a position of expectance before the empty hearth before Mrs. Younge entered the room. She looked very much as she had the last time Darcy saw the lady, except the quality of Mrs. Younge's clothing possessed less fashion.

"I thought Betsie lost her reason," she pronounced, "for surely Mr. Fitzwilliam Darcy could have no business with the likes of me."

"Again, you erred, Madam," Darcy said coldly.

The woman frowned, but her eyes still held the shrewdness Darcy once missed in his evaluation of her fitness as a companion for Georgiana. He would not make that mistake again.

"I see you have not lost any of your charm, Mr. Darcy." Mrs. Younge sat on a nearby chair without indicating they should sit also. "Speak your business, Sir. I have duties to perform."

Darcy ignored the woman's lack of manners, and instead, seated Elizabeth on a threadbare settle before joining Elizabeth there. He knew the tender care he displayed upon Elizabeth would not go unnoticed by Mrs. Younge. Thankfully, when Darcy captured Elizabeth's hand in his, she relinquished it willingly.

Unable to wait him out, Mrs. Younge asked, "Will you do me the favor of an introduction, Mr.

Darcy?"

Darcy realized the woman's curiosity would show itself.

"My wife," Darcy said simply. He felt Elizabeth's fingers wrapping around his, and he enjoyed how Elizabeth unconsciously responded to his declaration.

Mrs. Younge waited, but when Darcy did not conduct the introductions, she said, "I see. I did not know you married, Sir."

Elizabeth gave Darcy's fingers a quick squeeze to announce she would respond to the woman's query and for Darcy to trust her. Needless to say, Darcy long ago permitted Elizabeth Bennet his confidence. He returned Elizabeth's silent gesture.

"Our joining is a short duration," Elizabeth announced with the aplomb of a great actress.

"And as we do not move in the same circles, you would possess no knowledge of my private affairs, Madam," Darcy quipped. He meant to establish his authority over his former employee.

Darcy watched as Mrs. Younge's chin rose in defiance.

"Your business, Mr. Darcy. Speak quickly and then leave my house."

Darcy flicked an invisible piece of lint from his sleeve.

"I thought you would know my task before you stepped into this room: I seek the whereabouts of Mr. Wickham."

"Why would I hold knowledge of Mr. Wickham's activities?" Mrs. Younge asked in indignation.

"Because my former associate has few friends he

can continue to rely. I imagine both Mr. Wickham and I count you among Wickham's close associates."

"Then you will know regret, Mr. Darcy," Mrs. Younge denied in firm tones. "I hold no knowledge of Mr. Wickham's location."

A dark brow rose, and Darcy looked down his nose at the woman.

"Perhaps not, but you possess the means of learning Mr. Wickham's direction."

"And why would I aid you?" Mrs. Younge asked tautly. "You and I did not part upon the best of terms."

Darcy glanced about the dingy room.

"It is quite evident you require funds, Madam."

"Tell me why you seek Wickham," the woman demanded, but there was a hint of a crack in her armor resting in Mrs. Younge's tone.

Darcy stood and assisted Elizabeth to her feet.

"My business with Mr. Wickham is exactly that: *My* business." Darcy placed Elizabeth's hand upon his arm. "Come, my dear. We must provide Mrs. Younge private time to consider her options." To his adversary, he said, "I will call again on the morrow."

"No!" Mrs. Younge said with a start. "That is too soon. Nine of the clock on the second day," she bargained.

"I will not be pleased if you fail me," Darcy whispered in harsh warning, as he paused to tower over the woman. "And you know my nature when I am not pleased."

Chapter 5

"DO YOU BELIEVE MRS. YOUNGE will locate Mr. Wickham?" Elizabeth's uncle asked as he poured Darcy a brandy. Darcy returned Elizabeth to the Gardiners' home to encounter her uncle's anxious impatience.

It amused Darcy to observe Elizabeth drop her eyes and chin in response to Mr. Gardiner's chastisement.

"Lizzy, Edward Street is not a proper destination for a genteel bred lady," Gardiner said in a stern voice. Darcy wondered how often Elizabeth felt remorse at her impetuosity: He was quite certain she was a precocious child. "At least you had the good sense to take a maid with you."

Elizabeth shot a quick glance in Darcy's direction.

"I cannot claim such foresight," she admitted. "It was Mr. Darcy who commanded Gwenie to accompany us."

With Elizabeth's apology, her uncle excused

his niece before ushering Darcy into his study, but Darcy admitted, if only to himself, he missed Elizabeth Bennet's company. Although he knew her somewhere in the house, it was not enough: Now that they renewed their association, Darcy wished her within reach.

When they returned to the safety of his carriage, and he instructed Murray to place the Gardiner maid beside his coachman, Elizabeth hummed with excitement.

"You were brilliant!" she declared in enthusiastic tones. "I am greatly grieved I ever criticized your manners, Mr. Darcy. I was proud to know you would act to protect my…" Elizabeth quickly realized she came close to saying "my sister." In correction, she said, "To protect my reputation."

Darcy pretended not to notice Elizabeth's blunder.

"You approve of my inflexibility?" he teased.

Elizabeth studied him before choosing her response.

"I can acknowledge an appreciation for a bit of pompous glory upon extreme occasions, Sir, but I prefer the Mr. Darcy I see before me at this moment."

Darcy wished he held the right to catch her to him and kiss her senseless, but he would wait until this madness with Wickham came to an end, and then he would propose again and pray this time Elizabeth Bennet would agree.

"Mr. Darcy?" Her uncle's voice brought Darcy from his musings. "Is there reason to believe Mrs. Younge will lead us on a merry chase?"

Darcy shook his head in denial.

"The woman and Mr. Wickham are cut from the same cloth. Neither holds an allegiance to anything beyond the coins clutched within his palm. I made a few private inquiries regarding Mrs. Younge before I called upon your household this morning. The woman has four boarders, none of whom fit a description of Mr. Wickham; however, I received a report of a gentleman possessing Mr. Wickham's countenance calling upon Mrs. Younge three days prior."

Gardiner's eyebrow rose in admiration.

"My niece made a wise choice in seeking your assistance, Sir."

A smile tugged at Darcy's lips.

"Despite her propensity for obstinacy, I never knew Miss Elizabeth to act without logic."

"I see." Mr. Gardiner studied Darcy for several elongated moments, and Darcy had the feeling the man took his measure. "I should tell you that, I too, received information of Mr. Wickham. One of my warehouse employees came to me recently via Mr. Bennet's recommendation. Before making the trek to London, Tobias Dungle served in the Meryton militia. Upon my return to London, I sought him out to learn if Mr. Wickham ever spoke of his time in London. As Dungle is not the type to gamble away his hard earned savings, he was not part of Wickham's inner circle, but he did hear Wickham speak of praying often at St. Clement's. Dungle thought that fact odd for he did not consider Wickham a religious man."

"Did you learn anything of Mr. Wickham in the parish?"

Gardiner shook his head in the negative.

"Nothing useful, but I spoke to the rector and several others at the church. I asked them to send word if a couple..." Gardiner paused in awkward embarrassment.

"I know you do not seek Mr. Wickham upon Miss Elizabeth's behalf," Darcy said in confidence.

Mr. Gardiner released an exasperated sigh of relief.

"I am glad to hear it: I am not one to perfect a lie, and it pleases me to realize you would assist our Lizzy even when she foolishly places her reputation upon the line. Tell me how long you have known the truth."

Darcy chuckled in irony.

"Once my pride permitted my reason to return, I accepted the fact Miss Elizabeth would never succumb to a scoundrel like Mr. Wickham–more likely, she would ring Wickham's bell for attempting a seduction. I suspect from my observations of your other nieces, either Miss Catherine or Miss Lydia accompanied Mr. Wickham to London."

"Lydia," Mr. Gardiner growled. "The foolish chit brought havoc to the Bennet household. What I do to right this wrong, I do for her sisters. If not for Jane and Elizabeth, I would allow Lydia to slip into oblivion. Mrs. Bennet permits her younger daughters too much latitude." Another pause brought a second evaluation of Darcy's personage. "May I inquire of your intentions toward our Elizabeth, Mr. Darcy? I cannot imagine a gentleman of your consequence interfering in a private matter without a personal inducement."

Darcy sipped his brandy before answering.

"Once Miss Elizabeth's duty to her family

is resolved, I mean to propose to your niece." Darcy paused before adding, "Again."

"Again?" Mr. Gardiner's surprise spoke of Elizabeth's keeping secret the truth of their relationship. "You offered your hand to Lizzy, Mr. Darcy?"

"Twice." Darcy regarded Mr. Gardiner with respect. "Of course, the second time was upon our recent journey to London. Making the spontaneous proposal was part of my ruse to prove Miss Elizabeth meant to protect her family at all cost. Needless to say, if she accepted, I would count myself blessed. Yet, as your niece assumes I believe Mr. Wickham ruined her, she had no choice but to refuse. Miss Elizabeth is well aware of my history with Mr. Wickham, and if she were truly subject to Wickham's so-called charms, the possibility of her carrying his child would prevent me from claiming her to wife. What Miss Elizabeth forgets is Mr. Wickham is the beloved godson of my late father; therefore, I will never be truly free of him. All I can do is to shield the Darcy name by placing distance between my family and Mr. Wickham."

"Yet, if we are successful in saving Lydia, it would make Mr. Wickham Elizabeth's brother in marriage," Gardiner cautioned.

Despite his best efforts, Darcy felt his features tightened. He weighed the negatives of having a connection to Mr. Wickham against the pleasure of having Elizabeth at his side: His love for Elizabeth Bennet easily won out. He reasoned that Wickham would always be a shadow in Darcy's life. Therefore, it would be bacon brained for him to deny himself a contented life.

"Do we not all possess relatives we never see or only encounter once every decade or so?"

Gardiner chuckled with satisfaction.

"I can think of a few of mine I would avoid if possible." Darcy thought immediately of Elizabeth's mother: He imagined Gardiner's sister brought the man more than one regret. "What of your first proposal, Mr. Darcy?"

"In Kent, I declared my regard for your niece, but Miss Elizabeth took me to task for my participation in separating Miss Bennet from Mr. Bingley, as well as the skewed history of our relationship, which Mr. Wickham provided her. In truth, her charges brought me to a better understanding of my nature, and I found her criticism apropos. I have since made pronounced changes in my dealings, including confessing my perfidy to Mr. Bingley. My friend returned to Netherfield and Miss Bennet."

Gardiner regarded Darcy with mild amusement.

"Then you will be pleased to know that Lizzy recently described you as the one person she most trusted."

A note from Mrs. Younge came late on the first day, and after Darcy confirmed the accuracy of the information, he dispatched a payment to the woman. He suspected Mrs. Younge did not want her particular friend to realize she betrayed him to Darcy. Keeping Darcy away from Edward Street would be to Mrs. Younge's advantage for she catered to those on the fringe of disrespectability. Her boarders would not want a light shone on their activities.

"Miss Elizabeth." The maid showed Darcy into the morning room when he called upon the Gardiner household.

She glanced up from her tea.

"Mr. Darcy." For a brief second Elizabeth presented him the most welcoming smile Darcy ever experienced, and his heart leapt with hope. "You are earlier than I expected, Sir." She gestured to a chair across from her. "Join me. Uncle called in at his warehouse, something about a late shipment. I fear you must be content with my company." Gardiner's servant poured Darcy a cup of tea. "The gentleman prefers milk, but no sugar," Elizabeth instructed, and he thought it ironic Miss Elizabeth took note of his preferences. "Did you hear from Mrs. Younge?'

Darcy shot a quick glance to Gardiner's waiting servants, and Elizabeth perceptively excused them. When they were alone, he explained, "Mrs. Younge supplied the directions to a tavern with let rooms above in St. Clement's parish."

"Then Tobias Dungle had the right of it."

"Yes, your uncle would likely have learned something of Mr. Wickham without my assistance," Darcy allowed.

Elizabeth ignored Darcy's graciousness.

"But not with such speed of purpose," she countered. "How may my family thank you?'

Darcy shook off her suggestion.

"There is no need." Across the breakfast table was not the setting he wished to renew his proposal. "I mean to call upon Mr. Wickham this morning. Your uncle gave me permission to negotiate in behalf of your family."

A shudder of what appeared to be dread shook Elizabeth's shoulders. *Would this be the moment she would admit her perfidy?*

"You will act with honor, will you not, Mr. Darcy? I could not bear it if you and Mr. Wickham came to blows."

Tears misted her eyes, and Darcy could not stifle the question rising to his lips.

"Do you fear for my well being or that of Mr. Wickham?"

A single tear escaped before Elizabeth wiped it away.

"It would grieve me if this matter brought either of you to harm." Her diplomacy gave Darcy no comfort. He wanted Elizabeth to claim affection for him.

Darcy stood to announce his departure.

"I mean to call upon Mr. Wickham. As you hold a vested interest in what transpires, I thought you should accompany me. I would not wish to come to an understanding of which you did not approve."

Elizabeth's eyebrow rose in challenge.

"You thought of my company without my harassing you into serving as my escort?"

"Allow me credit, Woman, for making the effort," Darcy teased.

Elizabeth placed her serviette upon the table.

"I am proud of your progress, Sir." Her easy taunt almost made Darcy forget Elizabeth must soon speak of her purposeful deception. That conversation would determine whether they would travel into the future, hand-in-hand, or separate forever.

He waited another twenty minutes for her return, but Darcy knew the minute Elizabeth appeared upon the Gardiners' staircase, she arrived at a decision. He wished he read Elizabeth better while they were still in Kent, but something changed since her appearance at Pemberley. He recalled his illustrious father speaking of the late Lady Anne Darcy and George Darcy's connection to his wife. It was a week after he and his father stood in a cold rain to watch Lady Anne laid to rest.

"Your mother," his father said wistfully, *"was the only one who ever could anticipate my response before I spoke the words. And likewise, I with her. Lady Anne and I were often of one mind."*

At twelve years of age, Darcy could not fathom of what his father spoke, but the way George Darcy spoke of his late wife made the silent exchange of ideas an intangible prize awarded only to a few. Was it possible he and Elizabeth Bennet would know such understanding?

"Gwenie, Mr. Darcy and I have a matter of import to discuss before we depart. We shall only be a few minutes," Elizabeth announced when Darcy rose to greet her.

"Yes, Miss."

Without a word to him, Elizabeth strode into the nearby sitting room. Darcy followed, closing the door behind him before moving to intercept Elizabeth. Therefore, when she turned from what was likely anxious pacing, she walked into his embrace.

"Mr. D..." she blustered, but Elizabeth permitted Darcy to wrap his arms about her. "This is not what I planned." She sighed in resignation before burying her nose in his cravat.

"I know," Darcy whispered into her hair. Catching the bonnet she carried, he tossed it upon a table. Darcy stroked Elizabeth's back and simply enjoyed the way she fit snuggly under his chin.

"It is best you tell me what brings you such distress." Darcy meant to lift her chin with his fingers, but Elizabeth shook off his tenderness.

"I cannot." Elizabeth's voice caught on a stifled sob. "It will ruin everything."

Darcy leaned closer, the heat and scent of her fueling his desire.

"What will be ruined?" he encouraged.

"This!" she insisted. Elizabeth clutched at his lapels, nestling closer to him. "You and I."

Darcy's smile held a bit of devilment.

"Is there a 'you and I,' Miss Elizabeth?"

Tears misted her eyes when Elizabeth glanced up at him, and her bottom lip trembled.

"Of course there is no you and I, and after I confess my perfidy there never will be."

"Would you like there to be a 'you and I'?" Darcy lifted his brows in challenge.

Realizing what she admitted, Elizabeth shoved free of Darcy's loose embrace.

"My wishes are of no concern of yours, Sir," Elizabeth huffed. With her knuckles, she dashed away the remaining tears. "Mr. Darcy, I thank you for your intervention in this matter. My family is deeply in your debt, but at this juncture, it is best if Uncle Gardiner and I handle negotiations with Mr. Wickham." Her chin rose in customary defiance.

"No." Darcy declared. "You will not send me packing again, Elizabeth Bennet. Not after your confession of only a few moments prior. We will settle this now."

"There is nothing to settle, Sir," Elizabeth snapped.

Darcy closed the distance between them.

"There is the matter of your sister's ruination," he hissed.

"You know?" A look of bewilderment crossed Elizabeth's features before indignation arrived. "Yet, you allowed me to exact a pretense. Did you think to claim pleasure at my expense?" She turned her back on him. "Just leave, Mr. Darcy." A treble of embarrassment marked her voice. "You know enough glee from my foolhardiness."

Darcy ignored her protestations; instead, he placed his hands upon her shoulders and edged her return to his arms.

"You of all people know I would never claim joy from your mortification." He caressed her shoulders when Elizabeth attempted to shrug off his touch. Darcy bent to speak to her ear. "I admit to permitting my worst fears to claim my tongue. I meant to lash out at you for the thought of you–of the most magnificent woman of my acquaintance–choosing the man I abhor above all others drove me to Bedlam." He nuzzled Elizabeth's cheek. "Yet, by the time I settled into your uncle's carriage, my heart knew your tale impossible. You are too clever to succumb to the likes of Mr. Wickham."

"To whom should I succumb?" Elizabeth asked on a hiccup. Beneath his fingertips, he felt her anger fall away. Darcy wrapped his arms about her to line her back with his front. "You deserve a man who would cherish you above all others–one who would cater to your whims–one who values your intelligence as much as he does your beauty–one who wants you as his life partner and not simply the mother of a required heir. My revered father would often catalog things he loved about my mother. The way Lady Anne would straighten his collar before they entered a room full of guests. The odd manner in which she held a pair of scissors. The elegant style in which she snipped flowers for a bouquet. That is the type of man you deserve."

A shudder of regret shook Elizabeth frame.

"Your portrait is enticing, Mr. Darcy, but it is as futile as my attempt at deception. Lydia's flight from Brighton colors the future of all her sisters. The most I can hope is we save part of her reputation, but I ask myself why would any man choose a foolish wife with only a share of her mother's portion as dowry? Even if Mr. Wickham performs his duty to Lydia, a stain will follow the family."

"And you believe I cannot overlook this stain?"

"When I consider," Elizabeth lamented, "that I might have prevented this madness? I, who knew what he was. Had I but explained some part of what I learned to my family–had Mr. Wickham's character been known, this could not happen. But it is all, all too late now!" Her sobs intensified. "You opened my eyes to Mr. Wickham's real character, but I held my tongue.

Oh, had I known what I ought, what I dared to do! But I knew not–I was afraid of doing too much. Wretched, wretched mistake!"

"This business is not your fault to claim. It was I who begged your silence. I should have made Mr. Wickham's true nature known to those he meant to deceive."

"The truth cannot be denied: We both agree Mr. Wickham would not marry a girl whose lack of a substantial dowry would make it impossible for him to better his situation. How Lydia could ever attached him is incomprehensible." Darcy had his opinions, but he kept silent. "Although it grieves me to say so, for such an attachment as this Lydia might suffer charms. I do not suppose Lydia deliberately engaged in an elopement without the intention of marriage, but I hold no delusions that either my sister's virtue or her understanding would preserve her from falling an easy prey. Wishes are vain, and I possess no hopes of the connection you and I have claimed to remain after this matter knows a conclusion." Elizabeth sighed in acceptance of her words. "Gwenie has waited long enough for our return. Let us see the end to this farce. I am anxious for Mr. and Mrs. Bennet to know relief."

Darcy held different ideas, but Elizabeth was too upset to accept reason. Now that Elizabeth admitted she considered becoming his wife, Darcy was not inclined to permit her to walk away from his life.

"Then let us be about it," Darcy declared as he placed Elizabeth's hand upon his arm. He meant to grow old with Elizabeth Bennet by his side, and damn any obstacle placed in his way.

Chapter 6

"YOU ARE TO REMAIN CLOSE," Darcy whispered as he escorted Elizabeth into a bustling inner city tavern. Their appearance brought a hush to a busy room.

The beefy-built innkeeper hustled forward.

"Yes, Sir." The man attempted a bow, but his girth kept him off balance.

"The lady wishes to speak to her sister. I believe she is in the company of a dark-haired gentleman of a comparable height and build to mine." Darcy slipped a coin into the man's hand.

"Mr. Wiseman," the innkeeper confirmed. "Be there something amiss, Sir?"

Darcy shook off the suggestion. He did not want the innkeeper to drive Wickham from the inn and to force another search.

"The lady has news of a personal nature for Mrs. Wiseman. We will not remain long, and I promise no trouble will come your way. Now, would you kindly provide me Mr. Wiseman's directions?" A second coin earned the man's cooperation.

"Upstairs. Third door upon the right."

"Is there an empty room the ladies might use for their conversation?" One more coin produced a spare room key.

"Last room on the right." The innkeeper nodded his gratitude.

Darcy did likewise before directing Elizabeth's steps across the room to the stairs. He glanced back to make certain Gwenie followed. He knew from the stiffness in Elizabeth's form the degradation in which Lydia Bennet sank ripped at Elizabeth's sense of justice.

"I have you," Darcy whispered as they mounted the stairs. "Trust me. Mr. Wickham is a scoundrel, but he would never permit another to harm your sister."

Elizabeth nodded her understanding, but she walked as in a trance. When they reached the upper storey, Darcy halted her steps.

"Tell me you will not have a fit of the vapors." He bent to speak to her pale features.

As Darcy hoped, his words of challenge did the trick.

"I am not Mrs. Bennet," Elizabeth declared testily.

Darcy permitted himself a bit of a smile.

"Certainly not. You are the incomparable Elizabeth Bennet." He traced a gloved finger down Elizabeth's cheek to capture her chin in the palm of his hand. Lifting her chin where he might look upon Elizabeth's countenance, Darcy asked, "Are you prepared to encounter your sister? It is likely you will not approve of what goes on here."

"Yes. Yes, I am composed," Elizabeth assured.

"Then take this key. Last room on your right. I will send your sister to you."

Darcy waited outside of Wickham's door until Elizabeth entered the room. He noted her shudder of disgust, and as foolish as it sounded, her reaction only confirmed her as the one woman who would best complement his existence: Elizabeth Bennet would go to any lengths to defend their family. He knew no other woman who would even enter the premises.

Before approaching Wickham, Darcy placed Gwenie in the hall between Wickham's room and the one Elizabeth entered.

"If you hear anything unusual or someone attempts to enter Miss Elizabeth's room other than her sister Miss Lydia, you are to set up a caterwaul no one in these parts has ever heard before."

The maid sniggered.

"Yes, Sir."

With a deep sigh of satisfaction, Darcy rapped on Mr. Wickham's door. Within seconds, the door swung wide to reveal a half dressed Wickham.

"Darcy? What brings you to this fine establishment?" His former friend appeared surprised to see him. Evidently, Mrs. Younge did not warn Wickham of Darcy's inquiries. He worried that Mrs. Younge might tell Wickham of Darcy's claim of a bride–one Wickham would recognize from Mrs. Younge's description. Although Darcy enjoyed the idea of Elizabeth playing the role of wife, he did not want Wickham to thwart Elizabeth's efforts to save her family name.

"We have business," Darcy replied in cold tones. Over Wickham's shoulder Darcy spotted a disheveled Lydia Bennet. The fact the girl showed no shame at being caught in an intimate setting proved the power of Mr. Wickham's "charms." Darcy knew immediately Elizabeth's hopes of whisking Lydia away to the safety of her uncle's household would prove futile; therefore, it would be Darcy's task to force Wickham to marry the girl. With that purpose in mind, he said, "Tell Miss Lydia to don a wrapper and then go to the last room on the right. Miss Elizabeth awaits her there."

"Did you think to take up residence with Mr. Bennet's second daughter?" Wickham smirked. "I can attest to..."

Whatever Mr. Wickham meant to speak against Lydia Bennet's character was cut short as Darcy pinned his former friend to the back of the door, a forearm across Wickham's throat.

"You will not speak unkindly of Miss Elizabeth or her sisters," Darcy hissed. Without looking to the girl who acted so foolishly in giving her honor to a cad, he ordered, "Miss Lydia, you will join your sister immediately."

"But..."

"Immediately," Darcy barked. He waited until the girl grabbed a wrapper and scurried from the room before he released Wickham. "Have a seat," Darcy commanded, shoving the scoundrel toward a chair.

Wickham rubbed his neck.

"No reason to act with violence." Wickham

straightened his shirt. "As I *fully* understand that this is not a pleasant reunion, what business do we have, Darcy? I thought you never wished to see me again."

Darcy attempted to control his anger, but Wickham long since learned how to incite Darcy's response.

"You understood correctly, but the Devil has a way of rearing his ugly head at the most inopportune times."

"Why you, Darcy? Is this because of Miss Elizabeth? I long suspected you favored the woman."

Darcy ignored the question. If Wickham recognized Darcy's regard for Elizabeth, it would cost the Bennets more to claim Wickham's cooperation.

"In truth, Mr. Bingley asked for my intervention. A letter arrived in Derbyshire from Miss Bennet with hopes that Bingley could aid her family. Before Bingley rushed to Hertfordshire, he begged my assistance. Your own words told all of Meryton we held a contemptuous relationship. Bingley means to make Miss Bennet his wife, and her younger sister's actions brought harm to the family's reputation."

"And how did you connect with Miss Elizabeth?" Wickham studied Darcy searching for the holes in Darcy's tale.

What his friend did not realize was since their youthful days when Wickham easily read Darcy's thoughts, Darcy learned the fine art of negotiation at his revered father's knee: He schooled his features before answering. As partial truths served him well to this point, Darcy improvised his response.

"Miss Elizabeth and I renewed our acquaintance

in Kent. Before we parted, she told me of often spending time with her aunt and uncle in Cheapside. After learning of Miss Lydia's flight to London, I assumed Mr. Bennet would call in at Gracechurch Street; therefore, I made the necessary contacts. I was not surprised Miss Elizabeth accompanied Mr. Bennet to London. This situation caused Mrs. Bennet much anguish and affected the health of both of the Bennets. Miss Elizabeth feared seeing Miss Lydia brought low would harm the family patriarch, and so she convinced her father to permit her to reason with Miss Lydia first."

Wickham shrugged his shoulders in indifference.

"I hold no objections if Lydia wishes to return to Longbourn with her sister."

"Then you do not mean to act with honor?" Darcy forced his hands still: Other than personal satisfaction, it would prove pointless to beat Mr. Wickham senseless. The man possessed no scruples.

Wickham snarled a laugh.

"Why would I wish to marry Lydia? Even you would not wish me such a fate."

"You should have considered your options before you departed Brighton with the chit. The girl's family expects a marriage."

Wickham traced circles on a dusty table.

"I have expectations also, Darcy."

"Mr. Bennet is not a rich man, but he is willing to present you with the girl's share of her mother's portion."

Wickham did not look at him, which meant Wickham did not wish Darcy to note the scheming in his eyes.

"The girl's portion is not enough to cover my debts," Wickham responded matter-of-factly.

"That bad?" Darcy asked without sympathy.

"In Brighton and more in Meryton," Wickham admitted.

"I see. Your debts are the crux of the matter." Darcy calculated what it might cost to force Mr. Wickham to claim the parson's noose.

Wickham stretched out his legs before him.

"I require an heiress, so you are welcome to Lydia. She served her purpose."

"Which was to provide you a bit of coin to aid in your escape from your creditors," Darcy summarized.

Wickham continued to shrug his answers.

"What can I say? Desperation is necessity's mother."

"Taking the girl's coin did not necessitate ruining her."

"It was Lydia's idea for an adventure," Wickham offered in excuse.

Darcy sucked in a slow, steadying breath. "As no heiress is likely to come your way in this *fine* establishment and as you cannot be seen upon the streets of London's better addresses, I would suggest you consider other options. Surely accepting Mr. Bennet's generosity and claiming Miss Lydia to wife is preferable to debtors' prison. If your debts are as high as you indicated, you could be sentenced for each infraction–a very long term."

"Not if I choose to leave before the authorities discover me," Wickham asserted.

"I found you with little effort, and I am

certain the authorities will be quick to discover your whereabouts."

"And you would assist the magistrates?" Wickham charged.

"I will not protect you if you choose to run," Darcy said glibly.

"And if I choose to stay?" Wickham asked tentatively, but Darcy ignored the question. He wished his former friend to consider carefully his options.

Darcy glanced to the squalor in which Wickham dwelled. "Miss Elizabeth's uncle and I will call upon you tomorrow. Mr. Bennet asked Mr. Gardiner to act in his stead." He turned to go, but paused to say, "If desperation is truly a motive, consider my proposition. It is a viable solution."

Her sister's appearance shook Elizabeth to her core.

"Oh, Lydia!" Of its own accord, Elizabeth's hand came to her mouth. "Please tell me you did not greet Mr. Darcy dressed as such."

Lydia flounced past her to sit in a winged chair.

"How was I to know it was that stuffy Mr. Darcy at the door?" Her sister straightened her wrapper. "Filled his eyes though!" Lydia giggled foolishly. "You know what a curmudgeon he was in Meryton. Never smiled. Walked about like a constipated gentleman. And you have no idea what he did to poor Wickham. Mr. Darcy slammed Wickham against the door and ordered me from the room!"

Elizabeth prayed Mr. Darcy kept his temper under control. It would displease her immensely if Mr.

Darcy came to harm, and Elizabeth held no doubt Mr. Wickham would not fight with honor.

"What did Mr. Wickham say to Mr. Darcy to bring forth the gentleman's response?"

"What makes you think Wickham spoke from turn? We all knew Mr. Darcy to be a proud, disagreeable man." Lydia gestured wildly.

"What did Mr. Wickham say?" Elizabeth repeated.

With a flippant flick of her unstyled hair, Lydia said, "Something about you and Mr. Darcy taking up together." Lydia's gaze fell upon Elizabeth's features. "You do not have your sights set on the man, do you, Lizzy? He is rich, but…"

Elizabeth interrupted before her sister's accusations found a target.

"After your escapades, none of your sisters are likely to claim a decent marriage. How could you act so foolishly, Lydia?"

Her sister swung her legs over the chair arm.

"You are just jealous because Mr. Wickham found me more attractive than you."

"The man found you more naïve than other young ladies," Elizabeth asserted.

Lydia sprang to her feet.

"Mr. Wickham loves me."

"Has Mr. Wickham professed his regard?" Elizabeth charged. "Said he wishes to claim you to wife?"

"Not in so many words," Lydia admitted. She strolled to the window to glance out upon the noisy street. "But Wickham shows his affections in other ways."

"Did he ask you to marry him?" Elizabeth insisted. "You have set a date?"

Lydia did not turn to look at her, a fact Elizabeth knew to be more telling than her sister's words.

"We will marry when the time comes. There is no rush."

"There is a rush," Elizabeth said pointedly. "In addition to the very real possibility you could be with child, each day you remain unwed brings more doom to our father's door. Your mother and your sisters cannot go about in society because of the tarnish your actions brought to Longbourn's door. Mr. Bingley returned to Jane's side, but our eldest sister can claim no happiness because of you."

"Do not practice such drama," Lydia said with a nonchalant lift of her shoulders. "When Mr. Wickham and I marry all will be forgiven. You shall see. Society will pretend nothing of import occurred. I may be but newly sixteen, but I know more of the world than you."

Before Elizabeth could respond, Mr. Darcy tapped on the open door.

"Miss Elizabeth," he said in a strained tone. "If you are complete, we should depart."

She knew from his tight features Mr. Darcy's patience knew an end. Elizabeth glanced first to her sister and then to the man who held her heart. Her decision made, she accepted Mr. Darcy's proffered arm.

To her sister she said, "Convince Mr. Wickham to act honorably for the next time I come, I mean to bring Uncle with me. Mr. Gardiner will use every means possible to convince Mr. Wickham to speak his vows, including turning him over to debtors' prison if the gentleman refuses."

After returning the spare key to the innkeeper, they exited the building, followed closely by Gwenie. Elizabeth found she clutched Mr. Darcy's arm tighter. She looked up into his stone-faced expression.

"I am here," she said softly.

Evidently, her words penetrated Mr. Darcy's thoughts. The gentleman glanced down at her, and a smile slowly claimed the corners of his lips.

"I am blessed."

Mr. Darcy assisted Elizabeth to his waiting coach.

"Gwenie, Miss Elizabeth and I must hold a private conversation. If it would not be too much trouble, would you claim the seat above?"

Elizabeth noted the blush of embarrassment upon the girl's cheeks. She knew her Uncle Gardiner treated his servants well, but the notice of such a fine gentleman as Mr. Darcy had the maid's cheeks red.

"It be no trouble, Sir."

Being the perfect gentleman, Mr. Darcy assisted the maid to climb to the driver's seat before he joined Elizabeth in the carriage.

"Most kind of you, Mr. Darcy," Elizabeth teased.

Mr. Darcy tapped upon the coach roof to signal his driver.

"I have my moments, Miss Elizabeth."

Realizing they had only a short time to share what they learned from the imprudent couple, Elizabeth claimed the necessary conversation.

"Was it as bad as it appeared?"

Mr. Darcy sighed deeply.

"I would gladly pull Mr. Wickham's cork if he already married Miss Lydia, but I must wait until he speaks his vows before I run him through."

Elizabeth's lips twisted in amusement. She never thought of Mr. Darcy from control: It was an interesting possibility she would explore at her leisure.

"Certainly not. Before you make Lydia a widow, she should first become a wife."

Mr. Darcy's eyebrow rose in a test.

"Do not tempt me, Miss Elizabeth."

She chuckled.

"We have little time for challenges. Tell me what occurred with Mr. Wickham."

Darcy nodded his agreement.

"Mr. Wickham wished to know how I came to be involved in this situation."

"What was your response?"

He grinned.

"The truth."

"Which is?"

"Mr. Bingley asked for my assistance because Mr. Bennet knows little of Town."

"Very ingenious, Sir," Elizabeth said with a nod of pride. "What else?"

"It grieves me to say Mr. Wickham has no intention of marrying Miss Lydia. He is still insistent upon the need to eliminate his debts. That will be a major point of negotiation for Mr. Gardiner."

"I understand," Elizabeth assured. "Lydia is of the belief that Mr. Wickham means to marry her, but she says there is no urgency. I thought to demand her joining us, but I had the feeling Mr. Wickham would rejoice at Lydia's leave taking."

Mr. Darcy spoke bluntly. Despite the situation in which they found themselves, Elizabeth gloried in how the man treated her as an equal. That truth made it more bittersweet never to claim his affections.

"You have the right of it. If Miss Lydia leaves Wickham's side before a marriage is negotiated, Mr. Wickham will attempt to escape his debtors. Your sister will be left in ruin."

"Anything else?"

"I warned Mr. Wickham of the possibility of a long term in debtors' prison if he does not act with honor."

Elizabeth smiled knowingly.

"We are of a like mind, Sir. I said something similar to Lydia." Her comment appeared to please the gentleman. "I was thinking of how we might assure Lydia of a future. Could Mr. Wickham take up a position in the Regulars? Having a husband in the British Army would please Lydia, as well as Mrs. Bennet, and the position would provide them a steady income. I can think of no other occupation for which the man is suited"

Mr. Darcy appeared to mull over Elizabeth's suggestion.

"Resign his commission in the militia? You may have the right of it. Permit me to speak to Colonel Fitzwilliam regarding what may be available."

The carriage rolled to a halt before her uncle's house.

"Thank you, Mr. Darcy, for trusting me in this

matter." Elizabeth glanced to the busy street. "It is rare for a woman to be treated as an intelligent being." She knew from Mr. Darcy's expression he meant to profess his admiration again, but as the situation with Lydia held Elizabeth's hopes captive, she reached for the latch. Immediately, Mr. Darcy's footman set down the steps to assist Elizabeth from the carriage. Mr. Darcy followed her in the house.

The Gardiner children's appearance in the main hall surprised her. "You are back," Elizabeth called as they rushed to her side.

"You will play soldiers with us, Cousin Lizzy," said the eldest as the others surrounded her, bestowing hugs about her waist.

Elizabeth tousled the boy's hair.

"I have a guest at the moment, but when we are through, I will call in at the school room."

"Off with you," Aunt Gardiner ordered as she approached. "I need to speak to your cousin and Mr. Darcy."

As quickly as the children were from earshot, Elizabeth asked, "How are Mama and Papa and dearest Jane?"

Her aunt suggested. "Let us go into the sitting room." Once Mr. Darcy seated her Aunt Margaret, Mrs. Gardiner explained, "Your mother has not left her quarters, and Mr. Bennet remains in his study. I never knew your father so agitated. He asked you to return to Longbourn; he will send his carriage for you tomorrow. Jane requires your assistance; she cannot deal with both of your parents alone."

Elizabeth knew her aunt correct, but she did

not wish to leave Mr. Darcy behind. She might never possess another opportunity to spend time with him. Even if Mr. Wickham married Lydia, Mr. Darcy would be sore to claim Elizabeth to wife. How could Mr. Darcy accept Wickham as a brother?

"If you think it is best, Aunt."

"Then it is settled." Aunt Margaret turned to Mr. Darcy. "Would you care to join us for supper, Mr. Darcy. I am certain Mr. Gardiner will have questions regarding your outing today."

Mr. Darcy assumed his customary face of indifference, but Elizabeth learned to read the emotions behind the mask. He did not like the idea of her leaving any better than she did.

"I fear I have another engagement this evening, but I will come early tomorrow to bring Mr. Gardiner up to snuff. Please tell Mr. Gardiner I will require his company when I meet with Mr. Wickham. Our time is short if we are to convince Mr. Wickham to marry. I found him with ease and so may his creditors. If so, the authorities will whisk Wickham away before we can save the Bennet family's reputation."

Chapter 7

"MR. DARCY." MRS. GARDINER INTONED. "When you said 'early,' I did not expect you before we broke our fast."

"I was not certain what time Mr. Gardiner would call in at his warehouse," Darcy said in excuse. In truth, he called *early* because Darcy feared he might not have the opportunity to speak to Elizabeth before she departed for Hertfordshire. He met with Colonel Fitzwilliam last evening, explaining in detail his true purpose in seeking Mr. Wickham. Although his cousin disagreed with the extent Darcy chose to become involved in the matter, the colonel consented to assist Darcy.

"Then, by all means, come in." Mrs. Gardiner gestured toward the front sitting room, but the scent of lavender had Darcy turning to greet Elizabeth.

"I anticipated Mr. Darcy's unconventionality, Aunt. I shall entertain the gentleman while you finish with the children." The smile on Elizabeth's lips said she was waiting for him. It did Darcy's heart well to recognize Elizabeth's awareness of his choices.

"Not without a maid in attendance," her aunt warned. "One ruined reputation is enough."

Darcy's eyebrow rose in question, and Elizabeth chuckled.

"My aunt is well aware you are privy to my deception, Sir."

Mrs. Gardiner gave a satisfying nod before exiting. Elizabeth slipped her hands about his elbow, and Darcy tightened his arm muscles to bring her closer.

"I feared if I arrived later, I might miss you," he whispered.

"And you thought we had more to say to each other?"

Her cheeks reddened, and Elizabeth dropped her eyes.

"I did." Darcy directed her steps to the far side of the room when he noticed Gwenie hustling their way. They paused before windows, and Darcy turned where he might block Elizabeth from the maid's view. "First, please know Colonel Fitzwilliam searches for an appropriate opening in the Regulars." He smiled deviously. "My cousin's only concession was he meant to find a post as greatly removed from Derbyshire and Hertfordshire as possible."

Elizabeth's lips twisted up in amusement.

"Although Mrs. Bennet will find it vexing to have Lydia so far removed, please convey my appreciation to the colonel for his sensibility."

"I assume you relayed our conversations with the wayward couple to your uncle."

Elizabeth smiled mockingly.

"Uncle will still possess a galley load of questions when you meet this morning. Mr. Gardiner is a stickler for details. I imagine you hold other characteristics in common."

"And you remain satisfied with my role in this matter?" He would like to explore her comments on his personality, but time was short, and Darcy meant to make the best of these stolen moments.

"You were our salvation," Elizabeth admitted.

Darcy caught Elizabeth's fingertips. If Gwenie did not stand behind him, he would bring Elizabeth's ungloved knuckles to his lips. Instead, he lowered his voice to speak to her only. Hazel eyes carefully studied his.

"Then you will explain to your father how your sentiments have undergone a change since we first met?"

"I shall praise your benevolence to Mr. Bennet," Elizabeth dryly observed. "Is there another reason for my words of praise?"

"Impudent baggage," Darcy growled. "You know very well you blacked my name to your dearest family." Her eyes leaped with startled amazement. "And so when I call upon your father, I would prefer Mr. Bennet not be predisposed to deny my plight."

"Mr. Darcy! You cannot!" Elizabeth protested.

Darcy's eyebrows snapped together in a scowl.

"And why not? Would you refuse me a third time?"

Elizabeth's chin notched higher in non-cooperation.

"Any woman would call herself blessed to claim your regard. You, Sir, are a man of honor and compassion, but I cannot permit you to bring Mr. Wickham into your family. It would be unconscionable of me to place my desire before your good name. Please do not sacrifice your principles for me."

He heard the approach of heavy footfalls. Darcy wished to argue with her, but he knew the time short.

"You have several weeks to change your mind. Just know, when this madness is finished, I plan to call upon Mr. Bennet at Longbourn. For a man known for his intelligence, I can be quite bacon brained when he comes to you."

Kissing her gloved hand in parting, with regret, Darcy placed Elizabeth in her father's coach. When Mr. Gardiner interrupted their conversation, Darcy joined her uncle in the breakfast room while Elizabeth oversaw her packing, and so they had no time for another private exchange before she bid her relations farewell.

"Until we meet again, Miss Elizabeth," Darcy said as he bowed over her hand.

"Adieu, Mr. Darcy. May God bless you." Then Elizabeth departed; even so, Darcy felt the satisfaction of having Elizabeth turn to look back at him before the carriage veered off toward the roads leading from London.

"Three weeks," Darcy told his foolish heart. "It will take a minimum of three weeks from the time I secure Mr. Wickham's agreement until I can call upon the lady again." The realization provided Darcy impetus to be done with the negotiations.

And so he settled into the task.

"I am not certain it is best for you to view the conditions in which your niece dwells," Darcy said in caution as he and Mr. Gardiner entered the tavern.

Elizabeth's uncle appeared taken aback.

"Do you think me incapable of controlling my temper, Sir?"

Darcy's appreciation for the man grew each day of their acquaintance.

"In truth, I would not mind your taking a whip to Mr. Wickham, but I was thinking of an observation from Miss Elizabeth. Your niece thought to force Miss Lydia to leave with us, but chose otherwise because of the likelihood of Mr. Wickham's welcoming his release from responsibility."

Gardiner nodded his understanding.

"Our Lizzy is most perceptive."

The man would find no argument from Darcy.

"Perhaps Mr. Wickham would speak more candidly if we ask him to join us in the common room."

Gardiner glanced about the room.

"Not much ambiance, but I will secure a private table while you promote Mr. Wickham's participation in this business."

Within minutes, Darcy returned with Wickham. Part of Darcy wished he had not included Gardiner in the conference for he feared Wickham would demand more than the Bennets could afford, and Darcy already decided he would pay Wickham to marry Miss Lydia.

"I believe you previously were given the

acquaintance of Mrs. Bennet's brother, Mr. Gardiner," Darcy said by way of introduction.

Gardiner gestured them to seats.

"I find the need for these negotiations beyond the pale," Elizabeth's uncle announced in what Darcy assumed was the man's "business" voice. He noticed Wickham flinched from the hardness in Gardiner's tone, and Darcy smiled inwardly. Gardiner would prove a worthy opponent for Mr. Wickham.

Darcy's former friend removed a soiled handkerchief to wipe his brow.

"I am sorry things have come to this," Wickham said in his most amicable voice. Although Wickham attempted to disguise his wariness behind a cough; again, Wickham grimaced. "I suppose we should be about it. Mr. Darcy, what do you have in mind?"

Darcy swallowed his mirth: Mr. Gardiner provided Wickham with no opportunity to voice his demands.

"In addition to Miss Lydia's portion, I assume you will require assistance *again* to clear your debts. If not, the authorities would continue to seek retribution. Do you possess an accounting of who holds your vows?"

Wickham shot a tentative glance to the scowling Gardiner.

"I could construct a list."

Another cough had Darcy questioning, "Are you unwell?"

"No. It is just London's foul air," Wickham assured.

"Then perhaps we should see you away from

Town," Darcy responded in skepticism. "We will require the list of those in Meryton and in Brighton to whom you owe money." Wickham nodded his agreement in reply. Darcy continued, "I also explored an opportunity in your behalf. There is a position in the Regulars available. You could resign your position with the militia and receive a comparable post in King George's service. The post would remove you from censure in the South, as well as to provide you with a steady source of income and appropriate living quarters."

He watched as Wickham weighed the information carefully.

"Who will purchase the commission?"

Darcy sent a knowingly glance to Mr. Gardiner, one asking for the man's cooperation. They would dicker over the expenses later.

"The commission will be part of Miss Lydia's settlement."

"What if I choose a different course?" Wickham ventured.

Stone faced, Gardiner warned in harsh tones, "I will pay someone to stick your spoon in the nearest wall, then send Lydia to Scotland until we know whether she is with child, and eventually purchase her a gentleman farmer as a husband. All of which would cost the Bennets far less than what Mr. Darcy just encouraged you to accept."

Wickham swallowed hard.

"Lydia has expensive tastes. We will require something to sustain us once my proposed service ends. I have no skills to earn my living." He glanced to

Darcy. "Perhaps the living at Kympton?"

"A living is a pledge for life,' Darcy reminded his former chum. "When you refused my father's gift to his godson, I presented the living to another. While you are in service to the King, you must cultivate other opportunities. You will be in contact with many minor sons. If you perform honorably in your role, others will recognize your worth, and rewards will follow."

Gardiner brought the first of the negotiations to an end.

"There is little else we can accomplish today. Mr. Darcy and I will call again tomorrow. Please finalize a list of your creditors before then. I would prefer to see the marriage settlements drawn up as quickly as possible." Gardiner stood to indicate their exit.

Darcy followed the man to his feet. He knew Wickham well enough to know the son of Pemberley's steward would press for a larger settlement, but Gardiner showed Wickham he would not act the fool. Claiming a large dowry for marrying Lydia Bennet was not in Mr. Wickham's future.

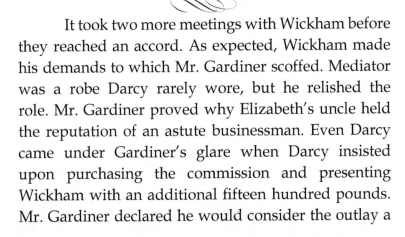

It took two more meetings with Wickham before they reached an accord. As expected, Wickham made his demands to which Mr. Gardiner scoffed. Mediator was a robe Darcy rarely wore, but he relished the role. Mr. Gardiner proved why Elizabeth's uncle held the reputation of an astute businessman. Even Darcy came under Gardiner's glare when Darcy insisted upon purchasing the commission and presenting Wickham with an additional fifteen hundred pounds. Mr. Gardiner declared he would consider the outlay a loan, but Darcy meant to claim the Gardiners as family. If his actions brought Elizabeth closer to accepting his proposal, then Darcy would count the expense more than worthwhile.

Finally, ten days after their arrival in London, Darcy set a course for Pemberley. In biding farewell to the Gardiners, he made the promise to return for the wedding. Despite Mr. Wickham's signature upon the settlement papers, Darcy still did not trust Wickham not to attempt an escape. The Gardiners brought Miss Lydia to reside with them until the marriage, while permitting Mr. Wickham to call upon his betrothed regularly. Darcy marveled at how well the Gardiners conducted themselves throughout this ordeal, and he was most grateful it was not necessary for him to contend with Mr. and Mrs. Bennet. Elizabeth's mother would advocate for Mr. Wickham to be presented a larger share, and Mr. Bennet would agree simply to reclaim his quiet study and his books.

"You are home at last," Georgiana called as she rushed down the stairs to greet him.

Darcy breathed easier. The first part of his plan knew success. Now, it was just a matter of time until he could call upon Elizabeth at Longbourn. He brushed a kiss across Georgiana's cheek.

"I must return to London at month's end, but I will explain all later. For the moment, I would welcome my bed. I slept little on this journey."

Georgiana wrapped her arm through his.

"Then most assuredly you should claim your chambers for you never complain." She walked with Darcy up the stairs to the family quarters. "We shall speak over supper. I am most anxious to know of your success."

Several hours later, Darcy entered the dining room to discover his sister waiting for him.

"Where is Mrs. Annesley? Pray say the lady is not ill."

Georgiana motioned the footman to serve the soup.

"Nothing of the kind. The lady's nephew welcomed a new son and tomorrow is the child's baptism. I permitted Mrs. Annesley to join her family for several days. You do recall that Vicar Annesley resides but thirty miles north?"

"Yes," Darcy said distractedly. "Now that you mention it, I do recall the lady prosing upon the young cleric's merits." He made himself smile at Georgiana. In truth, if he did not promise his sister that they would speak of his journey, Darcy would take a tray in his room and stay in bed. He doubted he slept more than four hours on any of the nights he was away from Pemberley. His initial turmoil over Elizabeth's insinuation of having known Mr. Wickham wreaked havoc with his composure, which was followed by the glory of a renewal of his hopes. "It was kind of you to consider Mrs. Annesley's happiness."

Georgiana blushed, and Darcy thought Georgiana and Elizabeth would make a delightful pair with their heads together in complementary mischief. It was a shame all Darcy's thoughts always came back to Elizabeth Bennet.

"My actions were nothing more than simple Christian goodwill." Georgiana sipped her soup course.

"Now, tell me of your days in London."

Following a sigh of resignation, Darcy motioned Murray and Lawson from the room.

"First, I believe you should learn what occurred between Mr. Bingley and me." He presented Georgiana a succinct account of his and Miss Bingley's actions to separate Bingley from Jane Bennet.

His sister appeared shocked, but Georgiana did not condemn him.

"Surely there was some circumstance, which spurred you to interfere with Mr. Bingley's life."

"I told myself I meant to protect Bingley, but in hindsight, I realize I meant to protect my tattered emotions."

Georgiana's features crunched up in confusion.

"I do not understand."

Darcy chuckled with irony.

"Neither did I for a long time. You will be surprised to learn I was as smitten as Bingley by a Bennet daughter." Darcy paused, but Georgiana looked upon him in complete disbelief. "Not Miss Bennet," he added, and his sister's features relaxed. "Miss Elizabeth. Yet, I termed the lady's connections far below what to expect as the next Mistress of Pemberley."

"But Lady Anne greatly outranked our father's status. True, papa was a wealthy gentleman, but as the daughter of an earl, our mother could claim a titled gentleman. Is not Miss Elizabeth a gentleman's daughter?"

"She is," Darcy admitted. "But at the time of our initial acquaintance I was too top-lofty to overlook Mrs. Bennet's connections to trade."

Georgiana clucked her tongue in disapproval; the gesture was one he heard their mother practice more often than the late Lady Anne would have ever claimed. Odd that his sister mimicked a woman she never knew.

"Yet you pronounce Mr. Bingley as a close acquaintance."

"I am well aware of my shortcomings," Darcy said with good-natured self-chastisement. "Nothing I did could be called 'reasonable.' I permitted my pride to rule my head. I came to the conclusion I could not attach our family name to the Bennets; therefore, I practiced a ruse to keep Bingley from Miss Bennet. I did not trust myself to be often in Miss Elizabeth's company. I told my troubled heart if I did not act with perfidy, I would lose Bingley's most excellent friendship forever."

While he thought on how to explain the remainder of his tale, Darcy permitted his servants to serve the fish course. Under Mrs. Annesley's tutorage his sister had learned to act as hostess, and so Georgiana waited until Darcy's footmen stepped into the servants' hall before she continued their conversation.

"Was this desire not to encounter the lady again the source of your reluctance at assisting Miss Elizabeth when she appeared upon Pemberley's threshold?"

"No, dearest one." Darcy placed his utensils upon the table and turned to his sister. It was important for Georgiana to know the whole truth. "Miss Elizabeth learned that Mr. Wickham ran off with her younger sister." He would not disclose to his sister his misplaced accusations regarding Elizabeth's culpability. "Miss Elizabeth wished my assistance in locating Mr.

Wickham."

Georgiana's bottom lip trembled, but not from fear of encountering Wickham. Darcy found her courage remarkable.

"How terrible for Miss Elizabeth's family." Darcy could read his sister's thoughts: If he did not interrupt Wickham's plans, Lydia Bennet's fate would be hers. "I realize you held no desire to associate with Mr. Wickham, but please say you knew success."

Darcy squeezed the back of her hand.

"It was not easy, but I possessed the direction for where I sent the last of Mrs. Younge's wages. The woman knew of Mr. Wickham and Miss Lydia's whereabouts. I am sorry to say Wickham held no intention of marrying Miss Lydia, but Mr. Gardiner and I threatened debtors' prison if Wickham did not act with honor toward the lady. The marriage settlements were drawn, and I will return to Town to assure that Mr. Wickham speaks his vows."

"I am certain Miss Elizabeth is quite relieved," Georgiana assured.

"Before the papers were signed, the lady returned to Longbourn to assist in the care of her family, but I assume the Gardiners kept Miss Elizabeth informed."

Georgiana was very quiet for several minutes before she spoke again.

"William, I possess a question."

"Then ask it. I am at your disposal."

"We assumed part of Mr. Wickham's attentions to me were because he wished revenge upon the Darcy name. If that is true, and it is also true the Bennets are not so well placed, why did Mr. Wickham choose to run off with Miss Lydia? What was his motive?"

Darcy added quickly, "Mr. Wickham's debts caused him to flee Brighton, where he held residence with the Meryton militia."

"Meryton? Is that not the name of the village close to Netherfield? Was Mr. Wickham in Meryton when you visited with Mr. Bingley?"

"Not at the outset," Darcy explained. "He appeared in the village a few days after Miss Bennet and Miss Elizabeth returned to Longbourn, once Miss Bennet recovered from her illness. I did not wish to tell you because I feared it might upset you."

Georgiana paused for responding.

"I would not welcome the news, and I understand your caution." She cleared her throat. "Did Mr. Wickham recognize your interest in Miss Elizabeth?"

"Mr. Wickham filled Miss Elizabeth's head with his version of what occurred since our time at Cambridge."

Georgiana shook off his explanation.

"That is not what I asked. I would expect nothing less from Mr. Wickham. However, do you think it possible Mr. Wickham chose to ruin Miss Lydia because of your attentions to Miss Elizabeth? Could our father's godson think to best you by destroying your chances with Miss Elizabeth?"

His sister's analysis took Darcy's breath away.

"I thought of many possibilities, but not that particular one. Miss Bingley took note of how I studied Miss Elizabeth, while Mr. Wickham had fellows such as Captain Denny to keep him abreast of my actions at public gatherings in the neighborhood. It would seem quite possible for Mr. Wickham to realize my interest in the lady. We spent much of our youth together. I would expect Mr. Wickham could read me as easily I read him." Darcy paused before adding, "If such was Wickham's purpose, he sorely erred. Miss Lydia is inferior to her elder sisters. Moreover, I plan to propose to Miss Elizabeth when this matter is finalized."

Georgiana's smile lit her countenance.

"I knew you the better man."

"If I marry Miss Elizabeth," Darcy cautioned, "Mr. Wickham's ties to this family will never be severed."

"Pooh," Georgiana declared. "Miss Elizabeth may keep her relationship with the future Mrs. Wickham without either of us accepting Mr. Wickham as part of the family."

"My thoughts exactly."

Georgiana called for Murray to serve the next course.

"Now tell me more of Miss Elizabeth. I enjoyed your accounts of her while you were at Netherfield. I always desired a sister. Do you believe she will take to me? Our brief encounter in Lambton only served to pique my interest. Mr. Bingley praised the lady when we returned to his carriage."

Darcy laughed for the first time in weeks.

"I thought this would be a difficult conversation, but you, my girl, made it exceedingly comfortable. You are growing into a extraordinary young lady. Our parents would be quite proud."

"None of your flattery, William. As a woman I want to know about what is important in life: the romance." A girlish giggle followed, and with a like smile, Darcy relaxed into his tale.

Chapter 8

A FORTNIGHT PASSED SINCE Elizabeth returned to Longbourn, and not a day went by that she did not pray Mr. Darcy would be good to his word and come for her.

"It is too soon," Elizabeth warned her foolish heart as she stared out upon the familiar pastures easily viewed from the bedchamber she shared with Jane. Her sister had gone below to greet Mr. Bingley. Although the family had yet to receive a confirmation of Lydia's marriage, some three days after Elizabeth's return to Longbourn, Uncle Gardiner sent an express to Mr. Bennet outlining the terms Uncle Edward and Mr. Darcy drafted as the settlement's terms.

Four days later, Elizabeth received a lengthy letter from her Aunt Margaret informing Elizabeth of the wedding details, as well as of Mr. Darcy's departure for Derbyshire and of the gentleman's promise to return for the wedding. Elizabeth was half tempted to beg her father to permit her return to the Gardiner's household just so she might encounter Mr. Darcy again.

"But what if once Mr. Darcy returned to Pemberley he realized the foolishness of aligning the Darcy family with his worst enemy?"

The present unhappy state of her family rendered any other excuse for the lowness of Elizabeth's spirits unnecessary; nothing, therefore, could be fairly conjectured from that, though Elizabeth, who was by this time tolerably well acquainted with her own feelings, was perfectly aware that, had she known nothing of Mr. Darcy, she could have borne the dread of Lydia's infamy somewhat better. It would spare her, Elizabeth thought, one sleepless night out of two.

Several days after her return, with Elizabeth's encouragement, Mr. Bennet joined his daughters at tea. Only then did Elizabeth venture to express her sorrow for what he endured over the past several weeks.

"Say nothing of that," her father declared. "Who would suffer but myself? It was of my own doing, and I ought to feel it."

"You must not be too severe upon yourself," replied Elizabeth.

"You may well warn me against such an evil. Human nature is so prone to fall into it! No, Lizzy, let me once in my life feel how much I was to blame. I am not afraid of being overpowered by the impression. It will pass away soon enough."

Then, after a short silence, he continued, "Lizzy, I bear you no ill-will for being justified in your advice to me last May, which, considering the event, shows some greatness of mind."

Miss Bennet, who came to fetch her mother's tea, interrupted them.

"This is a parade," cried Mr. Bennet, "which does one good; it gives such an elegance to misfortune! Another day I will do the same; I will sit in my library, in my night cap and powdering gown, and give as much trouble as I can, or, perhaps, I may defer it till Kitty runs away."

"I am not going to run away, Papa," said Kitty, fretfully; "if *I* should ever go to Brighton, I would behave better than Lydia."

"*You* go to Brighton! I would not trust you so near it as East-Bourne, for fifty pounds! No, Kitty, I have at last learnt to be cautious, and you will feel the effects of it. No officer is ever to enter my house again or even to pass through the village. Balls will be absolutely prohibited, unless you stand up with one of your sisters. And you are never to stir out of doors till you can prove that you spent ten minutes of every day in a rational manner."

Kitty, who took all these threats in a serious light, began to cry.

"Well, well," said he, "do not make yourself unhappy. If you are a good girl for the next ten years, I will take you to a review at the end of them."

Elizabeth, who looked on in sympathy for both her father and her sisters, considered Mr. Bennet too hard upon poor Kitty, but she had become accustomed to her parents' extremes: Mrs. Bennet's "nerves" were well known in the area, as were Mr. Bennet's joy at making sport of his neighbors and family. It much as Elizabeth loved her parents, of late, she wished, more than once, that they saw the peril of their choices.

As the days crawled by, Elizabeth found that she cursed her headstrong reply to Mr. Darcy while in Kent.

"I could have claimed months of happiness if I knew not prejudicial blindness. At least if Mr. Darcy sent me away after learning of Lydia's misplaced affections, I could claim the memories of our short-lived marital felicity to sustain me." Although Elizabeth wished otherwise, she imagined an impassable gulf between her and Mr. Darcy. "Had Lydia's marriage been concluded on the most honorable of terms, Mr. Darcy's affection could not outweigh his family's objections to an alliance with me. Lady Catherine would never be pleased to have her plans for Miss de Bourgh foiled by an upstart such as I, and I am certain other members of the gentleman's family will speak out against a joining. If nothing less, Mr. Darcy must take Miss Darcy's feelings to heart. How could Georgiana Darcy welcome a sister who holds a familial connection to Mr. Wickham?"

Such was the debate Elizabeth experienced several times each day. She assured herself that his feelings could not in rational expectation survive, and her loss humbled and grieved Elizabeth. She became jealous of Mr. Darcy's esteem, when she could no longer hope to claim it. She wanted to hear of him, to see him, when there seemed the least chance of gaining intelligence. She began to comprehend he was exactly the man who, in disposition and talents, would most suit her.

"Should not we have heard from your Uncle

Gardiner of dear Lydia's marriage by now?" her mother pleaded.

Elizabeth and Mary tended Mrs. Bennet. Their mother had not known her parlor for nearly a month.

When news came of the impending marriage, Mrs. Bennet thought to leave her bed and make the short journey to Meryton to spread the news of Lydia's "engagement," but Mr. Bennet refused his wife the use of his carriage with a warning, "We will not speak of this among the neighbors until our youngest claims the title of 'Mrs. Wickham.' Engagements can be broken; marriage vows cannot. I am not proud of the makeshift joining, and neither should you be. Lydia shamed this family and ruined the prospects of her sisters, and I refuse to celebrate her depravity. That is my final word on the subject."

And so, Mrs. Bennet grudgingly returned to her bed, rather than to assume her role as mistress of the manor.

"Sunday next would be the third calling of the banns," Elizabeth explained for what felt the hundredth time. "Uncle meant to have the service on either the Monday or Tuesday following, as quickly as the vicar could accommodate Lydia and Mr. Wickham." Elizabeth learned all the details of the arrangements from her father. Even though her mind told her Darcy would not come to Hertfordshire as he promised, Elizabeth pressed her father to know the day when her most feminine hopes would die.

"Would you like tea, Mama?" Mary asked.

"Yes, if you would so kind, and ask Mrs. Hill for a bit more of my tonic. I am feeling most anxious again." Elizabeth turned away to disguise a frown of disapproval; her mother's growing dependence on laudanum could not play well in the family's future.

While Mary absented herself to tend the "supposed" illness, Elizabeth distracted her mother with one of the fashion plates she brought specifically for Mrs. Bennet's amusement. She realized early on Mrs. Bennet held little interest in anything beyond fashion and gossip.

"What do you think of this one, Mama?" Elizabeth placed the book of plates in her mother's hands before she plumped the pillows to support Mrs. Bennet's back. "A more fitted waist would accent both Jane's and Kitty's forms. Do you not think?"

Her mother studied the sketch of Town fashion before extrapolating upon which cloths would be required for the design, as well as holding a sensible discussion on which colors best served each of her daughters. Mrs. Bennet's vast knowledge of such things took Elizabeth by surprise. Certainly, she heard her mother speak incessantly upon such matters in the past, but she never appreciated Mrs. Bennet's expertise previously.

"The next time I require a new gown, I must seek your excellent advice," Elizabeth said with a genuine smile.

In spite of her mother's insensibility, Elizabeth understood that women of her mother's generation held few opportunities to improve their minds. She was certain Grandfather Gardiner paid little attention to his two daughters, focusing his limited income and attentions upon his only son: Edward Gardiner. Aunt

Phillips excelled where Mrs. Bennet never applied herself to books. Although both sisters loved gossip and entertaining, Mrs. Phillips followed her husband's lead. Uncle Phillips always said a man who studied the law required a woman with sensibility

"I so wanted to oversee Lydia's bride clothes," her mother half whined. "I am certain my Sister Gardiner did not treat our dearest Lydia in the manner your sister should know as the wife of an officer in the Army."

Elizabeth straightened the blanket across her mother's lap.

"Jane and I gathered several items for Lydia when Mr. Gardiner sent word of locating her. Mr. Bingley generously agreed to permit one of his grooms to deliver the trunk to London."

"Yet, Lydia would show better in a new clothes," Mrs. Bennet protested.

Elizabeth patted the back of her mother's hand.

"I am certain the Gardiners extended their best toward Lydia, and do not forget that Uncle Gardiner knows the brunt of the cost of the marriage settlements. Papa and my uncle assumed Mr. Wickham's numerous gaming debts, as well as making Mr. Wickham a promise of one hundred pounds a year."

It was a statement to her mother's acceptance of Society's preference to gentlemen that Mrs. Bennet never once expressed her disapproval of Mr. Wickham's depravity: Mrs. Bennet thought it normal for Mr. Wickham to gamble away his future. Elizabeth withheld the mention of the expense of the commission purchased for Mr. Wickham, for she feared Mr. Darcy stood in honor in the matter. If so, her family owed the gentleman much.

"I know you do not approve of this marriage," her mother asserted.

Elizabeth responded with sympathy for her mother's aspirations for her daughters.

"I do not much care for Lydia's manner in finding a husband; yet, that fact does not make me love my sister less."

Mr. Bennet chose not to share with his wife Elizabeth's deception or her active involvement in the search for Lydia. Otherwise, Mrs. Bennet would be insisting upon Mr. Darcy making a match with their second daughter. In some ways, Elizabeth would celebrate being forced to marry the gentleman, but she did not think it fair to burden Mr. Darcy with her family's trials. It would not be fair punishment for the kindness Mr. Darcy showed her.

Their conversation came to an end when Mrs. Hill entered with a tea tray and a brown bottle containing a mixture of bilberry juice and laudanum.

"I will sit with your mother," the family's long time servant announced as she set the tray on a small table. "Once Mrs. Bennet has her tea, I will brush the mistress's hair." Elizabeth thought that a useless task if her mother was to return to sleep, but she knew Mrs. Hill's kindness would please Mrs. Bennet. "Your father, Miss, asked me to send you to him if you be finished here."

Elizabeth stood immediately: Perhaps her father held additional news on the marriage arrangements and the return of Mr. Darcy to London.

"Do you require anything else, Mama?"

Mrs. Bennet dismissed Elizabeth with a flick of her wrist.

"Mrs. Hill shall tend me well. When Mr. Bingley departs, send Jane up to sit with me."

"I shall call again a bit later," Elizabeth promised as she made her way to the door. "Rest well, Mama. This madness will soon know an end."

Elizabeth found her father in his study.

"You sent for me?"

"Yes. Come in, Lizzy, and close the door behind you." He appeared so grave that Elizabeth felt her heartbeat hitch higher.

"Has something amiss occurred?" Her father leaned heavily into his chair. A look of devastation crossed his features.

The underlying quiet in his tone stole Elizabeth's breath when he said, "You should read your Uncle Gardiner's latest message." He gestured to an open letter upon his desk. Her father closed his eyes and sighed deeply.

As if the letter were a venomous viper prepared to strike, Elizabeth inched her closer to it. Catching it up, she read: *The marriage must be postponed.*

"How can this be?" she pleaded. "What brought upon such a change of circumstances?"

"Read the entire letter, Child," her father instructed. "Just know Fate does not intend to be kind to the Bennets."

Elizabeth shoved her growing panic aside and concentrated upon the letter.

I should have considered the cough Mr. Wickham presented during our interviews an indication of what was to come, but I took no note. On Monday last, Mr. Wickham called upon Lydia, as he has done every day since signing the marriage settlement. Although I do not care for the man's morals, I did appreciate how he embraced our agreement. He appeared to accept his future with good grace. Unfortunately though, we may never see the fruits of our negotiations for Mr. W took quite ill. In truth, since Elizabeth's departure for Longbourn, a measles outbreak claimed St. Clement's parish. Without knowing of the spread of the disease, Mr. W came for supper and never departed: Mrs. G. attends him in one of the bedrooms above stairs. He called upon Lydia, but was too ill to leave.

Worse still, either Mr. Wickham or I carried this illness to Gracechurch Street. Two of the children are ill, as are several of my servants and workers. Needless to say, my employees could have come into contact with the illness elsewhere, but I feel personally responsible.

All that being said, Mrs. G is doing all she can to tend both Mr. W and our children. It will not surprise you, I am certain, to learn Lydia, although not in danger of knowing the illness for she experienced the disease as a child of four, is of little use to Margaret. Lydia is more concerned with whether the measles pustules will leave scars upon Mr. Wickham's cheeks and chin than she is the real possibility the man could die from the fever or the cough. I fear my niece does not understand the danger of the illness to adults, especially to males.

That brings me to the crux of this letter. Margaret is near exhaustion from her nursing duties. As four of my servants also succumbed to the illness, our house is an infirmary and my wife the chief caretaker. If it would not be an imposition, Brother, would you permit Elizabeth and Mary to come to us? Along with Lydia, Lizzy and Mary knew the disease when measles swept through Meryton some twelve years past. I believe both girls would be of great assistance to my dear wife. Hopefully, if we practice cleanliness and diligence, the disease will run its course within a month, and all should be well once more. It is imperative that we see Mr. Wickham to health. Heaven forbid the man should fall victim to his infection before he speaks his vows to Lydia.

E. Gardiner

"Oh, Papa!" Elizabeth exclaimed when she finished reading. "Will this farce never know a final curtain?"

"As you were long removed from London and Mr. Wickham, I assume you did not carry the disease to Longbourn."

"From what I know of the disease from Mama's

cousin, it shows itself within ten days to two weeks," Elizabeth assured. "I have been at Longbourn for over a fortnight, and while in London, I did not meet with Mr. Wickham. Only with Lydia."

Her father rolled his eyes heavenward.

"Mrs. Bennet will not take well the news of further isolation from her Sister Phillips," he said in mocked sincerity.

"I am most grateful you prevented Mama from announcing Lydia's engagement to the village," Elizabeth observed. "This situation will be a disaster if Mr. Wickham does not recover." After a brief pause, she asked, "Will you permit me and Mary to assist Aunt Gardiner?"

Mr. Bennet steepled his fingers upon his abdomen before answering,

"After all your uncle did to bring about a solution to this situation, I would not think to deny him. You will leave in the morning. While you explain the changes in this situation to Mary, Jane, and Kitty, I will attempt to reason with your mother."

"Mrs. Bennet knows her tonic," Elizabeth explained.

"A small blessing," her father said as he stood to straighten his waistcoat. "If I am truly fortunate, Mrs. Bennet's lack of understanding will be attributed to her overuse of the opiate rather than her customary insensibility."

⌒⌒⌒

"Miss Elizabeth?" Mr. Wickham murmured. When she and Mary arrived at Gracechurch Street, Elizabeth sent her aunt to bed for a much needed rest.

Tending to Mr. Wickham profoundly upset Mary's sense of propriety; therefore, Elizabeth insisted that Mary nurse the two ill Gardiner children while she saw to the gentleman. "How blessed I am!"

Elizabeth bathed his fevered brow with lavender water.

"You may not think so once you encounter my less than maternal touch," she warned. Despite her best efforts, Elizabeth examined his once handsome face, now sporting patches of red scabs. It was uncharitable of her to think Mr. Wickham might have turned out better if God did not give the man a pleasing countenance.

"Your aunt is a termagant," he explained with the hint of a smile. "Pray my commanding officer will possess a softer hand."

Elizabeth gently washed his arms from the elbow to his wrists.

"Most women run their households with military efficiency. Did not your mother perform as well?"

Mr. Wickham motioned to the glass of water upon a side table, and Elizabeth spooned several mouthfuls across his parched lips before he responded.

"Mrs. Wickham left when I was quite young– shortly after my father came to Pemberley. I do not remember her except for a miniature my father carried with him for the remainder of his days." He spoke slowly as if half in pain and half exhausted.

Although Elizabeth knew Mr. Wickham the master manipulator in speaking half-truths, she could not help but wonder who tended the young Wickham. It was not unusual for a woman to pass after childbirth: She assumed such was the case with Lady Anne Darcy.

Yet, Georgiana Darcy knew fortune in a loving father, brother, and cousin. But what happened to a child whose mother simply walked from his life?

"It grieves me to learn of your unhappy event," Elizabeth acknowledged softly. She could think of nothing more to say. Crossing to the windows to adjust the drapes so the sunlight would not irritate Mr. Wickham's eyes, she asked. "Do you think you could tolerate some clear broth?"

Wickham shook off the suggestion.

"Perhaps later." Glancing to where Elizabeth stood looking back at him, he remarked, "The breeze is refreshing."

"My mother's cousin is a surgeon in the Americas. Mr. Pantier treated many cases of the measles, among other unnamed diseases, while in the West Indies. He swears one of the surest means to assure recovery is to air out the sick room. Mrs. Bennet follows her cousin's instructions explicitly."

Mr. Wickham's eyes narrowed.

"I assume if you are in my room, you previously knew this scourge. How came you to contract the disease?'

As she busied herself with tidying the room, Elizabeth chuckled.

"When I was eight, Mrs. Bennet came to London to visit the drapers. While she was from home, a measles outbreak claimed many in Meryton. Before my mother could return, Mary, Lydia, and I took ill. Mrs. Bennet blamed my father for permitting Sir William Lucas's children to bring 'an epidemic' to her door. Mama swears Sir William carried the disease from London to Hertfordshire when he was honored at St. James. Needless to say, Mr. Bennet has not permitted his wife such a long stay in London since, for he fears another 'disaster' while on his watch. In view of that particular fact, when the disease revisited the neighborhood again, Mama insisted upon following Doctor Pantier's advice: Patients isolated; where permitting, windows opened for fresh air; and the area scrubbed clean. We have avoided another disaster by following Mama's instructions."

"Mayhap your family did not know an infected person since that first incident," Mr. Wickham suggested.

"True," Elizabeth agreed. "But is not part of the healing the belief in the physician's instructions?"

Wickham closed his eyes as if in discomfort, and for a few brief seconds, Elizabeth wondered if she should summon her uncle.

"Loss of belief in a person's word is a high price indeed," the gentleman observed in grave tones. He slowly opened his eyes to study her carefully. "It makes me most unhappy to know I lost the friendship you once offered."

Elizabeth wished she could despise the man, but she was not built for hatred. Disapproval? Most definitely. Perhaps even a bit revengeful. But not hatred, for it was an all-encompassing emotion. Hatred, in her opinion, was as irrational as the passion of love.

"Some day soon we shall be more than friends, Mr. Wickham," she assured. "When you recover, we shall be brother and sister."

"Mr. Darcy!" his butler called, but Darcy was too weak to even raise his head. For three days, he made himself complete the necessary paperwork for Mr. Wickham's joining with Miss Lydia, as well as to oversee the administration of his estate, but each day Darcy found the duties more difficult to perform. Earlier, when he stood to return to his quarters, the floor rose up to claim him. Surprisingly, Darcy welcomed the position he claimed upon the Turkish carpet. "Murray! Jatson! Lawson!" Mr. Nathan bellowed; yet, Darcy ignored the sound of urgency in the butler's voice.

Rushed steps announced his footmen's arrivals. Above him, hushed whispers spoke of exigency, but it was not until his servants lifted him from the floor that Darcy considered a protest; yet, the words would not form upon his lips.

His servants jostled him as they carried Darcy to his suite.

"Mr. Darcy?" Mrs. Reynolds pleaded as she rushed ahead of him. *Did his housekeeper not realize he was too exhausted to speak?* Darcy's only wish was to claim his bed and never come out. "Put him down gently," Mrs. Reynolds instructed. The familiar drape of the four-poster appeared above Darcy's head, and he sighed with contentment.

However, within seconds, the footmen exited the room, and his valet, Mr. Sheffield's worried face blocked the view of the overhead drapery.

"Permit me to remove your boots and jacket, Sir." Without Darcy's permission, Sheffield wrestled

Darcy to a seated position while his valet, his butler, and Mrs. Reynolds undressed him.

Darcy made no move to halt their efforts; it was too much to ask of his willpower.

"My stomach," he groaned.

Mrs. Reynolds claimed the clean chamber pot from beneath the bed and shoved it under Darcy's nose. Without preamble, Darcy emptied his breakfast into it. With cool efficiency, Mrs. Reynolds set the pot aside, wrung out a damp cloth to wipe his face, and retuned to the buttons upon his waistcoat.

"How long has Master William known illness?" she demanded of Mr. Sheffield.

The valet tugged upon Darcy's boots as Mr. Nathan lowered Darcy's head to the pillows. Sheffield grunted his response, "Two, perhaps three days." The first boot gave way. "Mr. Darcy refused my suggestion for assistance."

"Not Sheffield's fault," Darcy instructed in a weak tone he did not recognize.

Mrs. Reynolds wiped his face again.

"Then pray tell whose fault is it that you were discovered upon the floor of your study."

Darcy sighed when the comforting coolness claimed his skin. With eyes closed, he smiled in irony.

"Who else? Mr. Wickham."

Chapter 9

"MRS. REYNOLDS, IS MY sister unwell?" Darcy could recall little of the previous two days. Even now, his head throbbed from the slightest movement, but it was important he learn the extent of the illness he unknowingly carried to Pemberley.

His housekeeper bathed his arms and chest.

"Miss Georgiana took to her bed yesterday eve, Sir, but I do not think Miss Darcy will know your pain."

"Any pain Georgiana suffers at my hand is too much," Darcy insisted. "What of the others?"

"One of the footmen, Mr. Nathan, and two maids."

Darcy closed his eyes to digest the extent of what occurred since his return to Derbyshire.

"You saw to the staff?" he asked even though Darcy knew Mrs. Reynolds would act without his instructions. "Was a message sent to Darcy House?"

"Yes to both questions," Mrs. Reynolds

responded without censure. "I wrote to Mrs. Wells yesterday."

Darcy thought to nod his acceptance, but changed his mind when a thunderbolt of pain ricocheted between his temples. He squeezed his eyes shut and grimaced. Slowing his breathing, Darcy spoke in a husky whisper.

"I have one more message you must send. This one must go out today. Send it to Edward Gardiner at Gracechurch Street in Cheapside, London. The direction is in my ledger."

"To the couple that visited Pemberley?" Mrs. Reynolds asked in what sounded of disbelief. "If any of the recent visitors to the estate were to know the disease, it would be the Bingleys."

Darcy could not think clearly enough to speak a detailed explanation.

"Mr. Gardiner and I sought Mr. Wickham in London. My father's godson swore he was not ill when I found him, but Mr. Wickham's perfidy continues. Tell Mr. Gardiner what occurred here. Ask him to protect his wife and children and Miss Elizabeth. Nothing must happen to the lady."

"I do not understand, Master William, but I will see to your wishes immediately. Now, you must rest."

Darcy sighed heavily.

"Just see to Elizabeth Bennet, and I will be the most cooperative of patients."

⚬⚬⚬

"Yes, Miss?" Elizabeth realized she broke every rule of Society by calling upon Mr. Darcy's Town house, but it was imperative for her to know if Mr.

Darcy succumbed to the disease carried to St. Clements parish by two Chinese sailors. London officials ordered the parish into quarantine, and the military took unprecedented actions by assisting the local constables in securing the area.

"Yes, Sir. I am Miss Elizabeth Bennet." She shot a glance to Hannah, one of her uncle's maids. Hannah accompanied Elizabeth because Gwenie was one of the causalities of the measles at Gracechurch Street.

"My uncle, Mr. Gardiner, is a business associate of Mr. Darcy. My parents are Mr. Bingley's closest neighbors in Hertfordshire, and Miss Darcy and I hold an acquaintance." That last bit was an exaggeration, but Elizabeth did not wish the butler to send her away before she learned something of Mr. Darcy. "Mr. Darcy was to call upon my uncle at week's end, but it grieves me to inform Mr. Darcy that some of Mr. Gardiner's household knows the illness sweeping over many in London."

Elizabeth thought it telling that the butler did not recoil when she mentioned the possibility of measles. Many would shun her, fearing she might carry the disease.

"What is amiss, Thacker?" a familiar voice called.

"A young lady, Colonel, with a message from a Mr. Gardiner."

"Colonel Fitzwilliam?" Elizabeth spoke the gentleman's name before he appeared in the open door.

"Miss Elizabeth." The colonel glanced up and down the street, and Elizabeth realized he meant to protect her from Society's gossips: No lady of merit would call upon a bachelor household. "Please come in."

Elizabeth stepped into Mr. Darcy's London home, and despite her best efforts her breath caught. The entryway was magnificently stylish.

"I apologize, Colonel, I did not mean to interrupt your day."

"You require no invitation," the colonel assured, but Elizabeth assumed the colonel spoke to quiet any gossip among the servants.

When the butler stepped into a servant hall, her eyes took in the simple grandeur of the space: It so spoke of the man she had come to know that Elizabeth's eyes misted with joyful tears. She possessed another image in which to picture Mr. Darcy.

"I know you are aware of the business Mr. Darcy held with my uncle. As your cousin meant to return to London for the conclusion of the settlement, I thought it best to warn Mr. Darcy that the gentleman in question carried measles to my uncle's house."

"Is Wickham at Gracechurch Street?" the colonel asked in what sounded of relief. "I attempted to ascertain whether the cad remained at St. Clements, but those in charge of the quarantine could tell me little. I feared the scoundrel took flight."

"Mr. Wickham became ill on Friday a week prior. My aunt tended him and two of her children until my sister Mary and I arrived yesterday. Although not healed, Mr. Wickham improves. The wedding cannot proceed as planned, and I did not want Mr. Darcy to call at the Gardiners only to know a postponement."

The colonel frowned.

"I came to Darcy House last evening to discover

four of Darcy's servants ill. I have not seen to Darcy's servants, but I assume they know the measles." As much as Elizabeth admired the colonel, she found his *laissez faire* attitude toward the working class a bit disconcerting. "Knowing Darcy's recent business in St. Clements, I suspected as much for your uncle's household," the colonel asserted. "I intended to examine Darcy's ledgers for Mr. Gardiner's directions. We are of a like mind, Miss Elizabeth," he declared.

Elizabeth glanced about the entrance foyer once more. Sunlight flitted across the polished brass, and for a few brief second she saw the perfect mate for Mr. Darcy, but it was not she. The woman was tall and fair and expertly coiffed. Elizabeth glanced down at her drab day dress. Regret filled her heart. She would never be judged as an appropriate match for the gentleman; therefore, it did not matter how others viewed her. Her family owed Mr. Darcy a debt of gratitude, and she would repay the gentleman's loyalty with a like allegiance.

"If there are measles at Darcy House," Elizabeth questioned, "what is being done for Mr. Darcy's servants?"

The colonel appeared shocked by her impertinence.

"I am not certain, Miss Elizabeth."

"May I speak to Mr. Darcy's butler?"

"Thacker!" the colonel called. A smile of bemusement turned up the corners of the man's lips, but Elizabeth ignored the gesture. She meant for Mr. Darcy to think upon her with fond remembrance for her care of his servants.

"Yes, Colonel." Thacker appeared immediately.

"Miss Elizabeth wishes to be apprised of the treatment being given to Darcy's ill servants," the colonel said with a condescending smile.

The servant raised a disapproving eyebrow, but he responded in a respectful tone.

"The housekeeper removed the patients in the attic quarters, Miss. Mrs. Wells also consulted a physician."

Elizabeth realized she held no right to give Mr. Darcy's servant orders, but she ignored that detail.

"I wish to see them, Mr. Thacker."

Mr. Thacker shot a glance to the colonel who nodded his agreement.

"This way, Miss Elizabeth."

"Come along, Hannah," Elizabeth instructed. "I shall require your assistance."

Elizabeth followed the very proper butler to the attic quarters. Unfortunately, she knew immediate disappointment with the conditions.

"This shall not do, Mr. Thacker," she announced when Elizabeth first beheld the space. "I cannot imagine Mr. Darcy employs a physician who would consider this adequate care."

The butler cleared his throat with embarrassment.

"Doctor Davis did not call upon the household. Mrs. Wells thought it best if the good doctor not carry the disease to others."

"If the 'good doctor' practices cleanliness," Elizabeth insisted, "he will not bring death to others."

"What must be done, Miss Elizabeth?" The colonel abandoned his amusement for what appeared to be genuine concern.

"First, the idea of keeping the room dark is excellent, but we must move the patients into rooms where there are windows. My mother's cousin is a physician upon the American continent. He says a person carries the disease to others, but it also is transported through the air. For example, if I am inflicted with measles and cough at the same time as you inhale, you would suck in the disease with your breath."

"As with consumption?" the colonel asked.

"Yes, but not as severe," Elizabeth assured. "Even so, it is essential to open the windows so the illness can be carried away with the breeze. Moreover, Mr. Darcy's house must know a thorough scrubbing, even the wooden surfaces, Mr. Thacker. Once everyone claims health, then you may polish the fixtures again. Mr. Darcy would never place the property above the safety of his employees."

The colonel exchanged a knowing look with Thacker, but Elizabeth kept her shoulders stiff and her chin lifted.

"Mr. Darcy would expect you to follow Miss Elizabeth's suggestions," the colonel declared, and Elizabeth appreciated the gentleman's support.

"If you have a moment, Mr. Thacker, I will gladly share how best to proceed with you and Mr. Darcy's housekeeper."

"Certainly, Miss. We should return below, and then I will locate Mrs. Wells. It shan't take long."

Elizabeth returned to the foyer, where she joined Hannah upon a bench. The colonel offered to show Elizabeth into one of the sitting rooms, but she adamantly refused. She knew both embarrassment and exhilaration after her performance in the attic. Would Mr. Darcy despise her cheekiness? She entered his home uninvited and presented his servants orders. Her manners were deplorable. Within a few minutes, Mr. Thacker returned with the housekeeper, whose expression denounced Elizabeth upon first glance. However, Elizabeth stood tall, pronouncing a series of improvements for the care of Mr. Darcy's servants.

"You will see that Miss Elizabeth's suggestions are put into place until you hear otherwise from Mr. Darcy," the colonel instructed.

"Yes, Sir," Mrs. Wells said grudgingly before exiting.

"We should be going," Elizabeth declared with a blush of embarrassment. "I apologize for my brashness, Mr. Thacker. I meant no offense."

"We appreciate your loyalty to the master, Miss."

The colonel escorted Elizabeth to the door.

"If I hear from Darcy, I will send word to Gracechurch Street."

"Thank you, Colonel." Elizabeth departed Mr. Darcy's home with news of the gentleman's London staff, but not of the man himself. She decided during a hackney ride to Cheapside that she would permit one more day to pass before she broke another of Society's rules and wrote to the gentleman to inquire of Mr. Darcy's health.

"Lizzy, might I have a moment?"

Elizabeth looked up from where she sat reading the latest newsprints to Mr. Wickham. Upon her return to Gracechurch, Elizabeth assisted Mary with the children, who were restless after being indoors for so long. She made puppets from old stockings, and she and Mary performed a puppet show for the children's entertainment. It did Elizabeth well to observe Mary's kindness to their cousins, as well as the creative ideas her sister added to the impromptu play. Since opening her eyes to what she missed in Mr. Darcy's personality, Elizabeth discovered how mistaken she was of others.

"I believe Mr. Wickham will excuse my absence," Elizabeth announced as she stood to fold the pages.

"Politics put me to sleep," Mr. Wickham asserted with a hint of his former affability.

Elizabeth grinned mischievously.

"Which is why I choose the articles on Parliament. You know improvement, but additional rest can do you no harm."

Elizabeth closed the door behind her and followed her aunt into the nearest sitting room.

"Is something amiss?"

The frown upon her Aunt Margaret's lips spoke of disapproval. Elizabeth swore Hannah to secrecy, and she prayed the maid kept silent regarding their call upon Darcy House.

Her aunt handed Elizabeth a letter marked from Derbyshire. Elizabeth did not recognize the script, but she knew it not Mr. Darcy's for she read his letter so often Elizabeth could recite it from heart.

"This arrived by express for your uncle. Mr. Gardiner wished you to read it."

Elizabeth nodded her understanding and unfolded the single page to read…

Mr. Gardiner,

My employer, Mr. Darcy, instructed me to send you warning that he knows measles since returning from London. Miss Darcy has also taken low. The master expressed his concern for your wife and children and asked that if you do not know the disease, to do all you might to protect your family, especially the health of your niece Miss Elizabeth.

I do not understand this business, but Mr. Darcy charged me with the task. I might also share the fact Mr. Darcy believes his illness is a result of your joint business with Mr. Wickham.

Mrs. A. Reynolds

Elizabeth read the note a second time.

"This does not say anything of Mr. Darcy's condition. Is his a mild case, such as what Michael and Cassandra know? Could the gentleman be dying? Many die from the consumption, which sets into their lungs." A third perusal of the note provided no relief. Elizabeth glanced to her aunt. "I must go to him," she pleaded.

"Such would be beyond the pale," her aunt cautioned. "And with the children ill, I cannot accompany you to Derbyshire to provide you respectability." She caught Elizabeth's hand. "You must understand that if you would travel to Pemberley, your reputation would be in tatters. As ruined as Lydia's."

"What if Mary...?" Elizabeth interrupted.

Her aunt shook off the suggestion.

"I am pleased with the improvements in Mary since she is removed from Longbourn, but your sister practices strict propriety. Mary would never approve of your calling upon Pemberley unsought."

Elizabeth grasped upon an idea.

"Mr. Darcy proposed to me," she declared. "We knew we could not claim marital felicity until this situation with Mr. Wickham found a resolution, but Mr. Darcy meant to call upon my father after Wickham and Lydia spoke their vows."

A look of skepticism crossed her aunt's features.

"Mr. Darcy spoke to your uncle of a previous proposal, which you refused? Is this a more recent plight?"

Elizabeth swallowed the anxiety rushing to her throat.

"The morning of my departure for Hertfordshire. Mr. Darcy arrived early to secure my agreement."

"And you presented the gentleman your affirmation?" Her aunt's tone continued to speak of dismay.

"I did." Elizabeth prayed her deception would not prove her undoing.

"Your uncle will not be pleased with this development," Aunt Margaret warned. "You cannot travel unescorted or without a maid. And what would we tell the others?"

"We tell Lydia and Mary that another of uncle's business associates took ill and required someone to manage his house until his wife returns."

"You construct fabrications with ease, Lizzy," her aunt observed. "Perhaps we have misjudged you all these years."

Elizabeth ignored the chastisement.

"Before he departed, Mr. Darcy informed me that his cousin would be at Darcy House and if we required anything, we should contact Colonel Fitzwilliam. Perhaps the colonel would agree to see me to Pemberley. As the colonel also serves as Miss Darcy's guardian, he will wish to see his cousins to health."

"What if the colonel has not known the disease?"

Elizabeth's mind raced, searching for excuses her aunt and uncle might believe.

"Certainly as Mr. Darcy and his cousin consulted often on Mr. Wickham's situation, it would be possible for the colonel to encounter the disease, but as Colonel Fitzwilliam served many years in King George's army, I would imagine an introduction to the illness came previously."

"And what of this proposal? Will Colonel Fitzwilliam recognize your betrothal to his cousin?"

"Mr. Darcy assured me his cousin is aware of all aspects of the search for Mr. Wickham."

Elizabeth knew relief when the colonel called upon her in the early afternoon. While Aunt Margaret conferred with Uncle Gardiner, Elizabeth dispatched a note to Darcy House.

"Thank you for coming so quickly," she said as she gestured the colonel to a seat.

"As your note spoke of urgency, I thought expediency required. Has Mr. Wickham left without notice?"

"No. No. Mr. Wickham remains above stairs," Elizabeth assured. "My uncle received this message today." She handed the note to the colonel and waited impatiently for him to read it.

"Darcy and Georgiana both ill," the colonel thought aloud. "I wonder why Mrs. Reynolds sent no word of this situation to Darcy House."

Elizabeth attempted to keep her anxiousness hidden from the colonel.

"I cannot say for certain. Perhaps the post knew some sort of delay. This message arrived by express."

"Thank you for summoning me so quickly, Miss Elizabeth. I must set a course for Derbyshire," the colonel declared as he gathered his gloves.

"My thoughts exactly," Elizabeth interjected.

The colonel's eyebrow rose in curiosity.

"Perhaps you should enlighten me, Miss Elizabeth. I suspect you hold plans of which I should be made aware."

"I wish to travel to Pemberley with you," Elizabeth announced with a lift of her chin.

The colonel studied her for several elongated seconds.

"You believe Darcy would approve of your appearance at Pemberley?"

"Colonel, I am certain Mr. Darcy told you something of our often misconstruing each other." The colonel nodded his agreement. "Yet, you may not know your cousin and I came to an understanding. Even Mrs. Reynolds' note expresses Mr. Darcy's concern for me."

"Yet…" the colonel began, but Elizabeth shook off his objections.

"I mean to travel to Derbyshire with or without your escort, Colonel. I would prefer to act with gentility, but I am not dissuaded from what is sometimes called my 'hoydenish tendencies.'" Elizabeth paused to consider how best to reason with the man. "If Mr. Darcy received news of my illness, he would move heaven and earth to reach me. I am certain your cousin would spit in the eye of propriety to know a return of my health, and I am equally devoted to the gentleman."

Once they made the decision to depart London, Elizabeth performed with efficiency. The colonel commandeered one of Mr. Darcy's smaller carriages for the journey. She knew from their return to London more than three weeks prior it would take two days of good weather for them to reach Mr. Darcy's home, and she spoke a special prayer for God's kindness in the matter. With a late start, her party traveled on the first day until well after dark before claiming rooms.

The second day's stretch brought them ever closer to Derbyshire. Elizabeth wished the multiple toll roads did not slow their progress, but she knew some relief when the colonel announce on Friday evening that they had perhaps three or four hours on Saturday to reach their destination.

At length, the carriage rolled past the gatehouse at Pemberley to enter the park. The first appearance of

Pemberley Woods brought Elizabeth some perturbation. *What would Mr. Darcy think of her deception?* As with her two previous visits, Elizabeth admired every remarkable spot and point of view.

"It be grand," Hannah said in awe. Aunt Margaret insisted the girl accompany Elizabeth.

"Just watch," Elizabeth whispered as the wood ceased, and Pemberley House instantly caught the eye. It was a large, handsome stone building, standing well on high ground and backed to a ridge of high woody hills. She never saw a place for which nature did more. The thought of being the mistress of such a great estate set Elizabeth's spirits in a high flutter. *Would Mr. Darcy renew his proposal when he learned how she sacrificed everything to be at his side?* She refused him so often that Elizabeth no longer held assurances of his continued affections.

"Oh, my," Hannah murmured, and Elizabeth seconded the maid's sentiments.

Soon the colonel led the way into the house.

"Where is Mr. Nathan?" the colonel demanded of the footman who opened the door to them.

"Mr. Nathan is down with the illness, Colonel?"

Colonel Fitzwilliam frowned his disapproval.

"How bad is it?"

"Not as many as could be," the footman explained. "Most of the master's people knew the disease previously, but we avoid those in the village."

"I would like to see my cousins," the colonel insisted.

"I will see you up." Mr. Darcy's housekeeper appeared upon the stairs.

The colonel caught Elizabeth's arm, and she was pleased there would be no need for her to fight him regarding Elizabeth seeing Mr. Darcy.

"Jatson, see that the lady's trunk and my items are brought in before you escort the lady's maid to Miss Elizabeth's quarters," the colonel instructed.

"The green chamber was recently aired." Mrs. Reynolds looked knowingly to the footman. "Now, if you will follow me, Miss Elizabeth, I will show you to your quarters. The colonel knows his way to the family suites."

Elizabeth shot a glance to Mr. Darcy's cousin before responding to the housekeeper.

"I appreciate your accommodations for this intrusion, Mrs. Reynolds, but I mean to call upon Miss Darcy and her brother before I claim my ablutions from our travel."

Although Mrs. Reynolds presented Elizabeth a pointed look, it was not one of censure.

"Very well, Miss." The woman led the way into a section of the house Elizabeth did not view previously. *Tasteful elegance.* Every detail reflecting the man Elizabeth had come to love.

"I will call upon Miss Darcy first," Colonel Fitzwilliam whispered as they reached the first of the private suites. "I know you will not rest until you see Darcy." Elizabeth nodded her agreement. "Mrs. Reynolds will remain with you." He entered the rooms belonging to Miss Darcy, and Elizabeth heard the colonel call, "Where is my beautiful Georgie?" as the door closed behind him.

"This way, Miss." Mrs. Reynolds directed

Elizabeth to the chambers at the end of the hall.

Mrs. Reynolds opened the door to "his" quarters, and Elizabeth's steps faltered.

"If Mr. Darcy is asleep, there is no need to disturb him. I just need…" Elizabeth swallowed hard while she searched for the right words.

"No need to explain, Miss." The woman smiled in encouragement. "Master William holds the loyalty of many."

At length, Elizabeth's eyes fell upon the form resting upon the bed. Even with the red patches marring his cheeks, she thought the man whose hair fell over his forehead from sleep the most striking man of her acquaintance. On silent feet, Elizabeth moved closer, claiming a chair by Mr. Darcy's bed, but never removing her eyes from his familiar features.

"How long has Mr. Darcy been ill?" she whispered so as not to disturb him.

"Nearly a week since the master collapsed in his study," the housekeeper explained.

Elizabeth nodded her understanding, but her attention remained upon the figure lying upon the bed.

"Most know exposure a few days less than a week before they become ill," she whispered in distracted concentration. "The disease takes seven to fourteen days to know an end. We must monitor Mr. Darcy's breathing. Even if he survives the measles, Mr. Darcy could still succumb to its after effects."

"I have many items in my stillroom if you care to examine them later," Mrs. Reynolds volunteered. "You appear knowledgeable of the disease."

"I appreciate your kindness, Ma'am. For now, I

would just like to sit here a few minutes. To keep Mr. Darcy company if it is not too much bother." Elizabeth reached for his hand to cup his larger one in her two smaller ones.

Elizabeth knew the housekeeper withdrew to the other side of the room, but she continued to study the steady rise and fall of Mr. Darcy's chest. She examined the lines about his eyes and the many patches of red peppering his skin. After some ten minutes of quiet inspection, Mr. Darcy's eyes fluttered open.

"Ah, you returned," he rasped.

Elizabeth knew Mr. Darcy was not speaking in his full senses, but she could not resist teasing him.

"Where have I been, Sir?"

Mr. Darcy's eyes opened and closed several times before he responded.

"Devil take it...if I know. You are always...with me...but the...laudanum...skews my dreams."

"Do you dream of me, Mr. Darcy?" Although Elizabeth meant her words as a thankful taunt, she found her heart stuttered to a halt waiting for his response.

"More than a sane man should."

"I am pleased to hear it." She shoved the hair from Mr. Darcy's forehead.

The housekeeper returned to Elizabeth's side.

"Permit me to wipe your face, Master William." The woman wrung out a damp cloth to cool his cheeks with soothing lavender water.

"Was I talking in my sleep?" Mr. Darcy asked the woman as she leaned over him.

"No, Sir." Elizabeth heard the bemusement

in Mrs. Reynolds' tone. "You were speaking to Miss Elizabeth."

Elizabeth watched as Darcy accepted the inevitable.

"Ah, You know my secret, Mrs. Reynolds."

Elizabeth could bear it no longer. She squeezed the hand she still held.

"As do I, Sir," she announced, but the gentleman's reaction was not one of welcome. Mr. Darcy jerked his hand from hers and began to shout.

"Elizabeth!" Mr. Darcy's eyes opened wider. "What the devil are you doing here? Mrs. Reynolds remove her immediately!"

Chapter 10

ELIZABETH STARED AT MR. DARCY in shocked horror before she bolted from the room, her heart shattering with each step she took. At the top of the stairs, she caught at the balustrade to keep from sinking to her knees in complete devastation. Looking about her, Elizabeth realized she made the worst mistake of her short life. Fighting back the tears, which meant to consume her, she rushed down the stairs. Elizabeth possessed no idea where in Mr. Darcy's great house her uncle's maid could be found. Or where the footman placed her trunk. She just knew if she did not escape the embarrassment of the scene of a few moments prior, she would not be responsible for what havoc she might incur upon Mr. Darcy and his elegant manor house.

A different footman opened the door as Elizabeth rushed through it. With a lift of her skirts, she set her steps toward the gatehouse she admired earlier.

"What the devil goes on in here?" the colonel demanded. Darcy's cousin glanced about the room. "Where is Miss Elizabeth? Did the chit upset you?"

Darcy glared at the colonel.

"The woman...is not a chit...and I would prefer...you spoke of her...with proper respect." A coughing fit claimed Darcy's next words.

The colonel folded his arms across his chest.

"So you are in love with her?"

Darcy struggled for a breath.

"Certainly...I am...in love...with her."

"Then where has the lady gone?" Darcy's cousin challenged with a smirk claiming his lips. "Miss Elizabeth demanded I bring her to Pemberley so she might tend you. I thought her so determined that it would be necessary to remove her by force."

"Master William ordered Miss Elizabeth from the room. The lady fled," Mrs. Reynolds added in disapproval.

Darcy threw the bed linens off his legs to rise.

"Only because...I did not...want her to...take ill."

"You are too weak, Darcy." His cousin caught Darcy's shoulders to prevent Darcy's standing.

"There were tears...in her eyes," Darcy protested.

The colonel lifted Darcy's legs to the bed.

"I will go after Miss Elizabeth. You rest. Concentrate on an apology while I am absent. I understand a gentleman's humbling himself is a sure means to a lady's heart."

"I fear...you do not know...Miss Elizabeth's... resolve," Darcy said on another round of coughing.

❦

Elizabeth would have made better time if she did not stop every few minutes for a soul-cleansing cry. In truth, she held no idea where she meant to go. She left her cloak and bonnet and reticule in Mr. Darcy's chambers.

"I cannot return there to retrieve them," Elizabeth declared aloud. She looked about her in despair: Nothing but the beautiful park and woodland. "It would serve the gentleman right if I became lost in Pemberley Woods, never to be seen again." A bit of anger claimed her thoughts. "I swear if I die out here, I will return to Pemberley and haunt the remainder of Mr. Darcy's days."

"I am certain my cousin deserves that and more."

Elizabeth spun around to find Colonel Fitzwilliam watching her. Ashamed to be caught arguing with herself, Elizabeth dashed away her tears with her knuckles.

"You shall receive no quarrel from me, Sir."

The colonel edged closer.

"Return to Pemberley House with me. I believe another of your and Darcy's misconstructions occurred."

The tears welled in Elizabeth's eyes again, but she swallowed hard against the bile rising to her throat.

"I shall return long enough to claim my trunk. Hannah and I will go to Lambton to claim the next coach."

"Did you not hear Jatson say the staff has orders

not to go into the village until the illness knows an end?"

Elizabeth's eyes grew in disbelief.

"Then Hannah and I shall walk to Lambton," she asserted.

"I cannot permit you to depart, Miss Elizabeth."

"Do you mean to provide your cousin a second chance to humiliate me?"

The colonel shook off Elizabeth's remarks.

"When we set a course for Pemberley, I chose a coachman and a footman from Darcy's staff who knew the disease previously. On the journey I paid the two innkeepers extra to clean the rooms we used thoroughly after our departure. I do not know how this illness spreads; and although we are no longer susceptible to the symptoms, how do we know we do not carry it to others? I will return to London after I am assured the Darcys will recover. You and the maid may again travel with me."

Elizabeth felt the anger seep from her body.

"I do not wish others to become ill at my expense. But know I shall not accept Mr. Darcy's charity. Hannah and I shall assist Mrs. Reynolds. I am not so fortunate as to turn my mind from being useful."

A frown crossed the colonel's features.

"I do not imagine Darcy would be pleased to know such circumstances."

"Then I suggest, Colonel, you do not inform Mr. Darcy of my decision."

"Did you...find her?" Darcy asked as the colonel reappeared in his chambers.

Darcy refused Mrs. Reynolds and Sheffield's attempts to see to his personal needs until he knew something of Elizabeth's safety. If he were not so weak, Darcy would have chased Elizabeth down himself.

"I did," Fitzwilliam said with a touch of humor. "Your lady is quite the walker: Miss Elizabeth was more than a third of the way to the gatehouse. If I did not take the path through the woods, I might have missed her."

Darcy was well acquainted with both Elizabeth's love of long walks and her determination.

"Yet, the lady...returned to Pemberley?" Darcy pressed.

"She has," the colonel confirmed. "But not willingly. Miss Elizabeth means to place distance between you and her."

Despite Darcy's best efforts the familiar pang of loss claimed his heart.

"Did you offer...an explanation...for my harsh words?'

"I believe the apology must come from your lips, but I did express my opinion on how Miss Elizabeth misconstrued your words. Even so, the lady was not in an understanding mood. I suspect you must grovel if you wish to win Miss Elizabeth's affections."

Darcy would gladly grovel if Elizabeth would permit him near her again.

"Would you sit...with me...for a few minutes? I would hear...how Miss Elizabeth...came to be at Pemberley."

The colonel led Elizabeth to her assigned chamber before he returned to the private quarters. The room was exquisitely done: a soft green upon the walls and forest green draperies against the walnut woodwork, along with gold accents upon the cording. Sachets of pine needles gave the room a clean, fresh scent. The counterpane was a creamy gold, but it was a seat built into the window, which claimed Elizabeth's interest, and she curled up in it. Her mind and body knew exhaustion from the earlier turmoil. Arms wrapped about her knees, she looked blindly out upon a view of the lake.

"How could I have erred so egregiously?" she asked the emptiness crawling into every corner of her soul. "Because that dratted man wanted me to believe he cared for me!" Elizabeth dug in her sleeve for the damp handkerchief she stuffed there earlier. "I walked into Mr. Darcy's perfectly constructed revenge," she chastised. "In Kent, I injured his pride, and Mr. Darcy repaid me fully. At least, I shall not need to encounter him over the next few days. By the time Mr. Darcy is well enough to leave his bed, I shall be on the road to London and then to Longbourn."

A fresh swell of tears claimed Elizabeth.

"I wished upon the stars like a addled schoolgirl."

A shoulder-racking sob cut off the remainder of her recitation of lost hopes. Elizabeth gave herself up to the sorrow.

How long she remained as such, Elizabeth could not say, but Hannah's entrance had Elizabeth springing to her feet.

"Did they treat you well below stairs?" Elizabeth asked as she dabbed at her eyes.

"Oh, yes, Miss. Most welcoming." The maid shifted her weight from foot-to-foot. "Were you able to see Mr. Darcy?" Hannah asked tentatively.

"Yes."

"Did the gentleman welcome your presence in his home?"

Elizabeth's expression took on iron grimness.

"I imagine what you wish to know is whether the tales below stairs are accurate." She sighed with resignation. "If Mr. Darcy's servants spoke of their master driving me from his quarters, then they spoke the truth. I am an intruder. Unfortunately, we cannot assume the responsibility of delivering the measles to unsuspecting innocents by returning to Cheapside by public conveyance. Therefore, we shall remain in Derbyshire until Colonel Fitzwilliam is prepared to return to London. Three or four days at most. You should know I refused Mr. Darcy's voluntary provisions, and I mean to be of use to Mrs. Reynolds and the gentleman's staff. I shall repay Mr. Darcy for every penny he expends to house us during this stay."

Hannah's eyes grew large with bewilderment.

"Oh, no, Miss. Mr. Gardiner would tan my hide if'n I permitted you to work as you describe. I shall act in your stead."

"First, we both know Uncle Gardiner is a fair master, and you have nothing to fear at his hand," Elizabeth insisted. "As to the work, I do not fear a few sore muscles, and I must act or be forever indebted to a man who would take great pleasure in bandying my name about at social gatherings. Rather than permitting Mr. Darcy the pleasure of bringing me low, I choose to act with aid. Then the gentleman cannot speak ill of me."

"Yours appears a great sacrifice, Miss, if'n you ask me."

"Are you new…to my staff?" Darcy asked in the kindest tone he could muster.

Darcy spent a restless night attempting to construct a means to make amends to Elizabeth Bennet, but he could think of nothing other than to intrude upon the privacy she claimed under his roof. Frustration settled into his bones when Darcy learned of Elizabeth taking her meals in her quarters rather than joining the colonel in the estate's dining room.

The maid backed from the bed.

"I apologize, Sir," she said with an awkward curtsy. "I did not mean to disturb you."

Belatedly, Darcy noticed the chamber pot she held.

"You did not…disturb me," Darcy reassured. "I simply did not…recognize you." He nodded to the chamber pot. "Mr. Sheffield…can handle that."

"I believe your valet assists the colonel, Sir." The maid's voice trembled.

Darcy sighed with an ache of annoyance.

"Very well…but tell me…your name. You possess…a familiar countenance…now that I…look closer. I make it…a point…to know the name…of all those…in my employ." A round of tear-producing coughs shook Darcy's chest. "I apologize...for forgetting your name. Surely, Mrs. Reynolds...told me of you."

"No, Sir." The maid bobbed another curtsy. "I am Hannah. You saw me a time or two at the Gardiners' house. I am assisting Miss Elizabeth with the sick." News of Elizabeth had Darcy shoving himself higher in the bed. "Miss Elizabeth is tending your servants, Sir. One of the grooms and his boy took ill today. She assumed their care while Mrs. Reynolds sees to your sister."

Darcy's lips tightened in disapproval.

"There are enough...among Pemberley's staff... to tend...the ill...without Miss Elizabeth...staining her hands."

It was the maid's turn to frown.

"Miss Elizabeth is the most openhanded of creatures, Sir."

"I am well aware...of Miss Elizabeth's...finer qualities." Darcy's mood darkened.

Realizing she overstepped her bounds, a blush claimed the girl's cheeks.

"Mrs. Reynolds set those who are healthy to cleaning Pemberley thoroughly so others do not become ill: Miss Elizabeth be doing her part."

The fact Elizabeth engendered the maid's loyalty did not surprise Darcy.

"Please tell...Miss Elizabeth...I wish to see her... when she completes...her duties." Each breath Darcy took rattled in his chest like the sound of old keys in an empty box.

The maid blushed a second time.

"I shall tell her, Sir, but I doubt it will do much

good. I overhears Miss Elizabeth tell Mrs. Reynolds that she would never enter Pemberley's private quarters again. Once was enough."

Darcy sent Sheffield to the attic to bring down a rolling chair Darcy's late father used when George Darcy slipped and broke his leg several years back. Darcy should be in bed tending the splitting headache, which lodged between his temples; he should know sleep, but instead Darcy dressed to call upon his sister and hopefully to encounter Elizabeth within Pemberley's passages. Waiting for the infuriating woman to come to him was like waiting to view the sun during the night sky.

"How goes the illness?" Darcy asked his sister. Mr. Sheffield wheeled Darcy into Georgiana's quarters before the valet sought out the presence of Miss Elizabeth to satisfy Darcy's curiosity.

Georgiana reached for his hand.

"I am pleased to see you. I missed you."

"And I you," Darcy claimed the hand she offered. " He noticed that Georgiana did not struggle to breath as he did. Perhaps, his sister knew less of the disease, as Mrs. Reynolds declared. Darcy prayed that the fact. "It grieves me...I brought illness...to your door."

"None of that, William," Georgiana chastised. Her smile spread across her lips. "We always share everything."

Despite Darcy's regrets, he returned her smile.

"I could have chosen new music instead," he teased.

"Yes. Mrs. Reynolds claims this particular 'gift'

comes to us via Mr. Wickham. I suppose I prefer the measles to the alternative."

Darcy squeezed the back of her hand.

"The lesser of two evils?"

A comfortable pause followed.

"The colonel says I remain beautiful," Georgiana shared, at length.

Darcy's curiosity piqued.

"You are never vain. Did you think the measles would scar like the pox?"

"No. No. Nothing of the kind." His sister's cheeks reddened with embarrassment. Georgiana quickly changed the subject. "Our cousin also says Miss Elizabeth came to Pemberley. I hoped the lady would visit with me, but perhaps she fears catching the disease."

"I do not believe...that is the lady's objection. Miss Elizabeth called upon me...but in my delirium... when I awoke...and saw her there...I ordered Mrs. Reynolds...to remove the lady. I could not understand... Elizabeth's being there...and I feared...the lady would become...as ill as you and I...that I might lose her... before I could claim her."

"Oh, William, surely Miss Elizabeth will understand."

"At this point...I am not certain," Darcy confessed. "She remains at Pemberley...but Miss Elizabeth refuses...to speak to me." He tapped the arm of the rolling chair. "Thus, I employed a means...of encountering her."

Georgiana's expression crunched up in confusion.

"Then what Mrs. Reynolds says is true. Miss Elizabeth tends the ill: Dispensing licorice tea for their coughs and ginger tea for their stomach disorders. Demanding that windows be open to permit in fresh air and all surfaces be washed clean with soap and water."

"Mrs. Reynolds has...not shared...as such... with me, but the colonel spoke...of Miss Elizabeth's... unanticipated visit...to Darcy House...where she upset Mrs. Wells...with like demands."

"Mrs. Wells is not as kind as Mrs. Reynolds," Georgian observed.

"I was not pleased...with the woman's... obvious disdain...for Miss Elizabeth's efforts. The lady meant...to protect my household...in my absence. Miss Elizabeth traveled...to Darcy House...with only a maid...to warn Mr. Thacker...to take precautions... against the disease."

"Risking censure for calling upon a bachelor household." Georgiana responded in awe.

"If the colonel...did not call...on Darcy House... when he learned...of an outbreak...in St. Clements parish...and knowing...I called upon...Mr. Wickham there. Mr. Thacker...might have turned...Miss Elizabeth away."

Georgiana's mouth stood agape.

"Miss Elizabeth must love you dearly, William."

Before Darcy could respond to his sister's assertion, Sheffield returned.

"I will call...again later," Darcy told his sister. "Rest now."

With Georgiana's wish for his continued health, Darcy permitted his valet to wheel him from his sister's rooms. In the passageway, he asked of Elizabeth.

"Did you find...Miss Elizabeth?"

"Yes, but you will not appreciate what the lady does," Sheffield warned.

Darcy braced himself for what he knew would be a confrontation; yet, even so, Darcy was not prepared for what he observed from the upper landing. Below him, on the stairs were three maids washing and drying the balustrade and the spindles of the hand railing. It took him several seconds before he realized one of the maids was Elizabeth.

"What the devil are you about, Elizabeth?'

The familiar voice had Elizabeth's spine stiffening. Earlier, she donned her least favorite gown and joined the two maids in their duties. Rest would come only after she departed Pemberley. Until that time, Elizabeth meant to drive away her broken heart with hard work.

"Did you hear me?" Mr. Darcy demanded from above.

Without turning to look at him, Elizabeth responded.

"I suspect the whole house heard you, Sir, but permit me to ask." To the younger of the two maids Elizabeth set her inquiry. "Did you hear the gentleman, Jorie?"

"Yes, Miss," the girl responded with downcast eyes.

"And you, Millie?"

A whispered "Yes, Miss" came from the older maid.

Elizabeth continued cleaning the spindles while Jorie dried.

"It is unanimous, Sir," Elizabeth said without emotion. "Each of us heard your question. Should I also ask the footman below?"

"I understand...your impertinence," Mr. Darcy growled in what sounded of frustration.

Elizabeth did not respond, busying herself with her task instead.

"Will you...not speak to me...in private?" the gentleman asked without the earlier rancor.

Elizabeth stood and picked up one of the buckets of soapy water. However, she did not answer Mr. Darcy's question. Instead, she spoke to the maids.

"I believe I shall begin our work in the dining room. When you finish, please join me there."

"Yes, Miss," the maids said in unison.

From above her, Elizabeth heard a commotion and the protestations of Mr. Darcy's valet; yet, she continued her descent.

"No, Sir. You cannot," Mr. Sheffield declared. "You will fall!"

It took all of Elizabeth's hard-earned control not to look back—not to rush to Mr. Darcy's side.

"Elizabeth, please!" Mr. Darcy pleaded.

She halted her steps, but Elizabeth did not turn to look at him. Viewing Mr. Darcy's features drawn up in urgency would destroy her composure.

"I never gave you permission to use my Christian name," Elizabeth said in bitterness. "We do not hold such a familiarity."

The household went completely silent.

"Will you not...have the decency...to call upon... Miss Darcy? At least...do me the favor...of treating my sister...with dignity," Mr. Darcy charged.

If not for her practiced willpower Elizabeth would toss the bucket aside and mount the stairs to box Mr. Darcy's ears. Yet, she remained still.

"There is no purpose in forming a friendship of one day. I shall depart Pemberley soon, and Miss Darcy will have no need of my acquaintance." With a stifled sob, Elizabeth strode away toward the dining room, while ignoring the splash of water upon her gown from where she clutched the bucket so tightly.

Chapter 11

THE NEXT TWO DAYS brought Darcy no relief: He returned to his bed, but his mind raced to discover a solution. When he fell asleep in an exhausted heap at midnight, Darcy slept all that night and the next day and into the next night's middle. He awoke with a start, his heart pounding in his ears. His eyes searched the darkness for the familiarity of his quarters, the ones he redecorated shortly after his father's passing.

Forcing conscious reality to claim him, Darcy sighed in resignation. This would be his life: Even if he married another, he would wake filled with a yearning for only one woman.

"How could it have gone so wrong?' he whispered.

The scene of Elizabeth's racing from his quarters replayed in his dreams.

"Why did I not simply catch her to me and claim the affection, which brought Elizabeth to watch over me?" Darcy turned on his side to bury his face in his pillow. "Because I was taught to protect those I affect," he admitted. "Yet..." Darcy punched the pillow. "Yet, only a fool would send away the woman he adores most in the world. If only I spoke with temperance."

The sound of Mr. Sheffield stirring had Darcy pretending to sleep. He wished no one's pity. His servants witnessed the scene of his argument with Elizabeth. Afterwards, even Sheffield diverted his eyes when his valet insisted upon Darcy's return to his quarters. Darcy humiliated himself before the people who looked upon him for their future. How were his staff to judge him if he appeared weak?

"Another example of my cursed tongue saying what I should keep private," Darcy murmured. "Why did viewing Elizabeth upon her knees rip my heart in two?"

Although Darcy chose not to give his thoughts voice, he knew his response to Elizabeth's acting the role of servant was based on the fear he felt when he searched for Wickham, knowing such would be Elizabeth's life of drudgery if he failed. Most assuredly, Darcy experienced the pain of seeing Elizabeth brought low and at her own hands. It was humbling to realize that she despised him so much she would prefer to scrub his floors than to accept even the smallest token of humanity from him.

Darcy could hear the house stir to life, but he kept his eyes closed to the world. Only behind the façade of sleep could he woo and win Elizabeth Bennet's affections. Only then did he speak words of love, rather than censure. Only then did Elizabeth look upon him with favor.

❧

Elizabeth again found her way to the window seat. It was a beautiful night, a starry night with a gentle breeze, but it brought her no comfort. After the confrontation with Mr. Darcy, the gentleman returned to his quarters. From what she overheard, Mr. Darcy sought his bed and had yet to rise from their encounter. To Elizabeth's relief, Mrs. Reynolds disclosed Mr. Darcy did not succumb to his illness again. She did not think she could bear to be responsible for Mr. Darcy knowing greater suffering.

"Master William simply requires his rest," the housekeeper shared while the woman and Elizabeth changed out the linens upon the servants' sick beds. Other than the two latest patients, the others progressed nicely. Despite Elizabeth's resolve to leave Mr. Darcy behind, she could not but be sorry to leave him.

Reluctantly, Elizabeth climbed upon her bed. She required sleep for the colonel announced that he meant to depart for London after the morrow's breakfast.

"Finally," Elizabeth spoke softly to the shadows as she drew the linens over her head. "I shall be rid of this madness and of Mr. Darcy."

❧

"Darcy?" His cousin's voice came close to Darcy's ear.

"What is amiss, Fitzwilliam?" Darcy kept his eyes closed, praying his cousin would leave him so Darcy might grieve for his loss.

"I mean to depart for London today. You and Georgiana will be well soon, and General Leigh-Hunt expects me to join him for supper on Friday."

Although Darcy thought he knew the answer, he asked, "What day is this?"

"Wednesday."

Darcy rolled to his back.

"Have a safe journey, and keep me informed of Leigh-Hunt's wishes."

Darcy knew the general often called upon Fitzwilliam for his most pressing assignments, a fact of which Darcy disapproved.

The colonel waited for him to say more, but Darcy refused to ask of Elizabeth.

"Should I inquire after Wickham when I return to London?"

"Not on my account," Darcy said in bitterness. "I could do nothing even if the scoundrel reneges upon his promise. I am not well enough to execute another search, and the Bennets would not welcome more interference upon my part. Mr. Gardiner will deal well with Mr. Wickham."

"As you wish," the colonel said with a lift of his eyebrow, indicating his concern. "And what of Miss Elizabeth?"

Darcy closed his eyes to ward off the inevitable rush of regret.

"Miss Elizabeth means to walk away from Pemberley and me. When she departs with you today, our connection ends."

In spite of his spoken resolve to permit Elizabeth to leave without another confrontation, after the colonel departed to call upon Georgiana, Darcy donned a favorite banyan over his wrinkled shirt and breeches and slowly made his way to Elizabeth's door. Bracing his weight against the frame, he knocked lightly and waited for her appearance.

When the door swung wide, his heart stuttered to a halt. A silky wrapper covered her night rail. Her toes peeked from under the hem, and her hair–those glorious unstyled locks, which he viewed only once on the day Elizabeth walked from Longbourn to Netherfield to tend her ill sister–hung about her shoulders, draping to her waist. Auburn curls caressed her cheeks. Darcy wished to claim fistfuls of the fire-touched strains.

"Mr. Darcy," she hissed. "Why are you here? And at this hour?" She pulled the wrapper close about her. "Do you mean to ruin me?"

"I would never," Darcy said in defense. As he made his way to Elizabeth's quarters, Darcy rehearsed his apology, but her reaction to his appearance had him swallowing the words he meant to say. "I thought we held unfinished business." It was all Darcy could do not to reach for her. He thought if he could only hold Elizabeth in his arms all would be well.

"We do not!" Elizabeth reached for the door to close it.

Darcy leaned heavily against the framing.

"Wait! Please wait," he whispered.

"Why?" Elizabeth spoke with cool indifference. "So you may humiliate me further? I understand: You spoke the words Society expects from a gentleman, but I am not one of those seeking a husband on the Marriage Mart. All I ever required in any gentleman was honesty."

"Yes. I am well aware of your brand of honesty, Miss Elizabeth. You prefer scoundrels such as Mr. Wickham to a man who offers you respectability," Darcy snapped.

Her chin notched higher.

"Leave me, Mr. Darcy. Claim your victory. I dared to rebuke a man of your consequence, and you successfully repaid my prideful act. You proved yourself superior to Mr. Wickham and to my family."

"Do I hear you correctly? It is your belief that I enticed you to follow me to Pemberley specifically so I might reject you as you rejected me in Kent. Explain to me, Miss Elizabeth, how I planned to contract measles so you would feel empathy for me. I have known convoluted thinking previously, but never to this extent," he charged.

They were nearly nose-to-nose, so close, Darcy considered kissing Elizabeth senseless.

"I never thought you 'enticed' me to Pemberley, but..."

"But what?" Darcy pressed. "I spoke promises that you denied possible, yet for which you secretly hoped." She flinched when Darcy traced a line across her cheek with a single fingertip. "Is that the way of it, Elizabeth?"

"No!" Her denial lacked conviction as Elizabeth's eyes drifted close: A familiar longing crossed her expression. They stood as such for several elongated seconds as their breaths came faster. Fascinated by the feel of her skin beneath his finger, Darcy hesitated in kissing her. Unfortunately, the pause rekindled Elizabeth's ire.

"Unhand me!" Elizabeth accused.

Irritated by Elizabeth's continued stubbornness, Darcy held up the finger with which he stroked her cheek.

"Unhand you?" His eyebrow rose in challenge.

Sarcasm laced Elizabeth's words.

"You win again, Mr. Darcy."

"There is no winner unless we are together," Darcy insisted. "Can you not see every move I make is meant to protect you? Even when I thought you knew Mr. Wickham..." The image of Wickham touching Elizabeth always tore of Darcy's soul, and Darcy searched for the right words to express his affections.

"You mean when Mr. Bingley demanded you act with honor?" Fury sparked in Elizabeth's eyes. "Do not speak to me of your devotion."

Unable to resist the urge to lash out, Darcy responded with his own unkind accusation.

"Did you know of Miss Lydia's elopement when you and the Gardiners came to Pemberley? When you walked along the riverbank, did you know regret not to discover me at home? Were your 'innocent' remarks to Bingley of Miss Bennet's pining for his homecoming a means to prove my early estimations in error? I know Mrs. Reynolds informed you of my expected return to the manor with the Bingleys in company. Did you wait for the coaches to pass through Lambton in hopes of drawing Bingley's attentions?"

"You knew I visited Pemberley; yet, you made no attempt to renew our acquaintance? What does your inaction say of your regard, Mr. Darcy? Were you at home when my family toured the estate? Did you spy upon me? Did you count the number of times I returned to your portrait in the gallery and recognize my susceptibility? Is that when you hatched the plan to humiliate me?" Elizabeth reached for the door again. "Perhaps you should know, Mr. Darcy, that when I tended Mr. Wickham at Gracechurch Street, that gentleman welcomed my presence in his quarters." With her pronouncement, the door closed in Darcy's face, and his heart plummeted into more despair.

Darcy watched from the gallery as Mrs. Reynolds and a weakened Mr. Nathan bid Elizabeth and the colonel farewell. It was pure torture to observe the kindness with which Elizabeth treated his servants and to know no such tidings were meant for him. Mrs. Reynolds' expression spoke of his housekeeper's approval of Elizabeth Bennet. His servant presented Elizabeth with what appeared to be a strip of crocheted lace. Elizabeth blushed from the notice and quickly added it to the pages of the book she carried before placing her arms about Mrs. Reynolds in a lingering embrace. With a glance about the foyer, she accepted the colonel's proffered arm. And then she was gone. Elizabeth walked from Darcy's life once again.

"How could what began with such promise end in misery?" Darcy whispered.

With nothing to which to look forward, he turned his dejected steps toward his quarters.

Although Elizabeth attempted to speak in all politeness to Colonel Fitzwilliam, it was all she could do not to deliver a waspish denouncement of the colonel's abominable cousin. Elizabeth wished to question Fitzwilliam upon what he knew of Mr. Darcy's insinuations, but she did not. At length, they parted, and Elizabeth knew instant regret at not having the opportunity to claim the colonel as family.

"You have returned!" Lydia called from where she sat beside Mr. Wickham upon a settle in Aunt Gardiner's favorite drawing room.

"Yes, I have." Elizabeth curtsied to Mr. Wickham, who rose upon her entrance. "I am pleased to observe a bit of health has returned to your person, Sir."

"I am not yet prepared to attempt a country dance, but I can claim a steadier stance."

Elizabeth gestured his return to his seat while she perched upon the edge of a nearby chair.

"Lydia and I could not help but notice that Colonel Fitzwilliam set you down from one of Darcy's coaches. I thought Mr. Gardiner said you tended his business associate." A lift of his eyebrow said Wickham was more than curious.

"I did. Mr. Hacker resides near All Hallows Church, and as Uncle Gardiner's coachman assumed the care of his children when we welcomed your illness to uncle's household, I sent word to Colonel Fitzwilliam at Darcy House. Mr. Darcy offered his cousin's escort if I required anything in his absence. The colonel delivered me to Hacker's door and retrieved me today. I am most grateful for his kindness, especially as he holds duties with General Leigh-Hunt later today."

Elizabeth smiled at Mr. Wickham before asking Lydia of the wedding. Oblivious to the contest, which just passed between Elizabeth and Mr. Wickham, Lydia perked up immediately.

"I wish it could be grander, but Aunt Gardiner says I 'cannot flaunt my fortune' before others. To which I said, 'Why marry if not for the notice of others?'"

Elizabeth heard the hint of frustration in Lydia's tone, and so she swallowed her "Why indeed?" response. Instead, she offered her sister an enticing alternative.

"Yet, even without a larger ceremony, you should rejoice for you shall be the first among your sisters to marry." Elizabeth knew Lydia well enough to know her youngest sister would enjoy the distinction among the Bennet daughters.

Lydia's countenance brightened.

"And perhaps my dearest Wickham will be permitted to wear his Regimentals."

"We may only hope," Elizabeth said with pleasure.

Lydia suddenly sat straighter. She worried her bottom lip, which told Elizabeth her sister had a confession of sorts to divulge.

"I pray you shall not be angry with me. I did not know when you might return, and certainly did not wish Aunt Gardiner to be my attendant. I would prefer Kitty, but Papa refused Kitty's coming to London." Lydia paused before saying, "I asked Mary to serve as one of our witnesses."

"I could not be more delighted," Elizabeth said with all honesty. "It was kind of you to involve our sister. Mary is quite special in her own way." Elizabeth held no desire to observe her youngest sister marry Mr. Wickham. She would say a prayer of thanksgiving not to be a part of the actual ceremony. When she stood, Elizabeth motioned Mr. Wickham to remain seated. "Now, if you will pardon me, I should find Uncle and inform him of my time with the Hacker household."

As Elizabeth climbed the stairs to her quarters, her mind drifted again to the look of devastation upon Mr. Darcy's countenance when she spoke of spending time in Mr. Wickham's quarters. Elizabeth meant to damage his pride, but she did not think the gentleman would know such pain. Witnessing it, she wished to reach out to him–to comfort him.

"Foolish chit," she murmured in self-chastisement. "It is all part of the act. The man cares nothing for you."

Ten days passed since Elizabeth departed with the colonel. Darcy returned to his duties, but without much enthusiasm. He sent Mr. Gardiner a note stating his and Georgiana's health required Darcy's remaining at Pemberley rather than returning to London to witness the wedding. Knowing Elizabeth would likely remain in Town for Miss Lydia's nuptials, Darcy absented himself from the ceremony.

"Odd that I would prefer to encounter Mr. Wickham more than the woman I love."

He ran his fingers distractedly through his hair while making a poor attempt in updating his ledgers. None of the symptoms of the illness remained, other than the occasional queasiness in his stomach, which Darcy suspected had more to do with the pangs of unrequited love than the measles.

"A letter, Sir." Mr. Nathan carried in the post

upon a silver salver before exiting.

Darcy caught up the thick letter and turned it over to read the direction. He recognized the script, and his heart fluttered in his chest: It was from Elizabeth's uncle.

"The deed is done; Miss Lydia has a husband," Darcy whispered as he broke the seal and opened the folded over pages.

Within, Mr. Gardiner elaborated upon the unrepentant attitude of the "happy couple," but the gentleman assured Darcy all the terms they negotiated with and upon Mr. Wickham's behalf were executed as promised.

> *Even though they have but a few days to spare, Mrs. Wickham insisted upon her and the newly minted officer calling upon her family before parting for the North. Mrs. Bennet was most anxious to greet her daughter's new husband, and so my brother Bennet sent his carriage for the couple. Naturally, Elizabeth and Mary returned to Longbourn also. Mrs. G and I will miss their sweet ways with the children.*

"So she returns to the bosom of her family," Darcy murmured. "I pray Miss Elizabeth finds happiness."

The next part of the letter praised Darcy's intervention in the Bennet family's trials and held a promised devotion to Darcy's self. Although Darcy thought that he did not deserve Gardiner's kindness, he expected such sentiments from Elizabeth's uncle, who was quite a remarkable gentleman. Yet, it was the last paragraph, which had Darcy's heartbeat hitching upward.

> *Our Lizzy has not been her customary vivacious self since her return from Derbyshire. Mrs. G. believes our niece concerned for your full recovery, and neither of us think it would be inappropriate if you wrote to Lizzy at Longbourn to assure E of your continued health. We would never have permitted E to travel to Derbyshire if Lizzy did not insist that you renewed your proposal and that, as a couple, you simply awaited the Wickhams' joining before you made the announcement public. As you are betrothed, an exchange of letters would be acceptable. There is no need to worry each other because of the necessary distance of the moment.*
>
> *E. Gardiner*

"Betrothed?" Darcy did not know whether to be angry at Elizabeth's conniving or to celebrate her creativity. "Needless to say, Mr. Gardiner suspects something of Miss Elizabeth's perfidy." Darcy shook his head in amused disbelief. "Even if I wrote to Elizabeth, she would burn the letter without reading it. No," he said as he placed Gardiner's letter to the side to return to his ledgers. "I will not provide Miss Elizabeth the pleasure of rejecting me yet again."

Darcy dipped his pen in the ink and began to add the transactions regarding Mr. Wickham's marriage to his books, but the recording had him thinking of the manner in which Elizabeth's breath caught in her throat when Darcy edged her into his arms.

"Elizabeth is not immune to me."

Distracted, Darcy returned the pen to the well. He leaned into the leather of his favorite chair while he examined the possibility.

"If I simply show up on Elizabeth's doorstep, the lady will call off the false betrothal without considering a lifetime together. Her pride would never permit Elizabeth to admit her error," Darcy reasoned. "Yet, Elizabeth risked everything to know more of my health. I cannot permit her to claim ruin simply because we argued over something insignificant."

Darcy allowed the idea to take root.

"I do express myself better in writing," he mused. "Perhaps I could woo Elizabeth without her knowing my purpose."

Darcy began to construct plans on how best to proceed.

"My initial letter should say nothing of my hopes of a reconciliation. I should simply state the obvious: The lady's family is under the assumption we are engaged, and before Elizabeth ends our acquaintance it would be best if we continued the farce for a time because too many people know of her coming to Pemberley under the guise of being my betrothed." Darcy liked that idea. "No manipulations. Simple logic. The honesty Miss Elizabeth claims she desires in a man. Elizabeth will respond with an agreement to continue the sham for a bit longer or demand my withdrawal." Darcy chuckled. "The ball returns to your court, Elizabeth Bennet. Shall you continue to play the game or forfeit?"

Chapter 12

"YOU SENT FOR ME, Papa?"

Elizabeth found her father buried behind a stack of books. Since Mrs. Bennet's returned to her duties at Longbourn, Mr. Bennet retreated further into his isolation.

"Yes." He pointed to a letter resting upon a stack of books. "You have an admirer."

With as much calmness as she could muster, Elizabeth crossed the room to snatch up the post.

"From Charlotte or Aunt Gardiner?"

Yet, before her father could respond, the familiar script set Elizabeth's hands trembling.

"From your reaction, I assume you know the sender, and you will not attempt to convince me the letter came from a female. A gentleman's script lacks the delicate touch of Mrs. Collins or your aunt." Her father did not chastise, but dissatisfaction laced his tone.

"It is from Mr. Darcy," Elizabeth said obediently.

"And the gentleman believes it acceptable to correspond with my unmarried daughter because..."

"I did not ask him to write to me," Elizabeth protested. "In fact, when we parted last, we spoke most ill to each other."

"And where did this ill parting take place?"

Her father did not move a muscle or raise his voice, which set Elizabeth's nerves off kilter. She knew immediately that in her rush to deny knowledge of Mr. Darcy's correspondence she admitted her latest deception.

"Pemberley."

"Pemberley? I see. And this parting occurred recently?"

"A fortnight before Mary and I returned to Longbourn."

A long silence had Elizabeth shifting her weight self-consciously.

"I suspect your being at Pemberley had something to do with the illness, which followed Mr. Darcy to Pemberley."

"Yes, Sir."

Her father shook his head in disbelief.

"I am confused, Elizabeth, in regards to your relationship with Mr. Darcy. For many months while the gentleman resided with Mr. Bingley at Netherfield, you decried Mr. Darcy's worth as a man, but after your journey to Kent, your disdain softened. Most recently you admitted Mr. Darcy proved to you the depth of Mr. Wickham's wayward tendencies long before this situation with Lydia occurred. Your Uncle Gardiner says Mr. Darcy proposed to you twice." Elizabeth's shoulders sank further with each of her father's assertions. "You permitted the man to think you carried Wickham's child in order to provoke Mr. Darcy into assisting us in locating Wickham. According to your uncle, you told the Gardiners, you accepted Mr. Darcy's most recent proposal so you might race off to tend to his health." With a sigh of resignation, her father added, "I always thought you the most intelligent of my children. Now, I discover you are more of the nature of Kitty and Lydia."

Disappointing her father brought Elizabeth as much pain as losing Mr. Darcy.

"Guilty as charged," she whispered.

Her father stood and crossed from behind his desk to catch Elizabeth up in his embrace.

"Tell me, Lizzy, if you care for this man. We all know him to be a proud, unpleasant sort of man, but this would be nothing if you really liked him."

The tears Elizabeth withheld from the time she walked away from Pemberley came pouring out.

"It would not matter," she admitted on a hiccup of sobs, "if I wished the acquaintance. A man once shunned…will not…seriously claim…a woman whose connections to Mr. Wickham would bring her shame."

"Even so, the man played with your affections." The hardness lacing her father's tone was not often heard at Longbourn.

"We argued." Elizabeth dabbed at her eyes with the handkerchief her father provided without her asking. "I appeared upon Mr. Darcy's doorstep, but the gentleman ordered me removed. Mr. Darcy wished nothing to do with me."

Her father set her at arm's length from him.

"Did you leave when Mr. Darcy sent you away?"

"No. Colonel Fitzwilliam pointed out I could not take a public coach for we all knew the sick room for several days. We were not ill, but who is to say if my presence on the public coach would not spread the disease?"

"How long did you reside under Mr. Darcy's roof?"

Elizabeth did not understand her father's questions.

"Some four days."

"I see." Her father returned to his desk. "What will you do with Mr. Darcy's letter? Will you read it?"

"If you prefer I return it unopened, I shall do so. Or I could burn it," Elizabeth offered.

Her father's features appeared grave.

"I know you, Lizzy. You wish to learn of Mr. Darcy's reason for writing to you."

A red flush crept up her neck.

"I do."

Mr. Bennet sucked in a quick breath.

"I will tolerate the correspondence for the time being, but we must keep your relationship to Mr. Darcy secret. If Mrs. Bennet learns of it, there will be no peace at Longbourn until I demand a duel to protect your honor."

Silence rose between them.

"I shall not disappoint you again, Papa," Elizabeth whispered into the quiet.

"Ask Mr. Darcy in the future to address his

posts to 'Mr. T J P Bennet.' Few know my full Christian name. I will know it is he and present the letter to you. Continue the correspondence or end it. The decision is yours, Lizzy, but know, either way, you remain my dearest child."

After assisting Mrs. Hill to tie and hang the herbs from the garden, Elizabeth made her way to the privacy of her chambers. She knew Mr. Bingley escorted Jane upon a ride in the gentleman's new gig, and she would be alone. Climbing upon her bed, Elizabeth placed the letter before her to examine the flow of Mr. Darcy's script. The gentleman wrote the way he lived: with confidence and pride. At length, she broke the wax seal to find two pages.

11 September 1812
Miss Elizabeth,

> *Although I am certain this is not a letter you welcome, I thought it prudent we have further conversation. From both Colonel F and your uncle, I learned you broke with propriety to come to my aid. For this kindness I am forever grateful. Even before the death of my parents, it was I who provided the care to those I most affect. I am unaccustomed to others seeing to my welfare.*

"Apologize," Elizabeth pleaded. "Explain what went awry if you are grateful for my attentions." Yet, the frustrating man did not speak more on her intrusion into his quarters.

> *For many months, I hoped to host you under my roof–to show you Pemberley's grounds–to entertain you in its music room and to share Pemberley's many vistas. Yet, the circumstances robbed us of those memories, leaving behind the taste of bitterness.*

"I did not come to Derbyshire to enjoy its splendor," Elizabeth whispered to her broken heart. "I came because I could do nothing less–because you were there and ill." She dashed away a single tear upon her cheek.

> *Recently you charged me with the duty of speaking honestly, and so I will. Although our relationship is often provoking, it also knew moments of tenderness and understanding. I believe the latter is grounds for a connection.*
>
> *In truth, the pretext you practiced to oversee my care is well known at Pemberley and in the Gardiner household. As such, many believe us betrothed. We might ignore those rumors if you did not travel with the colonel to Derbyshire and did not stay at inns often used by the Fitzwilliam and Darcy families–if my staff did not know of your previous visits to Pemberley–if you did not demand access to my quarters from my housekeeper–if I did not order Mrs. Reynolds and Mr. Sheffield*

to remove you from my sick room–if we did not argue before two maids and a footman–if you did not insist before others that you would never return to the private quarters–if I did not stubbornly refuse to see you upon your journey to London–if you did not deny a visit with Miss Darcy–if you did not swear to my offer of marriage before you set out for Derbyshire–and if I did not neglect to announce our engagement.

Even though you likely hold no desire to place your life under my protection, there are issues present, which demand our attention. Whether either of us cares to admit it or not, your reputation could be as tattered as Mrs. Wickham's if we do not act. Mr. Bingley is a devoted suitor to Miss Bennet, but Bingley still desires an entrance into Society. If Miss Bennet possessed two sisters who knew ruination, it would make it more difficult for my friend to act upon his desire. And what of your younger sisters? What future would they claim if another scandal plagues your family? More importantly, what would your ruination say to Society of Mr. and Mrs. Bennet? How will others judge your parents?

Therefore, I propose we continue the farce, at least for the time being. We will exchange letters regularly, an act only the betrothed are permitted. In doing so, we have the time to learn more of each of other. Perhaps at the end, we will discover we do not

suit. Yet, there is also the possibility we may
choose to join for life. I await your response.
                    FD

Elizabeth expected many circumstances, but not the one presented in Mr. Darcy's letter. There was no passion. No words of love or censure. Only one line where he spoke of the least bit of affection.

"Mr. Darcy proposes a marriage of convenience! What more did you expect after performing in such a gormless fashion? You squelched any affection the gentleman once held for you! Well, I shall not do it!" Elizabeth refolded the letter and stuffed it in a drawer so no one else might read it. She did not permit herself to recognize that if she truly meant to deny Mr. Darcy her response, she would burn the dratted letter. In truth, Elizabeth could no more part with this second letter than she could the first one.

Aloud, she protested the gentleman's injustice.

"I cannot spend a lifetime at Mr. Darcy's side and pretend my heart not engaged!" Elizabeth lay back upon the bed to close her eyes. "I would rather remain a social outcast than to know less than love."

Despite reading Mr. Darcy's letter more often than she would admit, Elizabeth did not respond. Like his previous letter, she was in a fair way of knowing this second one by heart. She studied every sentence, and her feelings toward its writer were at times widely different. When Elizabeth recalled their encounters at Pemberley, indignation claimed her; yet, his dedication to discovering Mr. Wickham and Lydia remained exemplary. Often Elizabeth's anger turned against herself for permitting her heart to lead her head–for destroying what once held great promise, and Elizabeth felt no inclination to see Mr. Darcy again.

"How could I face him? It is best if we hold no connections, and marriage is the deepest of connections," Elizabeth cautioned, but then as was her nature, she turned her thoughts to sarcasm. "Of course, a marriage of convenience would be the easiest means to avoid a disagreeable husband."

The thought had but taken root when Elizabeth turned a corner of the house to discover her mother bent forward at the waist and sobbing.

"Mama!" she rushed forward to place her arm about her mother's shoulder. "What is amiss? Are you ill? Is it your nerves?"

A flush of embarrassment claimed Mrs. Bennet's cheeks.

"I did not mean to frighten you, Lizzy," she said in apology. "It is just your mother being her customary insensible self." Her mother stood straighter, but Elizabeth noted the self-chastisement remained.

"Come sit with me in the arbor," Elizabeth encouraged. "We shall be insensible together. I sincerely miss the games you once invented to entertain us girls." She tugged upon her mother's hand.

Mrs. Bennet paused but a brief moment before following.

"I should return to the manor. There is much to be done," her mother protested.

"Nothing that cannot wait a few minutes. We so rarely have moments to reminisce," Elizabeth insisted.

"Look! There are patches of clover." She did not know what she meant to convey with pointless chatter, but Elizabeth knew something of import bothered her mother. "Do you recall how you made endless chains of flowers for Jane's and Mary's and my hair?"

Her mother stared off as if seeing the scene playing before her eyes.

"Jane adored them as if they were tiaras, but Mary found nothing whimsical in them."

"And what of me?" Elizabeth asked.

Mrs. Bennet patted the back of Elizabeth's hand.

"You preferred for me to form the flowers into chainmail. You were always the adventurer–the one who chose her own way. You reminded me of that particular fact most recently when you refused Mr. Collins." Her mother sighed heavily. "I should not have insisted upon your acceptance of Mr. Collins's hand. I knew you would not suit."

"Yet, the alliance would secure our futures," Elizabeth reasoned. "I acted with selfishness."

"I considered the matter much while I was abed with my nerves. Instead of you, I should have directed Mr. Collins toward Mary. Your sister would be a better match for Mr. Collins, and Longbourn would know a Bennet in its future." Elizabeth would not wish Mr. Collins on any of her sisters, but she would agree that Mary's nature was similar to Charlotte Collins's in many ways. Her mother added softly, "I failed to secure the estate by delivering an heir for Mr. Bennet."

"Oh, Mama." Elizabeth slipped her arms about her mother's shoulders. "You did not fail Papa or the estate. With no male heir, you have done the next best thing: Placing your efforts to securing your daughters' futures."

"At least, Mr. Bingley returned to Jane's side. If Jane can bring Bingley up to snuff this time, a flicker of hope exists that we shall not be destitute after Mr. Bennet passes, and the Collinses claim Longbourn." A small smile tugged at her mother's lips. "Although Mr. Wickham did not act honorably toward Lydia, they are settled in the North. I never worried for Lydia finding a husband for she is quite pretty and very inviting."

Elizabeth thought, *Too inviting*, but she said nothing.

"And I hinted to my Sister Phillips that perhaps Mr. Phillip's new apprentice, Mr. Robert Grange, might find a sensible wife in Mary."

"Perhaps soon," Elizabeth teased, "you will only need to contend with Kitty and me."

"What else may a mother do? It is her lot in life to put forward her daughters as good mistresses of an eligible gentleman's household. Naturally, I would wish you and Kitty as well placed as Jane. It would be a great imposition if only Mr. Bingley were to support us. I do not expect the Wickhams in a position to contribute to our comfort."

Elizabeth privately agreed for the couple was not built to know economy.

"Mr. Grange," her mother continued, "will be some time as an apprentice before he can claim a wife and home. All we can do is hope Mr. Bennet delays his passing until all our daughters are settled."

"Is there an urgency?" Elizabeth knew her father not always the most robust of men, but she held no news of possible complaints regarding his health.

Her mother shook off Elizabeth's worry.

"Nothing immediate," her mother assured. "But a man can be thrown by his horse or choke upon a bite of lamb stew or fall upon the stairs. Fate is not always kind."

Mr. Bennet said something similar in regards to Lydia's folly.

"I promise Kitty and I will plan our appearances in society with more care," Elizabeth said good-naturedly. "If we are successful, only you and Papa will remain at Longbourn. What shall you do then?" she teased.

As if the idea was not one Mrs. Bennet would welcome, her mother frowned.

"What we do now: Avoid each other. Any tenderness Mr. Bennet once felt for me no longer exists."

Elizabeth spent an hour in the orchard before coming to her decision. *What if Mr. Bennet passed this day? Where would they go? How would her mother and sisters survive? If their father passed, Jane could not marry Mr. Bingley for a year because of the required mourning period? Who would take them in? Uncle Gardiner could not stand the extra expense after all he did for Lydia, and Uncle Phillips could not support two households on his income.*

"But if I chose an alliance with Mr. Darcy, all would be well," Elizabeth reasoned. "I could tolerate the correspondence between us long enough to see Jane settled with Mr. Bingley, and then I could end it if we cannot come to some understanding."

With resolve, she marched into her father's

study.

"Papa, I decided to correspond with Mr. Darcy. I pray you shall permit this aberration from propriety."

"I see," Mr. Bennet said, but her father did not appear surprised by Elizabeth's declaration. He leaned into his chair and studied Elizabeth's features. "What brought on this change of mind? Only two days prior you swore you wished nothing to do with the man."

"I considered what you said and what Mr. Darcy freely states in his letter: My impetuous spirit led many to believe I claim an engagement with Mr. Darcy. Heaven knows this family cannot bear more shame. Mr. Darcy proposes a betrothal for appearance sake, and if we choose to remain together, the gentleman will honor the engagement." Elizabeth added quickly. "What I share will sound of a bit of lunacy: Despite our multiple disagreements, Mr. Darcy remains my most devoted friend, and such is more than many may claim in a relationship."

"Yes," her father said sagely. "A marriage based on friendship is preferable to one based upon passion."

It took a week for her response to arrive, but Darcy's instincts proved correct: Elizabeth agreed to accept the "fake" engagement he suggested. Finally, Darcy's breathing eased.

"I simply must employ the words, which will bring the lady into my embrace forever."

Darcy reread Elizabeth's response. It was even more carefully worded than his initial letter. He smiled when he imagined her scratching out words and rewriting passages to eliminate any display of affection.

"Nice volley," Darcy mused aloud. "The game continues."

He picked up his pen to write:

My dearest Elizabeth,

Chapter 13

MY *DEAREST ELIZABETH,*

Elizabeth rushed to her quarters to read Mr. Darcy's response. She spent hours purging any sign of the affection she felt for the man in her letter to him, but she prayed for a glimmer of such in the gentleman's response.

"My dearest Elizabeth," she read aloud. "Thank you for your thoughtful response. I imagine you were as cautious as I in choosing the correct words, ones which offered no commitment and no evidence of our previous interactions."

In spite of her best efforts to ignore Mr. Darcy's audacious confidence, Elizabeth smiled.

"It is a true shame the man and I are of a like mind. Such knowledge would make our joining an interesting endeavor."

Therefore, I propose another compromise. Could we simply speak honestly? Let us talk of politics, estates, books, the latest on dits, family…whatever is upon our minds. Tell me of your day: The frustrations and the humor and the tenderness. Likewise, I will speak of mine. Speak to me of Bingley and Miss Bennet, what has occurred in Meryton, and of the Lucases. I wish to know more of Elizabeth Bennet, and it appears imperative that you should know something of Fitzwilliam Darcy beyond the image of the Master of Pemberley.

"A bold move, Mr. Darcy," Elizabeth murmured. "Perhaps I shall discover more to despise than to admire."

Assuming you will agree, I would like to revisit our earliest encounters. In truth, your rebuke of my attentions at Hunsford Cottage was a slap to my pride, but upon reflection, I discovered you said nothing of me that I did not deserve, and although your accusations were ill founded, formed on mistaken premises, my behavior to you at the time merited the severest reproof. It was unpardonable. I cannot think of it without abhorrence.

I know you will offer your forgiveness, but I am not so easily reconciled. The recollection of what I then said, of my conduct, my manners, and my expressions during the whole of it, is now, and has been many months, inexpressibly painful to me. Your reproof, so well applied, I will never forget –'Had you behaved in a more gentleman-like manner,' those were your words. You know not, you can scarcely conceive, how they have tortured me; though it was some time, I confess, before I was reasonable enough to allow their justice.

"Could Mr. Darcy value my opinion so?" Elizabeth sat in awe of his early devotion to her. She could barely recall what she said in anger, but Mr. Darcy knew pain from her remarks, so much so that Elizabeth regretted her impulsive tongue.

"Proclaiming Mr. Darcy less than a gentleman stung the man's conceit. How did I not see that my retort would act upon Mr. Darcy's scruples so profoundly?"

At the time you thought me then devoid of every proper feeling. I am certain you did. The turn of your countenance I shall never forget, as you said that I could not have addressed you in any possible way that would induce you to accept me.

"Dare I tell Mr. Darcy that I have long been most heartily ashamed of my actions?" Elizabeth whispered.

I pray the letter I so unceremoniously pressed into your hands the morning after your rejection had you thinking better of me. Did you, on reading it, give any credit to its contents? I would know your opinion, Miss Elizabeth, if you would indulge me. I realize what I wrote must have given you pain, but I pray not so much pain that exculpation cannot be presented. I hope you destroyed the letter. There was one part especially, the opening of it, which I should dread your having the power of reading again. I can remember some expressions, which might justly make you hate me.

"Hate you?" Elizabeth murmured as tears flooded her eyes. "I learned to care most deeply for you, and as to the burning of that letter, it shall never happen."

When I wrote that letter in Rosings' chambers, I believed myself perfectly calm and cool, but I am since convinced that it was written in a dreadful bitterness of spirit. No doubt, you will speak to me of how you, too, acted in reproach, but I cannot place the blame upon your shoulders. You acted well in the matter.

"As noted previously, Mr. Darcy," Elizabeth observed, "you hold yourself to impossibly strict standards. Doing so makes the fall more overwhelming."

But with me, it is not so. Painful recollections will intrude, which cannot, which ought not to be repelled. I have been a selfish being all my life, in practice, though not in principle. As a child I was taught what was right, but I was not taught to correct my temper. To be more affable toward others. I was given good principles, but left to follow them in pride and conceit. Unfortunately, as an only son, (for many years an only child), I was spoilt by my parents, who though good themselves, (my father particularly, all that was benevolent and amiable) allowed, encouraged, almost taught me to be selfish and overbearing, to care for none beyond my own family circle, to think meanly of all the rest of the world, to wish at least to think meanly of their sense and worth compared with my own. Such I was, from eight to eight and twenty; and such I might still have been but for you, dearest, loveliest Elizabeth. What do I not owe you? You taught me a lesson, hard indeed at first, but most advantageous. By you, I was properly humbled. I came to you without a doubt of my reception. You showed me how insufficient were all my pretensions to please a woman worthy of being pleased.

"Oh, my!" Elizabeth's heart quickened. "Could it be so?" She reread the last few lines. "Whether I care to hear it or not, Mr. Darcy always speaks the truth. Is there a chance we might know happiness?"

As I look to my future–to our future–I wish not to know the regret of a million opportunities, which I permitted to pass me by, especially the opportunity to place you safely in my embrace.

Yours, Darcy...

And so it began. Elizabeth's next letter to Mr. Darcy contained her assurances that she long since accepted his innocence in his dealings with Mr. Wickham before adding that he spoke too harshly of his foibles, but did not speak of the expressions of affection obvious in the gentleman's letter. Instead, Elizabeth followed his suggestion. She wrote of her day. She did venture to tell him of her most recent insights regarding her mother and her sister Mary. If Elizabeth were to agree to marry Mr. Darcy, she wished him to know of the dire straits, which could plague her mother and sisters if Mr. Bennet passed suddenly. She would not deceive Mr. Darcy in such matters.

Unsurprisingly, Mr. Darcy offered his opinions of what she disclosed, but no censure, and then he shared some of the lessons he learned from his parents.

Over the weeks that followed they debated the value of "The Borough" by George Crabbe. While Elizabeth advocated for another form rather than the heroic couplet used by Crabbe, Mr. Darcy extolled the value of the couplet in bringing the stories to the reader. They both thought Crabbe's depiction of borough life held value.

Mr. Darcy's description of Lord Byron's "Childe Harold's Pilgrimage" had Elizabeth wishing she read it so they might discuss Byron's ideas upon life.

Surprisingly, Mr. Darcy was equally enthusiastic

over Sir Richard Colt Hoare's study of *The Ancient History of South Wiltshire*. When Darcy told her of Samuel Darcy, a famous archaeologist, being a cousin, Elizabeth, who had seen many of the gentleman's artifacts at the museum on a previous trip to London, knew admiration.

One rotation of letters held their thoughts of the May assassination of Prime Minister Spencer Perceval and the execution of John Bellingham, Perceval's killer. Both expressed their concern for England if the Prime Minister could be brought down.

But what Elizabeth cherished most were those moments when Mr. Darcy spoke of family and the possibility of their joining.

"I have thought much of the subject of late," he wrote. "And I believe loving another gives a person courage to face the world."

To which Elizabeth added, "I would think love makes a person strong when he encounters disdain."

As the weeks passed, Elizabeth found she looked forward to the arrival of Mr. Darcy's letters and knew disappointment when one did not arrive as timely as she expected. Often their letters overlapped.

"Another letter?" her father said with a lift of his eyebrow.

Elizabeth handed him her latest response to Mr. Darcy's correspondence.

"Yes. Please send it out in the next post."

The corners of her father's lips turned upward.

"Quite an expensive courtship your gentleman set before us."

Still feeling the glow of Mr. Darcy's flirtatious

words, Elizabeth smiled largely.

"I forgot to tell you: Mr. Darcy transferred funds to your man of business to cover the cost of the additional posts."

"He did, did he?" The amusement in Mr. Bennet's tone spoke of his affection for her. "Incidentally, how long am I to anticipate this *exchange* to last before one of you decides to end it?"

Despite her best efforts, Elizabeth frowned. She did not wish the letters to end, but neither did she wish to encounter Mr. Darcy again. In their letters, they were friends and real affection blossomed, but when they were face-to-face, they said ill things to each other.

"I fear I cannot say. It is not as if Mr. Darcy can call at Longbourn. Only you and I know the gentleman and I correspond."

"Have you not spoken to Jane today?" her father asked.

The change of subject confused Elizabeth.

"Not since we broke our fast. Is something amiss?"

"Nothing we did not expect. Mr. Bingley called upon me this morning. I must say I am pleased Jane brought her young man's toes to the line. The news sent Mrs. Bennet from the house to spread her joy about the neighborhood. I do not expect your mother's return until supper."

"I am delighted for the union!" Elizabeth exclaimed. "I must find Jane and wish her happy."

"You should know, Lizzy," her father said as she reached the door, "that Mr. Bingley means to ask Mr. Darcy to stand up with him. Your 'friend' will be returning to Hertfordshire soon."

Elizabeth felt the panic claim her breathing, but she kept a smile upon her lips.

"I am anxious to hear Jane's plans." She would not permit her father to shake her composure. Elizabeth turned back to deliver a challenge. "Have you thought, Papa, of what you will do when all of your daughters marry and settle elsewhere? Mrs. Bennet will no longer have a reason to go to Meryton. You will be Mama's entire world."

With that, Elizabeth made her exit, but she heard her father call after her.

"Elizabeth Bennet. I did not find your observation amusing!" A burst of laughter followed Elizabeth down the hall.

Darcy did not expect two letters arriving at the same time, nor did he anticipate the familiarity the shorter one held. In the first, Elizabeth shared more of the experiences, which marked the woman she had become. In this latest one, she told him of falling from a tree limb when she was nine and how she no longer cared for heights. She also shared information on a scar, which marked her knee–a result of the fall. Afterwards, Darcy fantasized on the delight of kissing the scar and enjoying Elizabeth's response. The woman tangled him into knots and brought out the desire Darcy never thought to know.

The second letter began with a familiarity not found previously.

Darcy

Reading the salutation, it was all Darcy could do not to shout with triumph. Nearly a month passed since they began this written wooing, and this was the first time Elizabeth addressed him with anything other than "Mister Darcy."

"It is a step," he whispered to his empty study before continuing to read…

> *Darcy,*
> *I suppose you learned of the engagement of my dearest sister Jane and Mr. Bingley. I am certain you share my good wishes for the happy couple; yet, you must know the prospect of your return to Hertfordshire frightens me.*

"A bit difficult to realize the woman for which you yearn does not look forward to the prospect of beholding you again," Darcy murmured in cynicism. "Yet, this is not the time to abandon the chase."

> *What if we find we do not suit? I do wish our discussions to end. What if when we meet again, we say things, which are meant to destroy each other? I could not bear it.*
> *E.*

Darcy knew his response must be carefully worded. "My words must win the lady's heart and her cooperation."

Elizabeth lingered in the passage near her father's study for two days before Mr. Darcy's letter arrived. While she waited, she cursed her decision to write of her qualms to the gentleman.

"What if Mr. Darcy terms me gormless? What if my letter proves I am not the woman the gentleman thinks me to be?"

At length, his letter arrived. Snatching it from her father's hand, Elizabeth raced to her quarters to read her fate. Settling on her bed, she ripped at the wax seal bearing the imprint of his signet ring.

> *My dearest Elizabeth,*
>
> *Your letter brought me great happiness for, like me, you recognize the beauty of what we have achieved in so short a time. You have no idea of the joy I receive upon the sight of your now familiar script upon the page. Each of your letters is unique, and I spend countless hours reliving the moments you describe and deciphering the meaning behind the words. I cherish them for they hold your scent and the warmth of your hand. And I am quite of the nature to think a person who can write a long letter with ease, cannot write ill.*
>
> *That being said, as enchanting as your letters are, we cannot continue this exchange forever. It would not be fair of me to claim such a hold upon you. You deserve a husband who reveres you. You deserve a family who*

looks upon you as the center of their world. Even if continuing our correspondence would not go against propriety, we both know we cannot communicate as such if no betrothal exists; and as much as I adore your tales, I hold a duty to my estate. A betrothal must lead to a marriage, or it must be broken.

Elizabeth knew Mr. Darcy correct, but the thought of losing what was now within her reach shook Elizabeth to her core. Could she abandon the hope of finding something few women of her time knew?

We are born alone, and for many of us we remain alone. Even when a hundred people surround us, loneliness claims our hearts. Yet, when I took your acquaintance, something inside me said, "You can find happiness here." In truth, it took me many days to cease hushing that inner voice, but since accepting the thread, which ties me to you, I know the thing for which my heart covets most bears the name "Elizabeth."

Surely you must know what we share is more formidable than any force upon this earth. It can transform two souls yearning to know each other.

"Yet, what of our disagreements, Mr. Darcy?" Elizabeth whispered through the tears forming in her eyes. She desired what Mr. Darcy described, but Elizabeth feared failure.

So, you must decide, Elizabeth, what you will choose. Even after my earlier perfidy, Bingley asked me to stand up with him, and I pledged myself to do so. I will not write again. Instead, I will await your choice at Bingley's festivities. I pray you will choose to replace the pain of our earlier battles with a loveliness that will forever remain in our hearts.

D.

Chapter 14

THREE WEEKS PASSED, but Elizabeth knew no peace. She went about her days as if nothing unusual occurred; yet, every breath she took held the sadness of losing Mr. Darcy, for Elizabeth was certain they could not know the perfection Mr. Darcy's letters promised. No marriage could sustain such excellence. She resigned herself to meeting him again at Jane's wedding, but Elizabeth planned to avoid Mr. Darcy as much as possible. She even planned a pretend illness if she could not evade the gentleman.

"Better we part with amiable feelings toward each other than to know the blemish of harshness again," Elizabeth repeated, hoping her caution would stick.

"Mr. Bingley means to host an engagement party at Netherfield," Jane announced Thursday last.

Elizabeth's breathing hitched tighter.

"What a lovely idea!" she exclaimed. "When?"

"Saturday next," Jane explained. "The weekend before our nuptials. A full moon is expected to aid Mr. Bingley's guests in their travels."

Elizabeth swallowed the rush of panic claiming her chest.

"But I thought Mr. Darcy could not return to Netherfield until the day before the ceremony. Would Mr. Bingley host a ball without his friend? The wedding is five days removed from the ball."

"I am certain Mr. Bingley does not require Mr. Darcy's permission to host a ball in his own house," Mrs. Bennet declared in disapproval. "Bingley wishes to claim Jane before his neighbors. I find Bingley's actions exemplary."

Elizabeth shot a pleading glance to her father who shook off her look of despair.

"Bingley told me again only this afternoon that Mr. Darcy had business in London and would not arrive until the wedding."

Mr. Bennet remained the only one who knew of Elizabeth's deep connection to Mr. Darcy, and even her father did not know of Elizabeth's greatest alarm: that Mr. Darcy would arrive and depart without her. One moment she feared the man would look elsewhere for a wife, and the next, Elizabeth convinced herself his withdrawal was for the best. All Mr. Bennet knew was the letters stopped: She supposed her father thought Elizabeth ended the understanding she held with the gentleman.

"Certainly we shall all celebrate our dearest Jane's triumph," Elizabeth insisted. "Our sister will be the most beautiful bride ever."

Much to Elizabeth's chagrin and her relief, Saturday and the ball arrived with no word of Mr. Darcy's presence, and she did her best to place a smile on her face for Jane's sake. Netherfield overflowed with the local gentry from miles around. Without either of his sisters present to serve as his hostess, Mr. Bingley pressed Lady Lucas into service. He pacified his future mother in marriage by telling Mrs. Bennet that she held great responsibility with the wedding breakfast and preparations for Jane's bride clothes, and he wanted Mrs. Bennet to enjoy the ceremony without the pressing difficulties of hosting a ball to complicate the matter. Elizabeth thought Bingley handled the situation quite well. She realized with Bingley and Jane only a three miles trek from Longbourn, Bingley would often know Mrs. Bennet's interference, and it was best for the gentleman to set a standard response.

Netherfield never looked finer. Lady Lucas, known for her financial efficiency, kept the decorations simple and classic. Gone was the ostentatious display of the previous Netherfield Ball. Elizabeth found she preferred Lady Lucas' taste to that of Caroline Bingley.

"Everything is splendid," she told Bingley as he bowed over Elizabeth's hand. "I am certain you and Jane will be most happy here."

"I am anxious to claim Miss Bennet," Bingley assured in his customary amicable manner. "I believe your sister will make an excellent mistress for Netherfield."

"As do I," Elizabeth assured.

Bingley nodded his agreement.

"Now, if you will pardon me, I must see to my other guests," he whispered. "You will save me the second set."

Elizabeth smiled easily; Mr. Bingley brought out the softer side of everyone, except perhaps his sisters.

"It would be my pleasure."

As she watched Bingley greeting other neighbors, Elizabeth sighed with envy.

"I wonder what a ball at Pemberley would entail?" she murmured.

For a brief second Elizabeth closed her eyes to bring forth an image of Pemberley's largest ballroom and its Master in all their glory. Despite her best efforts, a smile tugged at the corners of her mouth.

"Dreaming of anyone I know," a seductively familiar voice said close to her ear, as warmth claimed her back. The scent of sandalwood flooded Elizabeth's senses.

With a start, she turned to stare up at Mr. Darcy's chin. Elizabeth did not realize he was so close.

"What are you...?" she began before remembering her manners. "Mr. Darcy." Elizabeth dropped a curtsy. "I was unaware, Sir, that you would attend tonight. I understood you held business in Town until next week."

Even though Elizabeth did not offer it, Mr. Darcy claimed her hand and brought it slowly to his lips.

"I did not wish to disappoint Bingley." He placed a kiss on the back of Elizabeth's gloved hand, before adding, "Or you." She felt the warmth of Mr. Darcy's caress race up her arm.

"You are quite certain of your attentions, Sir." Elizabeth said in chastisement. She had no idea why she rebuked him for she was never happier to see anyone. Unfortunately, Elizabeth had the empty satisfaction of noting the mirth crossing Mr. Darcy's features.

"Do you wish me to leave forever, Elizabeth?" he asked softly. "Just say the words."

However, before Elizabeth could put thought to her answer, a bubbly voice came from behind her.

"You found her, William!"

Elizabeth turned to discover Miss Darcy on the arm of Colonel Fitzwilliam.

"Miss Darcy. Colonel." Elizabeth dropped a curtsy. "I am pleased to see you again."

"And I you." Miss Darcy said with a speculative glance to her brother. "Darcy permitted me to join in your sister's celebration."

Elizabeth noted the practiced smile on Mr. Darcy's lips. The gentleman thought Elizabeth would not send him away if his family accompanied him.

"I am certain Jane will be honored by your presence." With a hint of a grin, Elizabeth turned to the colonel. "And you, Sir, how went your business with General Leigh-Hunt?"

"It was much as I expected," Fitzwilliam said with a shrug. "Rumors exist that I am to the American front shortly to train some of the newer recruits. I must report to the Upper Canada frontier."

Miss Darcy wrapped her arm through her cousin's.

"I am not best pleased. How are we to exist without Fitzwilliam's sensibility?" the girl declared.

"As I always do, I shall worry every day the colonel is away."

Colonel Fitzwilliam brought Miss Darcy closer to his side.

"Well, I shan't be leaving tonight, and Darcy promised that I might claim at least two of your sets." The colonel glanced to Elizabeth. "Might I claim the third set, Miss Elizabeth? Bingley says he is to have the second, and I am certain Darcy means to claim the first."

"I do," Mr. Darcy said with the faintest hint of irony in the lift of his lips. "That is, if Miss Elizabeth will permit my doing so."

"Certainly she will accept, shall you not, Miss Elizabeth," Miss Darcy declared. "We may form a quartet."

Elizabeth blushed scarlet as she handed Mr. Darcy her dance card.

"I would be honored, Sir."

"Shall I sign for you, Colonel?" Mr. Darcy asked his cousin.

The colonel laughed easily.

"We might as well claim the attentions of two of the most handsome women in the room. I will sign for you on Georgiana's card."

"You think I am handsome," Miss Darcy asked wistfully, and Elizabeth wondered if Mr. Darcy's sister felt more than cousinly affection for the colonel.

"No fishing for compliments, Georgie," the colonel teased with a wink directed to Miss Darcy.

Mr. Darcy returned Elizabeth's card before placing her hand upon his arm. They followed the colonel and Miss Darcy to the floor, where the lines formed.

"Your sister is most kind," Elizabeth spoke for Mr. Darcy's ears only. "I am certain she knows of my open disparagement of claiming her friendship."

Mr. Darcy tilted his head where he might speak with privacy.

"I explained to Georgiana that it was I that you found revolting, not she."

"I never found either..." Again, Elizabeth could not say the words her heart pronounced. "Neither of us performs well in such situations. We both expect our words to know authority."

"Do you truly believe your declarations?" Mr. Darcy asked as he set her in the line of ladies before stepping away. "I am of a different mind." His smile widened, and Elizabeth's breath caught in her throat. Mr. Darcy was an exceptionally handsome man when he smiled. "We have proved ourselves congenial more often than not?"

Elizabeth made herself speak with lightness. She would not ruin a dance with Mr. Darcy by arguing as she did the one time they danced in this very room nearly a year prior. While she circled him, Elizabeth set her mind to being witty.

"Then we shall speak of something pleasurable, Sir. What say you to books?"

Elizabeth crossed behind the colonel, laughing at the gentleman when he wagged his eyebrows at her. With a girlish giggle, Elizabeth extended her hand to Mr. Darcy, who used his strength to bring her closer to him than propriety declared.

"I say we are a book in two volumes but with one tale to tell," Mr. Darcy pronounced seductively.

A shiver of delight ran down Elizabeth's spine. It was all she do to remember the next steps when Mr. Darcy guided her toward Mr. Bingley while Mr. Darcy accepted Jane's hand.

As Bingley spun Elizabeth in a tight circle, she turned her head often to watch Mr. Darcy with Jane. Even without hearing his words, she knew Mr. Darcy wished Jane happy. As the dance brought her to Mr. Darcy's side again, they caught hands over their heads and behind their backs to turn in place.

"And what of art, sir?" she teased.

Mr. Darcy's lips twitched in amusement.

"I would quote Aristotle: The aim of art is to represent not the outward appearance of things, but their inward significance."

Elizabeth thought immediately of Mr. Darcy's portrait hanging in the Pemberley's gallery. It spoke of the gentleman's inner goodness.

"What of music?" Elizabeth demanded as she skipped away toward Mr. Grange, who claimed Mary for the set. Elizabeth squeezed her sister's hand as they passed. Mary rarely danced at such functions, and it did Elizabeth well to see Mary's eyes glisten with the joy of recognition.

Returning to Mr. Darcy's side, Elizabeth waited for his response, but when none came, her eyebrow rose in proof.

"Have you employed all your witty remarks, Sir?"

"Not at all, Miss Elizabeth," Mr. Darcy said

softly.

"Then what of music?"

They repeated the first pattern, and Elizabeth accepted the colonel's gloved hand. She glanced up at the man.

"Your thoughts, Colonel?" she questioned.

"I am gathering memories to carry me through the dark moments ahead." He smiled sadly at Elizabeth. "I will remember this moment. I pray you accept my cousin before I receive orders to depart. I wish to stand with Darcy in his happiness. Doing such would mean I might some day know the same."

Elizabeth had no time to respond before the music and the pattern whisked her back to Mr. Darcy. His humor softened the lines of his face.

"Music can transform into loneliness or contentment. Into strengths or weaknesses. Into a joining or a tearing away."

Mr. Darcy's words were as if an omen of what was to come, and Elizabeth felt the dread of loss claiming her tongue. They did not speak again until the second dance of the set. The minuet permitted them a closer proximity and an easy conversation.

At length, Elizabeth gave in to finishing what they left dangling some minutes prior.

"I do not know how to start over." She dared a glance to Mr. Darcy. His steady gaze was as controlled as everything else about the man. A unconscience stirring of Elizabeth's hopes brought a frisson of awareness as it ricocheted through her.

"We do not begin again." Mr. Darcy's countenance spoke of his adamant refusal, and panic returned to Elizabeth's breathing. "We have taken the first step, Elizabeth. We must either halt our progress or walk into the future, hand-in-hand. Before this night is over, I mean to have an answer."

Elizabeth introduced Miss Darcy to many in the room, especially to her two younger sisters. As she expected, Elizabeth found the girl quite agreeable. Miss Darcy made a friend of Mary by sneaking off to the music room to share a duet, and Georgiana impressed Kitty with the girl's sense of fashion.

From a respectable distance, Mr. Darcy kept a close eye on his sister, and Elizabeth had the strong suspicion upon her, as well. The gentleman nodded his approval of Mr. Grange's claiming a set on Miss Darcy's dance card, but he shook off Mr. Lincolnton's offer.

Yet, her brother's disapproval did not seem to bother the girl. Miss Darcy chattered with many of the younger sect, making Elizabeth feel ancient. The girlish giggles and the red-faced youths held no interest for her: Elizabeth preferred the chiseled features of Mr. Darcy.

Bingley claimed Elizabeth's second set and Colonel Fitzwilliam the third. Bingley spoke extensively of Jane's merits, while the colonel apologized for his earlier maudlin. Yet, no matter where Elizabeth went or to whom she spoke, she felt Mr. Darcy's eyes upon her. She found herself turning often, seeking his gaze when it was not offered. As if by their own accord, Elizabeth's eyes would meet his. She would glance away, but each time she did, an urgency–a feeling of being bereft of Mr. Darcy's closeness–would bring her back to the one countenance that provided Elizabeth peace and that wreaked havoc on her emotions at the same time.

"Lizzy," her mother tugged at Elizabeth's arm. "Come with me." In reluctance, she followed Mrs. Bennet to a nearby alcove.

"What is amiss, Mama?" Elizabeth asked with a glance over her shoulder to see to where Mr. Darcy had gotten.

Her mother reached up to pinch Elizabeth's cheeks.

"You have an excellent opportunity to earn Colonel Fitzwilliam's interest if you would ply a bit of flirtation."

Mrs. Bennet followed the pinch with a tug of Elizabeth's sleeve to set it aright.

"And why would I wish to draw the colonel's attentions?" Elizabeth rubbed the spots her mother reddened.

Mrs. Bennet tutted her disapproval.

"He is a gentleman and the son of an earl," her mother reasoned. "The colonel is the desire of every young lady in the room, but you have an advantage: you hold the longer acquaintance. Mr. Bennet says the colonel is the nephew of Lady Catherine de Bourgh, and he was at Rosings Park when you were at Hunsford Cottage."

"Mr. Darcy is also Lady Catherine's nephew," Elizabeth countered.

Her mother's nose snarled in disappointment.

"Mr. Darcy is all that others say of him, but his father was not an earl."

Elizabeth wished she never disparaged Mr.

Darcy to her family. She wished she could speak to her mother of George Darcy's heritage and of Lady Anne Fitzwilliam connection to the Matlocks–of Mr. Darcy's steadfast interest in her, but putting the idea of Mr. Darcy as Elizabeth's suitor into Mrs. Bennet's head would spell disaster.

"Colonel Fitzwilliam is the second son of Lord Matlock," Elizabeth explained. "He has no fortune of his own, thus his service in the King's army. Therefore, the colonel must choose a wife with a large dowry."

"Nonsense!" her mother declared. "The Earl of Matlock would not leave his son destitute."

"Pardon, Miss Elizabeth." Elizabeth looked from her mother's anxious features to Mr. Darcy, who stood some three feet removed. "I believe this is our set."

Elizabeth glanced to her mother, who appeared displeased that Mr. Darcy interrupted her manipulations.

"I believe it is, Sir. I apologize. I did not realize the set was forming. We shall speak more at home, Mama," Elizabeth said in parting.

Elizabeth placed her hand on Mr. Darcy's proffered arm and walked with him toward the dance floor.

"You appear upset," Mr. Darcy said softly.

"It is nothing," Elizabeth assured.

Mr. Darcy led her upon a leisurely turn of the room before assuming their places in the line.

"When your hazel eyes change to a cross between dark honey and cinnamon, something is amiss."

Elizabeth frowned, but a fissure of pleasure claimed a spot in her stomach.

"How is it you know me so well?"

Mr. Darcy smiled with satisfaction.

"I made a study of you."

Elizabeth's eyebrow rose in dismay.

"I do not know whether that particular fact is a compliment or something of which I should know concern."

"A compliment," Mr. Darcy assured. "Now, speak to me of what troubles you."

"You shall not be pleased," Elizabeth warned.

"Yet, I would hear it, nonetheless."

Elizabeth shrugged her resignation.

"Mrs. Bennet is as she always is: She fears my father will pass before all her daughters marry. Although I do not approve of her proposition, I understand my mother's urgency."

Mr. Darcy studied Elizabeth closely.

"I assume Mrs. Bennet chose a potential suitor for you."

Glee claimed Elizabeth's lips.

"Yes. Mrs. Bennet believes with a bit of effort on my part, I could become Mrs. Fitzwilliam."

Mr. Darcy's frown lines deepened.

"Mrs. Fitzwilliam…?" he probed.

"Nothing more," Elizabeth teased. "Mrs. Bennet thinks your cousin a viable candidate."

Mr. Darcy's mouth formed a grim line.

"I do not find your mother's persuasion to my liking."

Elizabeth joined the other ladies in the line.

"Why does that fact not surprise me? You and Mrs. Bennet are both singular in your opinions."

"Do not argue with Mr. Darcy," her sister Jane admonished as she joined Elizabeth in the female line. "Charles and I require your good sense over supper. There are still many decisions to make for the wedding."

"Supper?" Elizabeth's voice squeaked in surprise. "This is the supper set?"

Jane patted Elizabeth's arm good-naturedly.

"Certainly, it is the supper set."

Elizabeth glanced to Mr. Darcy. Other than one set with Jane, Mr. Darcy had divided his attentions between Elizabeth and Miss Darcy, but the supper set was a different matter.

"I assumed you would see Miss Darcy to supper. If I realized, I would never have accepted your arm, Sir. Please think nothing of it if you must speak your regrets."

Mr. Darcy's eyebrow rose in challenge.

"I assure you, Miss Elizabeth, my name is on your dance card for this set, and as to Georgiana, I gave her permission to join your younger sisters and several of the young gentlemen for the meal. It will do Miss Darcy well to possess company of a like age. My sister knows my cautions in such matters." The devastating smile Mr. Darcy so often hid escaped. "Did you not look at your card this evening?"

"Lizzy does not attend to such frivolities," Jane teased. "My sister claims to possess a fine memory of all who request her attentions."

Elizabeth laughed self-consciously.

"I am never as tolerable as you, dearest Jane." She shot a knowing glance to Mr. Darcy, and the gentleman returned her look with one of bemusement.

"Not so," Jane countered. "You are quite lovely, Lizzy."

"The handsomest woman of my acquaintance," Mr. Darcy declared before assuming his place in the line.

Chapter 15

DARCY MEANT TO HAVE another private word with Elizabeth, but her sister whisked Elizabeth away before he and Miss Elizabeth could converse upon the possibility of their own happiness, rather than on the details of Bingley and Miss Bennet's nuptials.

"At least the lady no longer avoids my company," Darcy murmured as he watched Elizabeth and Miss Bennet with their heads together. "It appears I must risk it all to prove my affections true." Darcy imagined such a state of affairs only last evening. "Then so be it. Embarrassment or success? Painful memories or delightful contentment? My future rests in Miss Elizabeth's hands."

"I am pleased to observe how well you and Mr. Darcy are getting on," Jane hinted as they watched the after supper set forming. "Do you expect Mr. Darcy to renew his earlier proposal?"

Elizabeth found her eyes searching the room for Mr. Darcy's familiar steady gaze. He stood up with his sister. Without realizing her expression relayed her very intimate feelings for the man, Elizabeth looked upon the scene with fondness.

"Mr. Darcy's affections remain; the gentleman asked me to marry him," she confessed.

It was time Elizabeth sought the counsel of another. Perhaps Jane could sway Elizabeth's decision one way or another. In truth, Elizabeth would welcome the advice of another if it meant she would know her heart's desire.

"And am I to wish you happy?" Jane asked in curiosity.

"Mr. Darcy says I must give him an answer this evening or he will withdraw from my company forever." Elizabeth continued to watch the gentleman and his sister; she meant to claim every memory she could of him.

"Oh, Lizzy," Jane pleaded. "Please tell me you did not refuse Mr. Darcy again. Your countenance betrays your attachment for the man."

Elizabeth turned her gaze upon her sister.

"It is not as easy as permitting my heart to lead. I could not bear it if after we speak our vows that we become a poor imitation of a contended couple. Look at our parents. When Papa married Mrs. Bennet, he knew the passion of young love. How can I be certain not to make my dearest parent's mistake?"

"You and Mr. Darcy hold nothing in common with our parents," Jane countered. "Mama cannot compete with Mr. Bennet's sharp wit and desire for knowledge, whereas you and Mr. Darcy are both intelligent beings, who would never permit only passion to rule your days."

Tears filled Elizabeth's eyes.

"That is the part which frightens me. Mr. Darcy and I have flayed each other raw upon more than one occasion. Will our stubbornness destroy us?"

"Do not the majority of your arguments deal with your defense of Mr. Wickham?" Jane questioned. "Can you not place yourself in Mr. Darcy's stead in regards to his former friend?"

"I hold no allegiance to Mr. Wickham," Elizabeth declared.

Jane's features displayed her exasperation with the conversation, but Elizabeth clung to the hope that her sister would instruct Elizabeth to marry Mr. Darcy. Even so, she knew Jane would not go so far as to order Elizabeth to be happy: Marrying Mr. Darcy would be Elizabeth's decision alone.

"I see." Jane hesitated. "I cannot speak to what brought our parents together. Our previous conjectures all lead to Mr. Bennet being captivated by youth and beauty and the appearance of good humor, which youth and beauty generally gives. Certainly none of us experienced a very pleasing picture of conjugal felicity, and as unfair as it is, the fact that mama did not deliver an heir for Longbourn must lay heavy between them. It would be an unspoken accusation never upon our father's lips, but often within his mind." Elizabeth thought of the scene with her mother in the garden and knew Jane's speculations true. "Father's line will end with him, and that fact must give Mr. Bennet pause, and Mama must know failure smartly. Yet, even with knowledge of the failure of our parents' marriage, Mr. Bingley and I carve out a bit of happiness. Can you not do the same with Mr. Darcy? The man means to please you."

"What if we never know accord?" Elizabeth could not admit, even to herself, that she feared failure as strongly as did her mother. "The gentleman claims his temper too little yielding and that he cannot forget the follies and vices of others nor their offenses against him."

Jane's frown lines deepened.

"You make Mr. Darcy appear the ogre. Do you not think Mr. Darcy was considering the actions of those of Mr. Wickham's nature when he spoke thusly? Wickham, by your own accounts, betrayed every principle Mr. Darcy holds most dear. Look how Wickham displayed no regard for our futures when he seduced Lydia. It is only with Mr. Darcy's allegiance that my dearest Charles and I reunited. And you cannot ignore how Mr. Darcy attended to your criticisms in Kent. You spoke quite elegantly of the changes you noted in the gentleman when you returned from London the first time. Surely in all these facts, you could find something about the man to please you."

"Mr. Darcy pleases me quite well," Elizabeth admitted. "The question remains whether I might please him."

"Do you wish to please the gentleman, Lizzy?"

"Very much so," Elizabeth whispered. "I do not go more than a few minutes of the day without thinking of the Master of Pemberley."

Jane turned Elizabeth toward where their father watched the festivities with a bemused smirk upon his lips.

"Speak to Papa," Jane encouraged. "Mr. Bennet soothed my qualms regarding Mr. Bingley's return to Hertfordshire. As you are our father's avowed favorite, Mr. Bennet will be sore to part with you and will not be left quaking by Mr. Darcy's wealth; yet, if our father acts as I suspect he will, Mr. Bennet will encourage you to claim your happiness."

With a nudge from Jane, Elizabeth set her steps and her mind to the task.

"Why the long face, Lizzy?" her father asked as she slid in beside him. "Do you bemoan the lack of a partner? Shall I demand that Mr. Darcy claim your hand for the next set?"

Elizabeth denied the idea of her father placing her in an embarrassing situation, but she would enjoy a third dance with Mr. Darcy. She missed the gentleman's closeness.

"Mr. Darcy and I stood up together twice."

Her father's gaze remained upon the dancers, as did Elizabeth's.

"I believe it is quite telling, Elizabeth, that you did not rebuke my tease with the mention of another gentleman. I expected my very clever Lizzy to suggest that Colonel Fitzwilliam or Mr. Townsend would be equal to your liking as is Mr. Darcy."

"No," she said simply.

"So it is Mr. Darcy who claims your heart?"

Elizabeth smiled in rueful resignation.

"I am discovered as a fool."

Although she did not look upon him, Elizabeth knew her father's frown became a positive scowl.

"Why do you term yourself a fool, Lizzy? Do you doubt Mr. Darcy's affections? I found your young man most persuasive."

Although the impact of Mr. Bennet's words took an elongated pause to register in Elizabeth's mind, nonetheless, they had her turning to question her father. Annoyance claimed Elizabeth's features.

"When did Mr. Darcy speak to you of me?"

Her father's eyes abruptly softened when he looked upon her.

"You did not think I would permit any man to ruin your reputation, did you, Lizzy? Mr. Darcy wrote to me prior to the beginning of your correspondence. He explained what occurred between you and the gentleman expressed his fondness for my second daughter. Your young man asked my permission to woo you."

"But you never spoke of Mr. Darcy's intentions," Elizabeth protested.

Mr. Bennet's lips twisted in what appeared to be suppressed emotions.

"Mr. Darcy pleaded for my silence, but, in truth, I wished to observe with my own eyes your allegiance to the man. It spoke of the depth of your affections if you were willing to call upon Darcy's bachelor household to learn more of his health, as well as your rushing to Pemberley to tend him."

Elizabeth's mouth thinned with displeasure.

"You knew of my escapades before you demanded a confession from me on the incidents?" she accused.

"Mr. Darcy was *kind* in describing how you set both of his households upon their heads," her father declared with what appeared to be true respect. "The gentleman claims you will make a magnificent mistress for his properties–that many on his staff already hold you with great regard. Darcy claims you are cut from the same cloth as his late mother Lady Anne Darcy; needless to say, I prefer to think you are formed in the image of your Grandmother Bennet."

"You approve of Mr. Darcy's suit?" Elizabeth demanded in disbelief.

"I gave Darcy my consent to court you. He is the kind of man, indeed, to whom I should never dare refuse anything, which he condescended to ask." Mr. Bennet shrugged, a hint of resignation in his manner. "What I wish to know, Elizabeth, is of your feelings. Are you resolved on having him?"

"I fear what will become of our joining," Elizabeth admitted. "I could not bear..." She stifled her criticism of her father's actions in dealing with the gap of understanding in her parents' marriage.

"You could not bear to marry unless you truly esteemed your husband," her father completed Elizabeth's thoughts. "Unless you looked upon him as a superior. I understand your disposition, Lizzy. Your lively talents would place you in the greatest danger in an unequal marriage: you could scarcely escape discredit and misery." Mr. Bennet gave a rueful shake of his head. "Child, let me not have the grief of seeing you unable to respect your partner in life. Yet, I do not believe it would be so with Mr. Darcy."

With an effort Elizabeth gathered her composure. "You do not?"

"From what I know Mr. Darcy's affections are not the work of a day, but rather they have stood the test of many months' suspense."

"The man brings out my most shrewish tongue," Elizabeth protested weakly, her resolve faltering.

A hint of regret rippled over her father's expression.

"No marriage is without its disagreements. It is when a couple does not express their concerns that a marriage must end or it must take a different form."

Elizabeth thought Mr. Bennet spoke of his relationship with Mrs. Bennet. Her father and mother never argued. Even when Mr. Bennet teased his wife unmercifully, they did not speak in harsh tones to each other. Her mother would reprimand Mr. Bennet to which Elizabeth's father would offer another unbearable taunt. *Unbearable*, Elizabeth thought. Was it not better for her and Mr. Darcy to voice their differences and then consent to disagree than it was to pick at a sore, which never healed?

"Mr. Darcy would make me an exemplary husband." For the first time in months, Elizabeth knew she spoke the truth.

"Well, my dear," her father said softly, "if this be the case, Mr. Darcy deserves you. I could not part with you, my Lizzy, to anyone less worthy."

Acknowledging the fact she wished to claim Mr. Darcy's affections, Elizabeth wished to do so immediately, but when she turned back to the ballroom the gentleman was no where to be found. She spotted Miss Darcy and the colonel upon the far side of the room, but as the night was soon to know an end, the crowded ballroom appeared unrelenting in the barrier it presented. Continuing to search for the tall, imposing figure of Mr. Darcy, Elizabeth systematically made her way to where the colonel and Miss Darcy awaited the last dance of the evening.

Elizabeth wondered if Mr. Darcy meant to stand up with another or whether he took her desertion after supper as her answer.

To her frustration, multiple friends and neighbors halted her progress to offer felicitations to her family upon Lydia's and Jane's joinings. With each, Elizabeth responded with civility, but her mind was elsewhere.

At length, she reached the colonel's side.

"Pardon me, Colonel, Miss Darcy, but do you know the whereabouts of Mr. Darcy?" Elizabeth attempted to sound nonchalant, but her fear of losing Mr. Darcy's affections forever shook her to her core.

The colonel smiled with what appeared to be sympathetic humor.

"I believe my cousin meant to speak to his valet regarding Darcy's travel plans."

Elizabeth no longer bothered to disguise her agitation.

"Mr. Darcy means to leave?" Elizabeth's voice squeaked as a flood of emotions washed over her.

"As is customary with my cousin, Darcy rarely consults me in such matters. I am frequently at his disposal."

Elizabeth's lips parted in dismay.

"But my business with Mr. Darcy is not complete," she declared in growing anxiety. Elizabeth analyzed her options: She knew she could not storm the guests' quarters to confront Mr. Darcy. Elizabeth also realized she committed more than her share of rule breaking in the past, which she had yet to ask God's forgiveness. If Mr. Darcy meant to leave her, Elizabeth would not prostrate herself before him.

"What type of business?" A warm breath brushed the hairs along the back of Elizabeth's neck, and she spun around to find a rather odd expression upon Mr. Darcy's countenance.

She glanced to the engaging grins claiming the colonel's and Miss Darcy's lips. With an effort Elizabeth gathered her composure.

"Might we walk the room, Sir?" Her voice sounded breathy and unsure, but Elizabeth felt gratitude at being given a second chance.

Mr. Darcy tilted his head in a familiar fashion, as if he studied her every move, but he offered Elizabeth his arm.

"Fitzwilliam," he said to his cousin, "you will escort Georgiana to her quarters."

The colonel presented an expression of congeniality, as he winked at Miss Darcy.

"I intend to dance once more with my precious girl, and then we will make appropriate farewells. Does that meet your pleasure, Georgiana?"

What appeared as mischief marked Miss Darcy's eyes.

"As this is my first foray in society, I wish to claim every memory afforded me."

Elizabeth shot a tentative glance to Mr. Darcy, who smiled deep into her eyes. The gentleman turned their steps to a slow promenade of the room. For several minutes they said nothing.

Even so, Elizabeth could feel the heat of his strength claim her arm, while tingles of excitement rushed through her veins. She was so engrossed with Mr. Darcy's closeness that she did not realize he led her out into the darkness of the terrace.

"We cannot..." she began, but Mr. Darcy stopped just outside the open terrace doors.

"What business?" he demanded.

It surprised Elizabeth that Mr. Darcy offered no apologies for leading her into the darkness. If they did not return soon, her reputation would know another black tick.

"Could we not return to the festivities?" she pleaded.

Elizabeth meant to pull her hand free of his arm, but with a flex of his muscles, Mr. Darcy locked her arm to his side. Anyone who passed the door could view Mr. Darcy's profile, but Elizabeth doubted they could see her. Even so, she did not wish to encounter censure from her neighbors.

"What business?" Mr. Darcy repeated.

Elizabeth gave her arm a second jerk, and this time Mr. Darcy permitted Elizabeth her freedom.

"I cannot remain here," she insisted. "People will talk." Elizabeth started past him only to find Mr. Darcy's hand staying her retreat.

"There would be no gossip if you agreed to accept me." He whispered in Elizabeth's ear, as he played with a curl, which came loose from her chignon.

"Not here," Elizabeth implored.

"Then where?" Mr. Darcy insisted.

Elizabeth did not bother to deny her exasperation.

"I hold no idea, but I cannot begin a relationship based on scandal." The gentleman released his hold on her arm, and Elizabeth sidestepped him to return to the ballroom.

Darcy watched her go.

"Not well played," he offered in self-chastisement. "But the game does not know an end." He sighed deeply. When Darcy led her onto the terrace, he thought to steal a kiss. "The woman is by far the most confounding and the most enchanting creature I have ever known. Who else, other than Elizabeth Bennet, would risk calling upon me in my quarters one day and be afraid of joining me on a darkened terrace upon another?"

With a shake of his head, Darcy turned toward the ballroom.

"One more volley, Miss Elizabeth," he said with a twitch of his lips. "I will know your acquiescence this night or the world will declare me as doddy as Lord Byron."

Darcy noted the rush of color upon Elizabeth's cheeks when he stepped through the terrace door. She joined her two younger sisters, but Elizabeth's eyes met his. *Not entirely set against me*, he thought in triumph. Darcy arched an eyebrow, and Elizabeth pointedly turned her back on him, but only for a few seconds.

He adored teasing her; Elizabeth's contestations would keep him young.

From off to his right the musicians took up their instruments again for what would be the last dance of the evening. Darcy knew Bingley intended to lead Miss Bennet out first before the other couples joined them. It was part of his friend's surprise for his betrothed: To dance with all eyes in the hall upon them. Darcy thought it an admirable gesture upon Bingley's part, but when he heard Bingley's plan, Darcy considered himself too private to conduct such a show, but perhaps, he erred.

Sir William Lucas took to the dais to announce the last dance and to instruct others to permit Mr. Bingley to honor his bride-to-be with a few minutes alone on the dance floor.

Noting Mr. Lincolnton's approach to claim Elizabeth's hand for the set, Darcy moved to intercept the fellow, but Colonel Fitzwilliam was quicker. Darcy's cousin stopped Lincolnton with what was likely an inane question, but one which Lincolnton could not ignore coming from an earl's son. Darcy nodded his appreciation before crossing to Elizabeth.

"I believe this is our set, Miss Elizabeth," Darcy announced loud enough for those about them to overhear.

Something like disregard flashed in her eyes, but Darcy schooled his features to remain unconcerned. Mary Bennet whispered something in Elizabeth's ear, and Elizabeth nodded her understanding.

"There must be some mistake, Mr. Darcy. We shared two sets previously."

Darcy gave her a slow shake of his head.

"I err often, Miss Elizabeth, but never where sharing your company comes into place. You really must be more aware of your dance card, my dear. If you look at the card, you will clearly note my name for this set."

"But, we cannot," Elizabeth protested. "Unless…"

Darcy sensed several in the crowd edging closer so they might hear his exchange with Elizabeth Bennet. He knew many of them were privy to his "not tolerable enough" comment from the Meryton assembly. The onlookers would think his earlier attentions to Elizabeth during the ball were in his role as standing with Bingley for his friend's nuptials, but no longer. Darcy placed that particular fact from his mind and concentrated upon the expression of hope crossing Elizabeth's features.

"Unless, we two were engaged," Darcy finished her thoughts. Swallowing his anxiety, he continued, "You are too generous to trifle with me. If your feelings are still what they were last April, tell me so at once. My affections and wishes remain unchanged, but one word from you will silence me on the subject forever."

Elizabeth's eyes widened. She did not expect such a public proposal. Yet, she remained Darcy's customarily magnificent opponent.

"Tell me how you know we will suit, Mr. Darcy," she demanded.

"That is simple, Miss Elizabeth." His lady regarded him with suspicion. "Some things you see with your eyes. Some things you know with your heart."

Tears misted Elizabeth's eyes.

"Why must you always possess the perfect response, Mr. Darcy?"

"I await your answer, Miss Elizabeth," Darcy insisted.

The common awkwardness and anxiety of their situation must have impressed her. With a startled blink, a smile of delight claimed Elizabeth's lips.

"Very well," she said with a shift of her shoulders. "I shall not leave you to pubic disdain without joining you in the merriment." Darcy watched as Elizabeth swallowed her fears. "My sentiments, Sir, have undergone so material a change since the period to which you alluded, as to make me receive with gratitude and pleasure your present assurances."

Darcy's lips twisted with wry humor. He elicited a promise from Elizabeth before a crowd of witnesses. Something like embarrassment rippled over her handsome countenance as Darcy extended his hand in her direction, but Elizabeth accepted the symbolic offer.

"Finally," Darcy whispered as Elizabeth joined him. From the other side of the ballroom, a round of applause accompanied Bingley and Miss Bennet's entrance to the dance floor, but Darcy thought it could just as easily be meant for him: He won the game and claimed his prize.

Chapter 16

THE CROWD PRESSED CLOSE about them, and Darcy was most uncomfortable by the recognition, but Elizabeth thankfully took pity upon him. She set the mood for their courtship.

"Oh, Lizzy!" Mrs. Bennet appeared at Elizabeth's side. The woman's famous nerves were all aflutter. "Why did you not...?"

Thankfully, Elizabeth broke through her mother's effusions.

"No well wishes, Mama," Darcy's bride-to-be declared. "There will be time enough for your joyful congratulations when we reach Longbourn. This moment is Jane's, not mine. Mr. Darcy and I shall gladly wait our turn. Jane is the dearest of sisters, and Mr. Darcy is Mr. Bingley's most loyal friend. Neither of us wishes to rob our loved ones of the fondest memories of their joining."

Elizabeth spoke loud enough for those about

them to hear her determination. To the few who meant to ignore her caution, she added in firm tones.

"Mr. Darcy and I would take umbrage with anyone who did not accept our wishes."

Darcy certainly did not object. To no longer be the center of attention pleased him. For a brief moment, he wondered what those who sought his attentions in London would think of his public proposal to Miss Elizabeth. Most would likely term the rumors "impossible" for Darcy held the reputation of a man who kept his cards close.

Elizabeth turned her mother's shoulders to face the dance floor.

"Is Jane not lovely, Mama? She is the prettiest among us, and the most kind."

"The prettiest girl in the neighborhood," Mrs. Bennet declared with pride, and many in the crowd nodded their agreement.

Darcy was of a different mind, but he kept his opinions to himself. Miss Bennet's beauty was too perfect for Darcy's tastes. Moreover, the eldest Bennet daughter lacked the depth of character found in *his* Elizabeth.

"All our daughters possess great beauty," Mr. Bennet said as he joined his wife among the well-wishers. "And they will be excellent stewards of their husbands' households."

Mr. Bennet's eyes misted over, as he looked first upon Miss Bennet and then upon Elizabeth. The removal of the two eldest daughters from his manor left the gentleman visibly moved.

When Bingley motioned his guests to join him,

Darcy directed Elizabeth's steps to the dance floor.

"Thank you," he whispered.

"For what am I to know your gratitude?" Elizabeth teased with a beguiling smile.

"For making me the happiest of men." Darcy brought the back of Elizabeth's hand to his lips.

"Is that all?" Elizabeth's breath hitched faster.

Darcy set her in the line forming on either side of Bingley and Miss Bennet.

"And for realizing one public spectacle was enough for the evening." Darcy winked at her as he stepped to the gentleman's line.

The dancers nodded their heads in time to the music and when the pattern repeated, Bingley raised his hand to gesture their participation, and they each stepped into the form. Darcy and Elizabeth circled each other: Their eyes locked in a loving gaze. Darcy never knew such happiness: He claimed a priceless jewel as his wife to be. The barren pain of desolation would no longer shadow his existence. Of late, Darcy accepted the turmoil gnawing at his insides as love, but now a gentler emotion spread through his chest. The realization of loving Elizabeth Bennet was all that was delightful.

He and Elizabeth parted, and Darcy found himself opposite his sister. It startled him to realize he forgot Georgiana was even among the dancers.

"Your countenance glows with happiness, William," Georgiana said with a girlish giggle. "You truly love Miss Elizabeth."

He turned Georgiana in a tight circle.

"Elizabeth is *home*," Darcy told her. "I have no

other means to explain it."

When the first dance of the set ended, Darcy caught Elizabeth's hand and tugged her along behind him.

"I must assist Jane," she declared, but Elizabeth did not resist his machinations. "Where are we going?"

Darcy slowed their steps. He met Elizabeth's questioning gaze with a smile.

"To the terrace. We have unfinished business."

"Oh," she whispered as a flush of color claimed her cheeks.

"Come along," Darcy announced in firm tones. With a smile, Elizabeth nodded her agreement.

When they reached the shadows of the terrace, Darcy turned Elizabeth into his embrace.

"At last," he whispered as Darcy caressed the curls framing her face. "I missed you."

"And I you." Elizabeth laid her cheek upon Darcy's chest.

The early autumn night was cool, but when Elizabeth moved into his embrace, Darcy would swear the blackness vibrated warm around them. At length, Elizabeth raised her gaze to meet his. She shivered again, but this time Darcy thought it was from anticipation–from desire–from the knowledge they would step into the future together.

Darcy lowered his head to claim Elizabeth's mouth. A gentle kiss. Their breaths shared. A kiss to declare his devotion to her. She was the one woman to complete him.

Elizabeth moved closer, clinging to him. Her arms came about Darcy's neck. Fingers teased the length of his hair. She kissed him back. Tentative at first and then with more boldness. God, but he would live a blessed life with Elizabeth by his side!

Darcy kissed her as he dreamed of doing since those early days at Netherfield. He tasted her for the first time, sliding his tongue along the seam of her lips and delving inside when Elizabeth opened her mouth to him. Darcy tightened his embrace, one hand splayed across the small of her back and the other upon the fall of Elizabeth's hips.

The scent of lavender filled his senses. Elizabeth was his whole world. Yet, such perfection must occasionally claim a breath of air. The sound of boisterous laughter brought them apart while still clinging to each other. Their hearts pounding in complete accord. Elizabeth appeared dazed, and her breath came in ragged puffs.

Darcy's eyes stared down upon her upturned countenance; the desire dripped from him. His fingers sought hers, and Elizabeth intertwined their hold.

"I feel I waited a lifetime to know you," Darcy whispered.

"I feel I always knew you," Elizabeth admitted.

Her innocent response had Darcy smiling again.

"We should return to the ballroom," he pronounced with regret. "Even those who are betrothed are not permitted the latitude of intimacies."

Elizabeth came close to admitting to Mr. Darcy her dislike for propriety's restrictions for she despised losing his closeness, but she dutifully followed him to the ballroom. Inside, she assisted her father in gathering her family so they might all return to Longbourn, while Mr. Darcy accepted the well wishes of his sister and cousin. Still tingling from the intensity of Mr. Darcy's kiss, Elizabeth at first did not notice Kitty sitting upon a small bench in the main foyer.

"Papa says to wait for him here," Elizabeth said as she settled beside Kitty. Mr. Darcy assured Elizabeth he would call in the morning to escort her to church, and so Elizabeth rejoined her family.

"Does it matter?" Dejection laced Kitty's tone.

"What is amiss?" Elizabeth implored.

Kitty sighed heavily, her shoulders lifted in resignation.

"Jane will marry and then you. Even Mary holds the prospect of Mr. Grange. Only I will remain at Longbourn, and it is not likely Mama will relinquish all of her daughters. I shall be Mama's nurse until I am well upon the shelf."

"Oh, my darling." Elizabeth laced her arms about Kitty's shoulders. "Do not permit the blue devils to vex you."

"I shall be like one of those heroines in a Gothic novel, where the woman is locked in a cell until the hero comes for her. But for me there shall be no such rescue," Kitty protested.

Elizabeth hid her bemusement. For years, Kitty embraced the dramatics to claim a bit of attention from Lydia.

"If there is a heroine, then there must be a hero. It may take him longer to arrive upon the scene than you would prefer, but trust me dearest one, your hero will arrive when the time is right." Elizabeth thought of Mr.

Darcy and how she was slow to accept the perfection of what he offered.

"No one will even know I am hidden away," Kitty protested. "Papa says I may not stand up at assemblies unless I stand up with my sisters, but my sisters shall be no where near Longbourn, and who would choose such a dolt to mate?"

Elizabeth did not point out the fact that Netherfield was but three miles from Longbourn and if Mary chose Mr. Grange, the middle Bennet sister would be in Meryton; instead, she attempted to soothe her sister's doldrums.

"I wish you more happiness than dancing with your sisters. And I would extend an invitation to you to join me and Mr. Darcy at Pemberley." Elizabeth prayed Mr. Darcy would not object. They had yet to discuss such details. She knew Mr. Darcy would never accept Lydia and Mr. Wickham under his roof, but what of the other Bennets. It would be something Elizabeth must address with the gentleman at the earliest convenience.

"Truly, Lizzy?" Kitty's features brightened.

"I will require a bit of time to settle in at Pemberley," Elizabeth cautioned. "Yet, I think you and Miss Darcy would do well together."

Kitty caught Elizabeth in a tight hug.

"Oh, thank you, Lizzy. You are the best of my sisters!" Happy at last, Kitty insisted, "I shall find Mary. Mr. Grange has had enough of our sister's time for one evening."

Watching Kitty skitter away, Elizabeth prayed she did not err in her estimation of Miss Katherine Bennet. She thought it would be to Kitty's material advantage to spend the chief of her younger sister's time with her and Jane. In society so superior to what Kitty generally knew, Kitty's improvement would be inevitable.

"Kitty is not so ungovernable a temper as Lydia, and, removed from the influence of Lydia's example, Kitty will have the opportunity to become less irritable, less ignorant, and less insipid," Elizabeth whispered to the empty foyer. "I should also speak to Papa about keeping Kitty from Lydia's company, as well as to speak to Jane in assisting Kitty to a better way in society."

Within the Bennet coach, Elizabeth tolerated her mother's excesses of "Good gracious! Lord bless me! Only think! Dear me! Mr. Darcy! Who would have thought it? And is it really true? Oh, my sweetest Lizzy! How rich and how great you will be! What pin money, what jewels, what carriages you will have! I am so pleased! So happy! Such a charming man! So handsome! So tall! Oh, my dear Lizzy! Pray apologize for my having disliked him so much before. I hope he will overlook it. Dear, dear Lizzy! A house in Town! Everything that is charming! Three daughters married! Ten thousand a year! O Lord! What will become of me! I shall go distracted!"

No one in Mr. Bennet's carriage attempted to silence Longbourn's mistress. They learned long ago to permit Mrs. Bennet her moments. Yet, between the lady's exclamations, Elizabeth and Jane whispered their hopes of happiness.

"I noticed you and Mr. Darcy disappeared for a few discreet minutes," Jane teased.

"Do you think others noticed?" Elizabeth asked

in alarm.

"No one who would criticize," Jane assured. "Did you enjoy your first kiss with Mr. Darcy?"

Elizabeth thanked the darkness for hiding the red heat crawling up her neck.

"Did you enjoy your first kiss from Mr. Bingley?" Elizabeth countered.

"Very much." Jane giggled is a manner Elizabeth had not observed in some time. "And you?"

"I did not kiss Mr. Bingley," she taunted good-naturedly.

"Lizzy!" her sister pronounced in frustration.

A smile tugged at Elizabeth's lips as the image of Mr. Darcy's countenance filled her memory.

"Yes, very much. Very much indeed."

Mr. Bennet crawled into the carriage to sit beside Elizabeth. He laced his fingers with hers. Her marrying Mr. Darcy would take Elizabeth away from her family, and for a moment, Elizabeth fought the urge to call off the engagement so she might remain with those who loved her, but then she thought of the devotion written upon Mr. Darcy's features; and she knew the gentleman would never permit her to know loneliness again. *And there is the promise of children*, she thought. *A husband. A new sister. And children.* She would know happiness.

Darcy slipped the local vicar an extra coin so the man would agree to add the first calling of the banns for his and Elizabeth's joining to the vicar's third calling of the banns for Bingley and Miss Bennet.

"But the Pemberley vicar does not do the same in Derbyshire," Elizabeth protested.

"Who says Mr. Winkler does not perform his official duties?"

Darcy winked at her as he placed Elizabeth beside his sister and the colonel on the bench.

"Yet..."

Darcy caught her hand as he sat beside Elizabeth.

"Does it matter, Elizabeth? Your deceptions and my deceptions brought us to this time. I, for one, am glad to claim your affections after all the turmoil."

Elizabeth's eyebrow rose in bemusement.

"This conversation is not over, William."

The sound of his Christian name upon her lips drove Darcy to distraction. He lifted the back of Elizabeth's gloved hand to his lips.

"I look forward to *all* our conversations," he said seductively.

Elizabeth's frown lines deepened.

"We are in church, Sir."

"Yet, the sermon has not yet begun." Darcy countered, "Moreover, God meant for men to think upon the women they affect. I am following His strictures. Genesis nine and twenty says, 'And Jacob served seven years for Rachel, and they seemed unto him but a few days, for the love he had to her.'"

Even with the speedy calling of the banns, it was a month before Darcy claimed Elizabeth to wife. They stood with Jane and Bingley mid week after the engagement ball. While Bingley whisked his new wife off to London to celebrate their marriage, Darcy and Georgiana stayed at Netherfield, although Darcy thought for a time it would be necessary to remove to the small inn in Meryton.

Miss Bingley and Mrs. Hurst arrived, without notice, the day before Bingley's nuptials, and Miss Bennet pleaded with Bingley to accept his family for the ceremonies. Unsurprisingly, Miss Bingley's effusions to the colonel had Fitzwilliam recalling duties awaiting him in London. Darcy's cousin made his exit following the wedding breakfast.

Thankfully, Bingley's disgust for his sisters' machinations had Darcy's friend informing Miss Bingley and Mrs. Hurst that they were welcome to stay at Netherfield only until Friday. Bingley had not yet forgiven their interference in his life.

"Jane is the mistress of Netherfield Park, and until you prove to me your regrets for treating my wife with disdain, you are not welcome under my roof," Bingley pronounced when his sisters claimed dismay at their brother's eviction.

Mr. and Mrs. Bingley returned in time for Darcy and Elizabeth's joining. As he and Fitzwilliam promised each other years prior, Darcy asked the colonel to stand with him on Darcy's wedding day. Although he expected Elizabeth to choose Mrs. Bingley, Darcy's betrothed surprised them all by requesting her sister Kitty to stand as witness.

"Mary stood with Lydia and I with Jane. Kitty deserves to know the hope of marital felicity," Elizabeth declared when others questioned her choice. Elizabeth's gesture pleased the girl, who had become one of Georgiana's favorites, and Miss Katherine Bennet rose to the occasion. It was a refreshing revelation for Darcy.

Later in life, Darcy would declare the births

of each of his five children his happiest days, but on the morning when Vicar Williamson place Elizabeth's hand in his, Darcy knew completion: Elizabeth Bennet was his life's blood–the very air upon which he existed. Beautiful in the light gray satin and lace dress Mrs. Bennet designed for her second daughter, Elizabeth's beauty stole Darcy's breath when she appeared in the church's alcove upon her father's arm. For months, Darcy wanted Elizabeth with a passion he did not think possible–day and night, desire nagged at him. It was as if Darcy saw Elizabeth for the first time; yet, his heart knew her the moment their eyes met.

On a day a week prior to their nuptials, Elizabeth's spirits rose to playfulness, and she asked Darcy to account for his having ever fallen in love with her.

"How could you begin?" said she. "I can comprehend your going on charmingly, once you made a beginning; but what could set you off in the first place?"

"I cannot fix on the hour, or the spot, or the look, or the words, which laid the foundation. It is too long ago. I was in the middle before I knew that I began."

"My beauty you early withstood, as for my manners–my behavior to you was at least always bordering on the uncivil, and I never spoke to you without rather wishing to give you pain than not. Now, be sincere; did you admire me for my impertinence?"

"For the liveliness of your mind I did."

"You may as well call it impertinence at once; it was very little less. The fact is, that you were sick of civility, of deference, of officious attention. Women who were always speaking, and looking, and thinking of your approbation alone disgusted you. I roused and interested you because I was so unlike them. Had you not been really amiable, you would have hated me for it; but in spite of the pains you took to disguise yourself, your feelings were always noble and just, and in your heart you thoroughly despised the persons who so assiduously courted you. There–I saved you the trouble of accounting for it; and really all things considered, I begin to think it perfectly reasonable. To be sure, you knew no actual good of me; but nobody thinks of that when he falls in love."

Darcy gathered her to him.

"There was nothing reasonable about my loving you," he protested good-naturedly. "One thing women do not understand about men is we do not think of love. When we look upon a handsome woman, our minds do not say 'What would it be like to marry her?'." We enjoy the lady's company, but we often do not think of marriage, not in the manner women do."

"Then how does a man reconcile himself to marriage?" Elizabeth questioned.

"Males are still very much an animal in their preferences, but when a male comes across that one female who will be his other half, he knows only one thing: to reach out and claim her as his own. There is no prelude. No questioning of his emotions. No dreaming of romance and a life of contentment. Only the reality that if he does not claim that one particular woman, he will never be whole."

And so Darcy considered the public voicing of their vows only a preliminary, for Elizabeth belonged to him as permanently as the sun belonged to the sky.

After an elaborate wedding breakfast, Darcy and Elizabeth traveled to London for a few days at Darcy House before they would journey on to Derbyshire. Between them, they decided they wished to be at Pemberley for Christmastide and as it was already late November, Elizabeth insisted upon their returning to his manor. Darcy made arrangements with the colonel to see Georgiana to Lord Matlock's London home. His sister would return to Derbyshire with the Matlocks early in December.

"There is much to plan if we are to host my family and yours for Christmastide," Elizabeth insisted as she curled into Darcy's embrace.

Darcy ordered Mr. Thacker not to place the knocker on the door for he wanted no visitors to disturb those first days of marital bliss. He and Elizabeth dined in Darcy's quarters and shared many intimate kisses, but Darcy meant to end his wife's nervous chatter.

"The details will show themselves," Darcy whispered as he kissed Elizabeth tenderly. "For now, I am content to know but one thing."

He could feel the tension between them build. Her kiss was a taste of heaven, and Darcy's desire climbed higher.

He rose to lift Elizabeth to him.

"It is time you become my wife in more than name only," Darcy said as he walked slowly toward his bed.

Elizabeth buried her face into his shoulder.

"I must warn you, William, I hold only a little knowledge of this night."

Darcy could feel the heat of embarrassment warm her skin.

"A little?" He chuckled as he nibbled upon Elizabeth's ear.

"Mrs. Bingley," she rasped as Darcy lowered Elizabeth to the bed.

"It will be enough," Darcy assured. Following her down, their lips found each other's. The string of kisses had their breaths ragged when they parted. "I love you, Elizabeth Darcy." He brushed his lips across her silken cheek.

"And I love you, William."

What flowed between them was passion and need, but also trust and vulnerability-a bonding of two souls. A bond only those who truly love would understand.

Other Books by Regina Jeffers

Jane Austen-Inspired Novels:

Darcy's Passions: Pride and Prejudice Retold Through His Eyes

Darcy's Temptation: A Pride and Prejudice Sequel

Captain Wentworth's Persuasion: Jane Austen's Classic Retold Through His Eyes

Vampire Darcy's Desire: A Pride and Prejudice Paranormal Adventure

The Phantom of Pemberley: A Pride and Prejudice Mystery

Christmas at Pemberley: A Pride and Prejudice Sequel

The Disappearance of Georgiana Darcy: A Pride and Prejudice Mystery

The Mysterious Death of Mr. Darcy: A Pride and Prejudice Mystery

"The Pemberley Ball" (a short story in *The Road to Pemberley* anthology)

Honor and Hope: A Contemporary Pride and Prejudice

Regency and Contemporary Romances:

The Scandal of Lady Eleanor – Book 1 of the Realm Series (aka A Touch of Scandal)

A Touch of Velvet – Book 2 of the Realm Series

A Touch of Cashémere – Book 3 of the Realm Series

A Touch of Grace – Book 4 of the Realm Series

A Touch of Mercy – Book 5 of the Realm Series

A Touch of Love – Book 6 of the Realm Series

A Touch of Honor – Book 7 of the Realm Series

His: Two Regency Novellas (includes "His American Heartsong," a Realm series novella and "His Irish Eve," a sequel to *The Phantom of Pemberley*)

The First Wives' Club – Book 1 of the First Wives' Trilogy

Second Chances: The Courtship Wars

Coming Soon...

Meet the Author

Writing passionately comes easily to Regina Jeffers. A master teacher, for thirty-nine years, she passionately taught thousands of students English in the public schools of West Virginia, Ohio, and North Carolina. Yet, "teacher" does not define her as a person. Ask any of her students or her family, and they will tell you Regina is passionate about so many things: her son, her grandchildren, truth, children in need, our country's veterans, responsibility, the value of a good education, words, music, dance, the theatre, pro football, classic movies, the BBC, track and field, books, books, and more books. Holding multiple degrees, Jeffers often serves as a Language Arts or Media Literacy consultant to school districts and has served on several state and national educational commissions.

Regina's writing career began when a former student challenged her to do what she so "righteously" told her class should be accomplished in writing. On a whim, she self-published her first book Darcy's Passions. "I never thought anything would happen with it. Then one day, a publishing company contacted me. They watched the sales of the book on Amazon, and they offered to print it."

Since that time, Jeffers continues to write. "Writing is just my latest release of the creative side of my brain. I taught theatre, even participated in professional and community-based productions when I was younger. I trained dance teams, flag lines, majorettes, and field commanders. My dancers were both state and national champions. I simply require time each day to let the possibilities flow. When I write, I write as I used to choreograph routines for my dance teams; I write the scenes in my head as if they are a movie. Usually, it plays there for several days being tweaked and rewritten, but, eventually, I put it to paper. From that point, things do not change much because I completed several mental rewrites."

Every Woman Dreams https://reginajeffers.wordpress.com

Website www.rjeffers.com

Austen Authors http://austenauthors.net

English Historical Fiction Authors http://englishhistoryau-thors.blogspot.com

Join Regina on Twitter, Facebook, Pinterest, Google+, and LinkedIn.

Chapter 1

LONDON 1819

THE ODOR OF THE Thames as it wafted over the area beyond Greenland Docks caused Hunt's nose to snarl, but Sir Alexander declared that someone paid large sums of money for the privilege of a blind eye to unloaded contraband, and it was Hunt's duty to learn more of the people involved. The wig he wore itched, and he fought the urge to remove the offending item, and it did not slip his notice how his coachman, Etch, swallowed his amusement.

"Jist relax, Sir. It shan't be long," Etch cautioned.

Hunt grunted his response, attempting to disguise his own mirth. He slouched lazily against the back of the chair, just as the baronet taught him. It was not much, this bit of public duty he performed, but Hunt took a certain pride in doing more than being the Duke of Devilfoard's heir-more than being the Devil's cub. His ears perked with interest at the conversation, taking place nearby.

"I tells you," said the dark-haired man Hunt followed into the tavern. "The viscounty means to learn more of the earl. Then we be makin' a call upon His Lordship."

"And this Town lord knows of the earl?" the shorter of the two asked.

"That's wat the viscounty says. Says he's got an arr'ngement with the Highest. He also say we be keepin' the high lord company fer awhile 'til we's know fer certain he be easy pickin's. The viscounty be wantin' information on who the high lord shows his attentions."

The men rose to depart, and Hunt made to leave, but Etch placed a hand upon his sleeve.

"Wait." The coachman nodded to the door. "Is that not Lord Newsome? Doing business in this part of London?"

Hunt's expression screwed up in disbelief.

"The viscounty?" he wondered aloud. "This just became interesting."

"You are pure evil," she declared as he chased her through the intricate maze.

Dressed all in black, he stalked her, and Angelica's body heated from his brief touch, as he brushed her wrist with his fingertips. Catching her skirt tail, she skittered away from his slow pursuit.

"A copper for your thoughts," she taunted with a nervous giggle.

"I was considering the pure pleasure of

possessing my own personal angel." His deep resonant voice spoke of desire, but also of contentment.

"Am I that angel?" she rasped when he caught her shoulders and spun her to him.

"Forever."

"Miss Angelica." Her maid shook Angel's shoulder. "Wake up, Miss."

Angelica Lovelace rolled to her back and stretched. She hated to leave the dream behind. It was one of her favorites, and she particularly enjoyed how it always ended with her in the dark stranger's very masculine embrace.

"What is amiss?" she murmured. Angelica kept her eyes closed watching the scene's details playing out behind her lids. She could not remember a time when she did not dream of her dark lover. Even as a very young girl, she enjoyed his company. When she was a child, he was her best friend, but when she turned to womanhood, he became her secret lover, and although she never met him, he remained the man by which she judged all others. To her, he was her "dearest Devil," always dressed in black; his shaggy coal-colored hair streaked with hints of mahogany. Over the years, Angelica blamed her oft-spoken-of irreverent attitude on the mystery man with a wicked wit and a splash of deviltry. *If my critics knew of my sultry musings, they would agree I am quite beyond the pale.* The thought brought a smile to her lips.

"Your father, Miss," the maid encouraged. "Mr. Lovelace requests you attend him in the small drawing room. Baron Arden has called."

Angelica forced her eyes open.

"Baron Arden? What might the baron require?" She pushed herself to a seated position.

"Mrs. Watson be thinking the baron will make himself known as a suitor." The maid braced Angelica on the steps beside the bed.

"Do you suppose the baron consulted Mrs. Watson?" Angelica asked, with a bit of a tease.

The maid rarely understood Angel's light sarcasm.

"Oh, no, Miss. Mrs. Watson be creatin' a guess."

A chuckle slipped from Angelica's lips.

"And I thought an English upper servant worth her salt prided herself on knowing everything within the household."

"Mrs. Watson knows enough." The maid unlaced the ties on Angelica's night rail. "I thought the silver muslin, Miss."

Angelica fought the urge to roll her eyes.

"Another virginal gown. Why is it English ladies announce their marital state with their gown's color? What could be the harm in wearing a bright red or a royal blue?"

"You may choose whatever color most pleases you once you marry," the maid observed in severe tones. "Lady Peterson wears only shades of purple. Can you imagine, Miss? Purple dresses every day?"

Angelica frowned.

"I am not certain I could tolerate the monotony. Of course, it would simplify the need for accessories. A few pairs of slippers and gloves would match one's attire."

"You're so practical, Miss," the young girl

observed.

Twenty minutes later and without breaking her fast, Angelica swept into the room. She and her father had imposed upon the earl and her mother's sister Sarah by imploring upon her maternal relatives to open the earl's Town house for the Season and for Lady Mannington to assume the position of Angelica's sponsor in Society. Her mother's older sister married Lord Mannington some five and twenty years prior, long before Angelica's birth and before Lady Victoria Copley married Horace Lovelace and traveled to America.

"You sent for me, Sir?" She paused as her mother had taught her. *"Allow the man to take your full measure."* The words rang clear in Angel's mind: It was comforting to have a bit of her mother with her.

"There you are, my dear." Her father struggled to his feet.

Each day, Angelica became more aware of the man's mortality. That particular fact was one of the reasons she agreed to this venture. Her mother passed two years prior, and her father insisted on carrying out his wife's dying wishes. For years, Victoria Lovelace spoke of bringing her only daughter to England for a proper debut, but her mother succumbed to consumption before her wish knew fruition. Therefore, without the love of his life, Angel's father made the journey.

"Please come in." He gestured her forward. "You are acquainted with Baron Arden, I believe."

"Yes, Sir." She curtsied to the man standing aristocratically beside the hearth. "The baron and

I stood up together at the Breesons' ball on Tuesday last."

The baron executed a respectful bow.

"It is singular you have such perfect recall, Miss Lovelace."

"Angelica has a quick mind," her father remarked with pride, but then blustered. "Of course, my Victoria would say a learned lady was not a virtue by English standards." He winced when shock crossed the baron's features. "I apologize, Arden. I offer no censure. My late wife always accused me of acting a cake when speaking of our daughter. So many years away from my homeland must make me appear quite the heathen. I am accustomed to a freer speaking society."

"It is quite acceptable, Lovelace." The baron grasped the hand Angelica extended in his direction and offered the obligatory air kiss. "Despite the consensus to the contrary, many Englishmen prefer their wives to possess a sensible nature."

Angelica gestured to a nearby chair.

"But the author of *Pride and Prejudice* proved in her first novel that *sense* and *sensibility* are different from intelligence, my lord," she countered.

"I am surprised you have read the lady's novels," Arden remarked.

Angelica seated herself on the edge of the cushion and straightened her dress's seam.

"Would your *surprise* be because the author is British rather than American or because the author is a lady, and women should not trespass upon the male dominated world of authorship?" She did not wait for his response before adding, "Perhaps your astonishment rests in the fact *Sense and Sensibility* is a novel rather than a serious tome?"

She smiled prettily at the man. Her mother may have determined Angelica required an English aristocrat for a husband, however, Angel had decided only a partner who could accept her flaws, as well as her substantial dowry, would do.

Arden frowned. He clearly not expected a challenge to his opinions.

"I suppose all three, Miss Lovelace."

"But you hold no objection, Baron, to a woman who develops her mind through extensive reading?" Angelica chuckled internally at the familiar line from the British author's books. She was certain Arden possessed no idea of the remark's source.

"I would imagine my wife would oversee our children's educations. Therefore, I would expect a certain rationality."

"Which brings us to the reason for Baron Arden's visit, my dear," her father interrupted. "Arden has requested my permission to call upon you with the intention of a courtship. That is, if you are agreeable."

"A time to learn if we would suit?"

Angelica took a closer look at the baron. His thick dark brown hair had a tendency to curl about his collar. Barely six feet, the man's stature struggled to appear more than a walking block of wood, but he possessed a pleasant countenance.

"Customarily, such details are not discussed before the lady," the baron bristled.

Angelica forced her mouth into a straight line. Since making her debut a month prior, she had delighted in ruffling the feathers of a number of gentlemen who saw her dowry as an inducement to marriage to a hoydenish American. When her father suggested this journey, Angel reminded him, as she had often reminded her dear mother, Angel's ways would not sit well among the English elite: she spent too much time studying her father's book on antiquities, tending Horace Lovelace's growing string of thoroughbreds, and overseeing the health and happiness of her father's workers. Those were the things, which brought her contentment in her Virginia home, but they were not qualities most men of the English peerage sought in a wife.

"We Americans often take a divergent course. I pray that fact does not present a difficulty to our future felicity, Baron," she said with a practiced smile.

"Certainly not." Despite his words of assurance, Arden frowned. "I welcome your frankness, Miss Lovelace."

Angelica heard the man's insincerity, but she promised her Aunt Sarah not to make predisposed judgments.

"Then how should we proceed, Sir?"

"I thought I might escort you on daily outings," he began. "If it is agreeable, we could drive today during the fashionable hour. I also hoped you would consider accompanying me to the theatre tomorrow. My sister and her husband will join us."

Angelica stood to end the conversation.

"I am amenable, Lord Arden."

He followed her to his feet.

"Then I will call for you this afternoon."

"I shall anticipate it." She directed him from the room, but before Angelica opened the door to the main hallway, she paused. With her hand resting on the handle, she smiled innocently up at the man. "Might I ask one question before you leave us, Baron?"

He looked surprised and then assumed a cynical expression.

"By all means."

Angelica hesitated as if undecided, but, in reality, she meant to set guidelines before their courtship began.

"During this time where we determine whether we might suit, am I to limit my interactions with other gentlemen callers? I would prefer to understand our agreement."

The baron's eyes narrowed.

"I would expect your undivided attention, Miss Lovelace."

She smiled sweetly.

"Then I would expect the same from you, Baron."

"Of what do you accuse me, Miss Lovelace?" he huffed.

Angelica withheld a glare of disgust.

"I meant no offense, Sir." She schooled her features to portray politeness. With that, she opened the door and turned the baron over to the waiting footman.

"Was that necessary?" Her father grumbled as he poured himself a glass of claret.

She resumed her seat.

"I studied the list of potential candidates Uncle Lancelot provided us. Arden has a long-standing title, but he is deeply in debt. My dowry must appear quite tempting. The baron would accept a woman lacking in effeminate ways to salvage his estate. I mean to keep the baron off balance until I am certain of his motivations. Who knows? Perhaps we shall suit, but I shan't be his subject. When I marry, I wish a relationship as loving as yours and mother's."

"Lady Victoria Copley was one of a kind," her father said wistfully. "Your mother possessed a magnanimous heart. My Victoria deserved better than a minor son, but I am more than grateful she chose me from among her many suitors. You will find it difficult to discover a man of even half Lady Victoria's merit."

Angelica thought of her devilish dreams. A man of passion and compassion would do well for her.

"I require a man of vision, like my father," she said in earnest.

The slow carriage procession drove Angelica nearly to Bedlam, but she kept the smile upon her lips. She agreed to the craziness of the "Marriage Mart," as her Uncle Lancelot termed it, but she preferred to be anywhere else. The baron's gig crawled along behind a Stanhope. Every few feet, the man would slow the carriage to acknowledge another member of the *beau monde* before introducing her to his acquaintances. The *ton* practiced their pompousness with prescribed efficiency, and Angelica found it blatantly boring. With amusement, she wondered what *her devil* would say to such pretentiousness. Mayhap he would use it as a prime argument in defense of passion ruling the world. Not that Angelica knew anything of passion. In fact, she had never known even the most faithful of kisses.

"Woolgathering, Miss Lovelace?" a brittle voice

broke through her thoughts.

Angelica flushed as she looked up into the countenance of a frowning earl.

"I beg your pardon, Lord Townsend, I was simply enjoying the park's splendor on a spring day."

"You should always carry a parasol, Miss Lovelace," Lady Townsend warned. "We would not wish to see you become too brown from the sun."

Angelica doubted the woman's sincerity: She was certain the *ton* would celebrate any flaw Angel sported. She despised the British standard for unblemished skin. White pasty skin. Virginal white gowns. Proper manners, which hid prejudice and censure. A bland lifestyle wrapped in formality. She missed her American friends and her home in the picturesque Virginia mountains. Missed riding break neck across her father's land.

"I am grateful for the suggestion, Ma'am, and honored by your attention."

The carriage nudged forward, and she prepared to greet the baron's next acquaintance.

"What a crazy tradition!" she observed. "Would it not be wonderful to give the horses their heads?"

"A proper gentleman would never place his cattle in danger," Arden said in chastisement.

Angelica stiffened. His tone increased her often-quick ire: The baron's first thought was of his team. Should he not think of the park goers or her position in the high backed gig if safety knew his true concern?

"I never suggested you turn your team free; I simply made the observation it would be a pleasant experience to feel the wind upon one's cheeks."

"Acting such would age a woman," he said with another scowl.

Angelica considered arguing, but she stifled her words. It was useless to think she might find a mate who spoke to her soul. She apologized. This was her first outing with Arden, and she would not leave the man with a poor impression of her manners. She ignored his declaration, and instead focused on the families enjoying the park. *I wish for family,* she thought. *Children and a husband, who knows pleasure in me in my devotion. A marriage where love rules our reason.*

In resignation of what may never be, Angel turned her head and watched a tall figure toss a ball to a boy hefting a cricket bat. Even from a distance, she could tell he cut a fine figure. It was brazen of her to study one man when riding out with another; yet, she could not turn her gaze. Without realizing the reason, she extended her gloved hand in his direction, as if she wished to turn him toward her so she might look upon his features. It was the oddest of sensation; Angel swallowed hard against the rising constriction in her chest.

Huntington McLaughlin, Marquess of Malvern, ignored the continual line of carriages tooling its way along the lane leading to and from the Serpentine, as well as the Society mamas, who attempted to catch his attention. He never understood the *ton's* desire to be on display. In fact, Hunt could not recall the last time he suffered a drive through the park during the fashionable hour. Today, he brought Logan and Lucas, his sister's twins, to the park, but earlier, he spent hours pacifying his father's high dudgeon regarding Hunt's refusal of Lord Sandahl's virginal daughter, Lady Mathild.

"I want nothing of an innocent," he declared.

If his father forced him to marry, Hunt would consider a widow, but no green girl straight from the schoolroom: He wished for a woman to place her love for him above all others–a woman who shared his passions for life and adventure and learning.

"What is amiss, Uncle Hunt?" Logan called as he took a few practice swings. Hunt escorted his nephews to the park to remove them from Henrietta's way. His twin sister was heavy with another child, and with Viscount Stoke away on governmental business, Malvern promised to see to the twins' safeties, while permitting the boys to expend some of their unbridled energy.

"Nothing," he mumbled, but he brought his forearm across his eyes to block the sun. Despite standing in an open field and surrounded by many of Society's best, his loins tightened. From the long equipage line, he watched a slow moving carriage turning toward Rotten Row. A golden-haired beauty clung to the gig's side, the wisps of her hair alive with light, and she turned in the seat to stare at him. *Too young*, his mind argued, but his body reacted nonetheless. He hardened, and although he knew it a foolish act for the distance between them too far apart to distinguish each other's features, he lowered his arm so she might look upon him. "Bloody hell," he mumbled as the gig moved away.

"Come on, Uncle Hunt," Lucas encouraged.

He withdrew his eyes from the departing carriage, but not before he spotted what he thought was the woman reaching out to him. It was like nothing he ever experienced, and the movement set his body on alert.

"Right away," he said with little conviction. With the girl no longer in sight, Hunt turned to the seven-year-olds. "Are you prepared?" He tossed the ball in the air to catch it again.

"It will be a fiver," Logan bragged.

Hunt laughed as his nephew puffed out chest.

"No boasting until after you produce." Yet, while he tossed the ball to Lucas, Hunt thought only of the pleasure of greeting the unknown girl with an embrace she would never forget.

"Are you frightened to toss the ball to me?" She pranced around in a circle.

He smiled in deviousness.

"Your confidence exceeds your ability."

His words taunted her, but she knew he would treat her gently. So, when he wound up as if to burn her with his bowler, Angel anticipated the easy loft. He did not disappoint her. The ball sailed within her reach, and Angelica smacked it with the bat, sending it buzzing past his ear.

With a burst of pure joy, she ran to touch the post with her bat as he scrambled for the ball to tag her out. As they both raced toward the home post, he caught her about the waist and swung her around in a circle.

"No fair!" she protested between gasps of delight.

He placed her before him.

"I have no sense of fair play where you are concerned." His thumb caressed her bottom lip. "You are mine," he whispered. "You deserve to be more than a mere baroness."

Angelica assumed her seat beside the baron in the Arden family box. After last night's dream, she considered canceling her evening plans. Never before had her secret lover made such a bold statement, and it shook Angel's composure. Realizing the unfairness to Arden, as well as to her father, Angelica met her obligations; yet, the dream remained clearly in her memory. She reminded her weary heart she promised her extended family to deal honorably with her suitors, and so she smiled at the man of whom she already tired.

"Have you attended the theatre previously, Miss Lovelace?" Lady Wickersham asked as she waited for her husband to assist her with her wrap.

"Quite often, Your Ladyship."

"I am certain it could not be of the same quality," the baron's sister declared. The Wickershams had commented on the lack of proper roads, religion, and refinement in the Americas. "How often must you have encountered a savage!" The woman exclaimed from nowhere. "Daily, I imagine."

"Never once," Angelica corrected, but the trio ignored her protests. Their snickers spoke volumes as to their honest opinion of the Lovelace fortune, and Angel bit the inside of her jaw to prevent the retort resting upon her lips.

"Have you traveled to the Americas, my lord?"

she asked the newly minted Viscount Wickersham.

"Heavens, no!" he snapped. "Why would I care to place myself in such a hostile society?"

She wondered if Lord Wickersham held any notice of how patronizing he sounded. With hope, Angelica sought the baron's attention to intercede, but her supposed suitor turned his notice to the lower levels. Angel followed his gaze. The baron's eyes fell upon a dark-haired buxom beauty. Immediately, Angelica recalled observing the same woman near the park's gate yesterday afternoon. The woman dropped a curtsy as the baron's gig exited the park. *Coincidence?*

Suddenly, it became quite clear what bothered her about yesterday's excursion. Other than when he introduced her to his brief acquaintances, Arden never spoke to her except to instruct or to criticize. In the ninety minutes' outing, he generally ignored her. And the same occurred thus far this evening. He disregarded her in the carriage, spending his time discussing politics with his brother in marriage. Did he despise being around her? He required her dowry, but the baron seemed under the delusion he owed her nothing in return. She had shared her expectations with him, but Arden gave her request no care.

Irritated by his attitude, she whispered in the baron's ear.

"Do you find the lady interesting, Sir?"

Arden turned his head to glare at her.

"We are not yet betrothed, Miss Lovelace, but you show tendencies for jealousy," he hissed. "Should I be flattered?"

"You should be courting my favor; it is my hand

you seek," she returned. Angelica refused to look away. If Arden thought to have a biddable wife, he should look elsewhere.

Arden's cheeks flushed.

"I will treat you with respect, Miss Lovelace, but I will not dance attendance on your every whim."

"I see," she said guardedly. With great care, she turned to the stage and began silently to count to one hundred. The pause would provide her time to make a decision. At length, turning to her party, Angelica set her mouth in a straight line. "If you will excuse me, Arden, I shall step to the ladies' retiring room."

"Shall I accompany you, Miss Lovelace?" Lady Wickersham asked as she adjusted her seat to address the stage.

Angelica kept her voice calm.

"That shan't be necessary, Viscountess. I have noted a smudge on my gown, which I should address. Enjoy the opening aria."

The baron did not even honor her by rising when Angelica exited his box. Angel had never experienced such decided censure. *When had Arden's intent changed? Had he meant to teach me a lesson prior to my accepting his plight? If so, the baron erred.* Reaching the main entrance, she motioned to a footman.

"Might you assist me?"

"Certainly, Miss."

"I am not feeling well. Would you hail a respectable hack to see me to St. James Street?"

The man bowed.

"Immediately, Miss." He turned toward the nearest exit. Within moments, he reappeared. "Your ride awaits, Miss." He escorted her to the carriage.

She slipped a coin into his hand.

"One more task," she whispered. "Please inform Lady Wickersham I developed a headache. Her Ladyship keeps her brother Baron Arden company."

"As you wish, Miss." With that, he steadied her step into the public coach.

As the hack rolled from the curb, Angelica looked back to determine if Arden followed. Instead, on the corner stoop, she espied the same gentleman who played cricket in the park the previous day. She recognized him from his stance and by the way her breathing hitched tighter. He assisted a very enciente woman, who clung to his arm. *Two sons and another on the way.* With a deep sigh of regret at her loss, she refocused her attentions on London's busy streets. She was without a suitor once again. Baron Arden would be furious: She had ended their courtship with a dramatic period.

Hunt turned his head to survey the traffic, but his gaze locked on the hackney and the woman climbing into it. His arm tensed. *It is she,* he thought.

"Someone you know?" His sister asked as her gaze followed his.

"No," he murmured.

Henrietta tightened her hold on his arm.

"The girl? The one with the golden blonde hair?"

Hunt could not remove his eyes from the hack.

"Saw the lady yesterday when I escorted your boys to the park. At least, I think she is the same one." His voice trailed off as the hack pulled away from the curb.

"Who is she?" Henrietta's too sharp eyes followed the departing coach.

Hunt returned his attention to his sister.

"Obviously no one of any consequence. Otherwise, what would the lady be doing in a public coach and alone at this time of the evening?"

"Is she pretty?" Etta's expression lit with an interest Hunt recognized as his sister's meddlesome ways.

He rolled his eyes heavenward.

"First, I only saw the lady from a distance," he cautioned. "She likely has bad teeth and crossed eyes." His sister chuckled. "Secondly, I am in no humor to entertain a *girl*. If I share my time with a lady, I want one who can hold an intelligent conversation."

"Is that what Alexandra Dandridge provides, Hunt? Intelligent conversation?"

He heard the disappointment, which laced his twin's tone.

"As a genteel lady, you should know nothing of the likes of Miss Dandridge," Hunt warned.

"Every well-bred English woman knows of women such as Miss Dandridge. We just rarely speak of them," his sister asserted.

Hunt swallowed his amusement.

"Miss Dandridge was never known for intellectual repartee."

"Was?" Etta jumped on the past tense verb.

"Was," Hunt confirmed. "I released Zan several days prior."

Henrietta intertwined their fingers as he escorted

her across the busy street.

"I cannot say I am sorry to hear it, Hunt. I know Papa's schemes are tiresome, but you do require someone with whom you may share your life. It is a sin against nature for you to have no children of your own. You are the perfect uncle."

"Most certainly." He grinned. "I spoil my nephews and then send them home for their parents to discipline." They stepped from the way of the late arriving theatergoers. "I know my duty, Etta. I am well aware of my responsibility to the dukedom."

He stepped upon the stage, and Angelica's heart raced. The audience quieted, and everyone leaned forward in anticipation. Like the others spectators, she slid to the edge of her seat and waited for the opera's opening notes. Without ever hearing him sing, Angel knew he would be a compelling baritone, one to mesmerize every female in the theatre.

As he opened his mouth for the first phrases, he made a slow advance to the stage's edge and then down the side steps beyond the imaginary fourth wall of the stage. She knew he was coming for her: His gaze remained locked upon her countenance. It was as if she could feel the heat of his breath upon her cheek. As his voice rose to fill every corner of the house, he reached for her, and Angelica placed her hand in his.

CPSIA information can be obtained
at www.ICGtesting.com
Printed in the USA
LVOW01s1832190616
493259LV00039B/720/P